US
KIDS
KNOW

US KIDS KNOW

JJ STRONG

RAZORBILL®

An Imprint of Penguin Random House

RAZORBILL®

An Imprint of Penguin Random House
Penguin.com

RAZORBILL & colophon is a registered trademark
of Penguin Random House LLC.

First published in the United States of America by Razorbill,
an imprint of Penguin Random House LLC, 2017

Quotation on page 373 is from
"Everything Means Nothing to Me" by Elliott Smith

LIBRARY OF CONGRESS CATALOGING-IN-PUBLICATION DATA IS AVAILABLE

ISBN 9780448494173

Printed in the United States of America

1 3 5 7 9 10 8 6 4 2

Interior design: Eric M. Ford

for Mom & Dad
and
for Via

PART ONE

Cullen

BEFORE THERE WAS RAY, there was Ray's sister, Brielle. The first time I noticed her—for real noticed her—was at a school dance. A dance that, as a senior, I had no business attending. For freshmen and sophomores, of course, at a place like St. John of the Cross Preparatory School, these dances are gold. They're still corny and trite and mostly boring, and none of the first- or second-year guys admit to *wanting* to go, but they all go anyway. Because the dances happen twice a year—once in winter and once in spring—and these are the only times when girls—real girls, not a teacher or a mom or someone's little sister or whatever—actually step foot inside our school. So if you're a guy in the early stages of being imprisoned inside the walls of a single-sex Catholic high school like St. John's, you'd be a fool to miss out.

It's different for seniors, though. By the time your final

year arrives, you're supposed to have cultivated your own network of friends, and if that network doesn't yet include members of the opposite sex—assuming you're into that sort of thing—then you're pretty much out of luck as far as making up ground goes. Because no fifteen-year-old girl from St. Anne's or Marymount Academy is about to do anything but scoff at some creepy upperclassman prowling the disco-ball, slow-dance circuit.

But I wasn't worried about all that. Because I wasn't there for the girls. I was there because I had a trunk full of ice-cold, watered-down domestic light beer (two dollars a can, six bucks for ten) and three bottles of syrupy, cinnamon-flavored liquor (three dollars a shot, fifty-five for the bottle). And even though I was smart enough to park two and a half blocks away, in the driveway of Mark Martz's house—Mark Martz, who had gone on a college campus visit with his parents for the weekend and who therefore hadn't the slightest clue that I was using his driveway to make a few bucks—I still had to make the rounds at the dance to recruit thirsty freshmen.

My pursuit of customers led me to the cafeteria, where kids gathered to blow off steam when they finally grew weary of the hot-breathed, smothering darkness of the gym. It was there that I saw Brielle. She was carrying three Diet Cokes from the vending machine to two tiny blond girls. It's both easy and difficult to describe the sensation of that moment. There was all the predictable stuff: butterflies, heart speeding up, hair on end, et cetera, et cetera. It's not like I hadn't ever seen a pretty girl before. But Brielle was different. Her friends—the blondes—were pretty. *Very* pretty. But predictably so. It was like if you asked a hundred ordinary guys for a description of their perfect girl, fifty guys would describe one of Brielle's friends, and fifty would describe the other. But Brielle looked only like herself. And because of that, she shone.

Like me, she was from Rosewood, so I remembered her vaguely from elementary school. I suppose she remembered me well enough too, because while her two friends were wiping paper napkins across the lips of their soda cans, Brielle looked right at me and waved. She did this like she knew I'd been staring at her and was simply waiting for the right moment to acknowledge me. Like we'd been communicating before even looking at each other.

I waved back. Her cheeks were rosy and chubby, and her mouth was small and very red, and based on absolutely no tangible information whatsoever I felt like she and I understood something important that nobody else at this dance understood—or would ever understand. In that one quick moment—a look, a smile, a wave—we transcended the night. The giggles, fake flirting, sweaty palms, dudes in popped collars singing along to Nelly, girls in flower-print dresses throwing bony arms in the air and crying, "Will the real Slim Shady please stand up, please stand up, please stand up," the DJ with his thumb rings and orange-dyed soul patch, the trusting teachers who moved among us believing we were all having an innocent good time, the suspicious teachers who were on the scent for boozy breath at every turn . . . Brielle and I seemed to float above all that ordinary, predictable nonsense and meet on some rare, electrified plane. I decided in that very same moment that I would do whatever I could to meet her there again.

The next week I drove to Marymount after school to watch her at field hockey practice. Brielle was made to play field hockey the way pillows are made to be bricks. Her only potential strength was that her elbows flew around so awkwardly that nobody could get close enough to steal the ball without risking a black eye. She didn't have the ball often, though, and when she did, her twitching arms would fling it wildly out of reach before she could manage to do anything productive with it.

But off the field, when she wasn't forced to tighten up and move her body in a way it was never meant to be moved, she was a sight: on the sidelines, leaning on her field hockey stick, picking wet bits of grass from the back of her knee, swaying her long auburn ponytail from one shoulder to the other, silent and content and somehow totally unaware that she was outrageously beautiful.

I watched her every day for almost an entire season without speaking to her. To be honest, I was scared to death of her, and so for weeks I stood fifty yards away, leaning against my Buick, watching and wondering what to say to a girl like that. Sure, she was two classes below me, but you don't just walk up to a girl like Brielle O'Dell and plainly ask her out like it's nothing. And even though I nurtured some pretty serious delusions that she might approach me and break the ice herself, I also knew the occasion of our next meeting needed to be much more memorable than that. Ours was a story that wouldn't stand for the commonplace.

The first encounter had to be astonishing.

Had to be grand. Epic. Fierce.

Violent.

Bloody.

And so, after one month of watching her giggle with her friends after they'd showered and changed, and then following her home through the slippery, foggy, winding autumn roads of north Jersey—during which I learned that she rode right past my house every night between five forty-five and six P.M.—I decided that Brielle O'Dell and I were going to crash into each other's lives.

Brielle

BEFORE THE ACCIDENT, I recalled Cullen only vaguely from Rosewood. He'd been notorious at our public school before we each moved on to different high schools. He would wear the same pair of dilapidated jeans every day, and he was the first boy in school to grow his hair long and begin wearing oversized flannel shirts with black Doc Martin boots just like the high school kids were doing. It was a style he never really abandoned, even when the '90s look faded away and boys started wearing khakis and polos and expensive flip-flops. Rumors would circulate that Cullen was going to fight someone after school or that he'd been suspended for any number of transgressions—pocketing school supplies, keying the principal's car, burning the carpet in the library with hydrochloric acid pilfered from the science teacher's closet.

We all knew about Cullen Hickson.

So when he started showing up at our field hockey practices, I pretended I was just as creeped out by him as the other girls. He'd stand there in the parking lot, beside that oversized sedan he drove, just watching us. We had only three seniors on the team that year, and they all assured us he was a dirtbag—that he went to St. John's but that he worked at a gas station where he sold drugs and he wasn't even going to college next year.

It wasn't unusual for boys from the surrounding schools to drive over to practice, but most of them did so to see their girlfriends, and the ones without girlfriends were baby-faced enough that they posed no real threat; they were simply satisfying their own curiosity about the world of girls that their parochial schools had robbed them of. We were just as painfully curious about the male universe and so were happy to oblige.

But Cullen was different. He was tall, with sturdy shoulders, greasy, wavy hair, and a thick, obnoxious mustache stamped above his top lip. (St. John's forbade beards, and Cullen pushed that rule as far as he could.) He watched us like we were in a zoo. Girls would point at him and laugh, or tell him to go fuck himself, or honk their horns at him when they sped by. He'd just lean against his door with the strangest, slightest grin.

I caught him staring at me a few times and never thought much of it. Girls were always telling stories about the terrible ways Cullen had gawked at them. Scarlett Reed and Katie Kinney would stand on either side of me in the locker room, so thin in their underwear but strong from their sportiness, the two of them flitting and skipping about without a hint of self-consciousness, while I hid all my soft parts beneath a loose-fitting shirt and folded arms, and they'd inevitably proclaim how Cullen Hickson had ogled them yet again today, how awful and gross he was. I assumed the looks he gave me were the same he gave to us all. I was happy at least to be included in that group of the wanted.

I was terribly inept at most athletic endeavors, and field hockey proved no exception. Katie and Scarlett, meanwhile, were two beautiful blond girls from Short Hills who were ferociously adept athletes. I met them the first summer practice of freshman year when the three of us randomly gathered on the same spot of clover-patched lawn for a lunch break. Life is arbitrary that way. Had I not decided—despite a total lack of experience with field hockey or any evidence that I would be even remotely good at it—that athletic involvement was an indispensable component of any serious student's college application, and had I not sat down in that exact spot on that first day after only a few hours of practice—just short of the amount of time it would take Katie Kinney and everyone else to learn that I was the single *worst* player on the team—who knows how things would have unfolded?

I mentioned to them that I was excited to see *House of Mirth* on our English class reading list—I'd heard about the book and wanted to check it out.

"Absolutely," Katie said, holding her chin aloft, tucking

a stray piece of arugula into her mouth. "*House of Mirth* is Edith Wharton's tour de force."

I nodded excitedly. This is exactly how I'd hoped girls at Marymount would talk.

"Absolutely," Scarlett echoed, smiling, also nodding, obviously having no clue what we were talking about. "I totally agree."

Katie rolled her eyes to me, out of sight of Scarlett. I held back a conspiratorial grin and knew that she and I had suddenly become friends. Katie had this way of conversing as though she was the teacher and you were the student. When you landed on a correct answer, there was no better feeling in the world. I was so proud of myself.

First day at a new school and, having left the old Brielle behind—the public school one, the nerdy one, the shy one, the invisible-to-boys one—I'd thrust myself right into a promising new social circle. The only question was how long I could make it last.

Despite my struggles to master it, I stuck with field hockey for all of freshman year and joined up again sophomore year. It was one of the few sports where no cuts were made, and being on the team meant I stayed close to Katie, and staying close to Katie meant I ate lunch with her and Scarlett. Which meant I hung out with them after school. And on weekends. And at parties. Which meant I was *cool*. I was *popular*. And yes, I did enjoy those benefits. I'd be crazy to claim otherwise. But the more important truth is much simpler: I liked Katie. She was smart. And funny. And, yes, beautiful. And Scarlett was fun too. A little dim, sure. But fun. They both so effortlessly saw themselves as worthy and desirable. It made me believe I could feel the same way about myself.

From Katie and Scarlett I learned what kind of shoes to wear and how to rip off the top band of your jeans so they clung to your hips a full two inches below where your shirt ended. I learned how that shirt should either be a pastel-colored polo or a pastel-colored spaghetti-strap tank, even in winter when you should shed all your warm layers whenever possible—walking around the mall, for instance. Or waiting in the backseat of a car while someone ran into the store to try their fake ID and you were perfectly situated so the driver could peek down your shirt from the rearview mirror. Or in the back of a movie theater so some boy could more easily feel you up, even though afterward you'd never admit to being felt up in a movie theater, let alone purposefully wearing a shirt that facilitated it.

None of this seemed like anything I wanted to do. But there was an overwhelming feeling that I *should* want to do it all . . . and more. Popular girls were supposed to be tilting and leaning and covering and uncovering their bodies in all sorts of cunning ways I did not yet understand. I remained convinced that my mastery of such moves lurked just around some unseen corner.

The night of the accident, coincidentally, was the same night that the delicate thread binding me to the sphere of the worthy and desirable first started to fray. Coach Tanner put us through an excruciating practice. We'd just lost our final regular-season game to Summit High, and with playoffs on the horizon, she aimed to make sure we were ready for battle. After what seemed liked hours of dribbling, wind sprints, and loose-ball drills, we assembled for a standard pass-and-shoot exercise. Coach T. stood in front of the goal and called me out of line.

It wasn't purposeful. She didn't intend to put any pressure on me. She needed a player, saw my face, and called me out. Simple as that. Normally, I'd have been off in my safe haven with the JV squad and she'd have summoned one of the starters to model a drill—Meghan Ngyuen, junior captain and our best forward, was a frequent choice—but that day the JV and varsity squads practiced together. That day, she called me.

No big deal, I told myself while stepping out of line, still winded from the last round of sprints. *I got this.*

"Watch," Coach T. said. "We missed eight one-timers last week. *Eight.*"

She passed me the ball.

I missed it.

It hopped over my stick and squirted through the line of players behind me. Nobody chased after it for me. I squeezed between two girls who didn't exactly jump at the chance to let me by, retrieved the ball, and ran back into place.

Whatever, I thought. *Anybody can flub one pass. God, Bri, please, just relax.*

Coach T. backed up outside of the striking circle. "Hit me where I was just standing."

She ran toward the goal. My hands shook with panic. I swung short, and the stick kicked up a splattering of dirt and grass, and quickly I swung again and this time hit the ball so hard and cleanly that it sailed clear past Coach T.

Behind me: anger. My teammates didn't even mock or ridicule me. It was too late in the day, and everyone was much too exhausted for that. They wanted only to complete whatever tasks Coach T. wanted us to complete and then get home, because there was dinner to eat and papers to write and tests to study for and maybe six hours of sleep to grab before tomorrow morning, when it would all start again. And I was failing. Pathetically, tragically, pitifully failing. I heard the frustrated sighs. I sensed impatient shiftings of weight from one leg to the other.

Coach T. chased down the ball and knocked it back to me, harder this time. And again I missed it. And again I chased after it, having to hurry between two peeved teammates. I dribbled the ball clumsily back to my spot beside the goal, almost slipping in the wet grass before catching myself at the last moment.

I stood with the ball, awaiting further instruction. Coach T. bit her lower lip and glared at all of us. *Oh no*, I thought. *Please scapegoat me. Scream at me. Call me names. Shame me back into line and summon someone else. Please, please, please*, I thought. *Punish me. Only me.*

Coach T. spit and wiped her mouth and then, in a voice that was at once quiet and forceful, said, "On the line."

One or two girls groaned.

"On the line!"

We ran sprint after sprint, even as the sun went down and rain started to fall and the temperature dropped so low you could see your own breath. We ran until we were just short of collapsing, and then we ran some more. It was not lost on anyone that this was entirely my fault.

Practice went so late that nobody bothered to shower. With sticky hair and muddy knees, I hopped into Meghan Ngyuen's Jetta—the Jetta her parents had bought her for her seventeenth birthday and that she'd named, because of some inside joke I was never privy to, Chunky Tuna—and we pulled away, speeding home through a light drizzle so that Meghan could study for an upcoming AP European history test.

The trip took us from school to Green Valley Road in Rosewood through dark and forested streets. We didn't talk. It wasn't like we were very close friends, but we'd lived down the street from each other our whole lives, so on most nights we were at least friendly. Tonight she navigated the slick, winding streets without so much as looking at me. A Dave Matthews CD played quietly. I nodded my head like I was enjoying the song, in what I hoped was a subtle attempt at solidarity, but in truth, even though this music and all it suggested—carefree days, sunshine, flirting with boys, bonfires on the beach, green grass, bare legs—was almost a prerequisite for admission to Marymount, I couldn't help but find it frivolous.

The rain fell harder. As we sailed down the hill into the dark, quiet streets of Rosewood, a large figure materialized from under a street lamp for the briefest moment—too brief for Meghan to brake in time. Too brief for her to do anything but pipe out a terrified yelp and yank on the wheel as the figure—a man—collided with the hood, smashed into the windshield, and flipped over the roof, out of view.

The car was tossed across the slippery street, wheeling around what felt like a million times, then jumping the curb and skidding across a muddy, overgrown yard, slamming into the front stoop of a house and stopping, finally, thankfully, just before its front door.

This all became clear to me later, of course. At the time all I processed was the man, the whooshing of the sailing car, the quick crack of my skull against the window, and the hollow humming in my head that followed.

When it was over, Meghan was breathing heavily, looking at me, eyes wide and stunned. I wiped a trickle of blood inching down my temple and felt an odd calm. Adrenaline must have been surging through me, obscuring the pain I would later feel, but I wasn't panicked. I stepped out of the car and felt like I was in a dream. I eyed the obliterated stoop—which I would later learn was Cullen's stoop—and the ruined yard . . . Cullen's yard. And the man lying in the road? Cullen Hickson himself. He'd propped himself up on an elbow, legs crossed, like he was mocking the pose of a sweater model. His face was scraped and bloody, his jeans shredded, also bloody. One of his shoes was missing, and he was clutching his left wrist. He was in pain, anyone could see that, yet he looked somehow amused. He wasn't smiling, exactly, but he looked . . . contented. And not at all surprised. As though he'd been waiting for this moment his whole life.

Ray

AT SCHOOL, my locker was next to Nick O'Dwyer's—a stocky guy from the Ironbound section of Newark with a cauliflowered ear and a gold crucifix around his neck. One day during the second week of school—before Cullen and before the stolen-car business—Nick and a bunch of other guys were crowded around his locker before class.

As I approached, I thought about asking them to move, but at the last moment I chickened out and tried to squeeze through without so much as a whisper. I thought maybe they'd seen me coming and would clear a path. Instead, I ended up squirming between them, my face rubbing painfully against a canvas backpack as I tried to push through to freedom without disturbing anyone, worming my way forward, burrowing my head in my open locker to retrieve my books.

"Anyway," one of the guys was saying, "I'll catch you later."

"Where you headed?"

"Downstairs. Bible class with the boy fondler."

"Yo, Father Joe's my boy." Nick slammed his locker shut and checked the lock.

"I'm just messin' around."

"Whatever," Nick said. "Don't talk shit about him like that."

The group had started to disperse, so I lifted my head from the darkness of my locker.

"I like that class," I said.

I don't know why I said it. They were big guys who all knew each other from football—it's not like I thought we were all going to be friends. I wasn't even expecting a response. It was just a reflex. Early days at a new school— what was the harm in trying to engage with my fellow freshmen?

"Huh?" Nick said.

They were all looking at me. They had been seconds away from walking away to class without even noticing I was there, but now they were looking at me, waiting for a response. And I got the distinct impression that whatever response I gave would be the wrong one.

"Father Joe," I said. "I was just saying, I like that class too."

Nick gave a look to the other guys, who held back laughter. I turned to grab a history book. The locker door smacked into the side of my head.

"Oh shit!" Nick cried out. "My bad." He turned to his friends and grinned. "I tripped."

So that was the first time. There would be many more. Nick was very big—he had huge shoulders and rough hands and looked like he could grow a beard at a moment's notice. I weighed ninety-nine pounds, my voice sounded precisely the same as it always had, and my body featured very little hair in any of the places a freshman boy is supposed to have grown hair. These essential truths, as far as I could tell, necessitated that Nick kick my ass or otherwise humiliate me whenever I failed to escape his sights. Except not in any ordinary way. At an all-boys high school, kids like Nick O'Dwyer don't have to worry about what girls will think of the way they torment kids like me. So when I changed before gym, he'd grab my nipples until I screamed in pain and fell to the floor with everyone watching. He'd grab me by the back of my hair while I was pulling up my shorts and make me stand there while he slapped his enormous hand across my bare ass so violently I could hardly sit down for the whole rest of the day. Sometimes he'd sneak up on me in the hallway and smack me in the balls or just grab them really hard and squeeze. Maybe stuff like that happens at normal high schools too; I wouldn't know. It didn't happen in seventh or eighth grades, though, when I was still in public school. In any case, it was a shitty introduction to St. John's, and it resulted in a lot of strategic maneuvering through the halls on my part. I forced myself to be either very late or very early for every class so that I could arrive at my locker before Nick showed up to retrieve some forgotten book and administer his daily shot of abuse. I started wearing gym shorts under my khakis so I could change more quickly in the locker room, but once Nick caught on to this, it only gave him more reason to come after me.

That's when he started what he called his "warm-ups" for gym, which meant using me as a punching bag before class. With dozens of hot, purple bruises all over my arms, I resorted to changing clothes in a stall of the second-floor bathroom so I didn't have to show up in the gym locker room at all.

The funny thing was that even though I hated every second I spent in his company, for a while Nick was pretty much the only guy at school with whom I interacted. Everyone else ignored me. And so, finding myself without any friends at all, I was left with a lot of alone time. Time to aimlessly roam the halls. Time to watch one New Jersey town after another flick by on the bus back and forth from school. Time to hang around in my bedroom in the afternoons rather than meet up with the other kids in my grade who were out in the world doing things I could only imagine—creating mischief, drinking beer, going to parties, talking to girls, touching girls, kissing girls. And so in those halls, and on that bus, and in that room, all I did was think. I thought about myself. And the world. And the fact that I, like every other person in the world, was alone. And would someday die.

I thought about God too—the idea that some unseen Thing was watching me, was interested in me, and was reserving a place for me in a magical world where I would go when I died and disappeared from *this* world. And for the first time in my life, I realized I'd never actually been given a single satisfying reason to believe in all this.

In response to these developments, I quickly swore off any attempts at normalcy. I wasn't going to sit around and wait for the day when my dick would grow to a respectable size and my shoulders would fill out and my Adam's apple would finally surface (*From where?* I wondered. *Where in my xylophone neck was a thing like that hiding?*). I wouldn't seek out things that weren't meant to be mine—things that, probably because I couldn't have them, I decided were beneath me: Friends. Popularity. Girls. Sports. Sex.

I wanted more. If God was really out there, there had to be a way to find Him. So I started searching.

I read St. Augustine's *Confessions.* Augustine says, "If the things of this world delight you, praise God for them but turn your love away from them and give it to their Maker." So I tossed away my stereo and untacked the posters of Derek Jeter and assorted supermodels from my bedroom wall. I unplugged my thirteen-inch television and PlayStation 2 and left them on the curb, ripped up the carpet in the corner where I used to waste countless hours on *Madden* and *Gran Turismo,* and laid down a straw mat for meditating. Beyond these few possessions, it wasn't all that hard to rid myself of "the things of this world" because I only felt vaguely con-nected to them to begin with. Which was probably a big part of the problem in the first place: If I were more interested in what other kids were interested in—Britney Spears and Eminem and *TRL* and hemp necklaces and cell phones and whatever else—maybe none of this would have ever happened. But even when I listened to that music or watched those shows, whatever sensation I was supposed to feel never arrived. They seemed to be speaking a language I didn't understand and had no interest in learning. Like I was missing the part of my brain that made me a real teenager. Mom said once that until me, she'd never known a kid who didn't like candy. And as for cell phones, well . . . who was I going to call?

I started reading this book, *Zen Mind, Beginner's Mind.* Every day after school, I tried and failed over and over to balance on my head, to keep my back tree-trunk straight during hour-long attempts at meditation. When I finished with *Zen Mind*, I moved on to the Bible. Augustine says, "We are too weak to discover the truth by reason alone, and for this reason you need the authority of sacred books." So I read for myself all those Sunday school tales that I'd never really paid attention to the first time around, and I found that God in the Bible was loud and certain. Some agreed with his words and some disagreed, but I couldn't stand how everyone *heard* the words. I turned to Buddhist texts and found the same problem. God was this and God was that, but God was, in all of these books, *around.* I couldn't find a word about the silence I encountered every time I propped up on my mat and listened for Him.

I moved from Augustine to Thomas Aquinas. Even though I could hardly understand what Aquinas was saying—I usually read one paragraph six or seven times before I could make out even a glimpse of a clear idea—I still liked reading it. Sometimes I just liked to hold the book in my hands. It made me feel like whatever I was doing mattered. Like I wasn't crazy and I wasn't a loser, because someone else had once done what I was doing.

Still, Aquinas's answers, when I could make them out, didn't help all that much. "As fire," Aquinas said, "which is the maximum of heat, is the cause of all hot things . . . there must also be something which is to all beings the cause of their being, goodness, and every other perfection; and this we call God." *Must*, he says. Yeah, okay. *Must*.

But where?

I'd always been a reliable student, mostly out of a willingness to do exactly what I was told rather than because of any profound, earth-shattering intellect, but when I started listening for God, I pretty much stopped doing my schoolwork altogether. So it wasn't all that surprising to me when an early progress report showed four Ds and two Fs. It certainly came as a shock to Dad, though. He did that thing he did when he was upset, pressing his lips together and avoiding eye contact, leaving you there to stew in the silence.

We were sitting at the kitchen table, Dad fiddling with the report card in his hands. When I couldn't take the silence anymore, I asked him why I couldn't study what I *wanted* to study rather than what some group of people who didn't even know me and who would never meet me had decided I *should* study.

"What do you want to study?" Dad said.

"God," I told him.

He put the report card on the table, lining up its edges with the table's corner. I suddenly felt like I'd said too much. I didn't want to be there anymore, and I didn't want to discuss all the things I was thinking about with him.

"Okay," he said. "Explain why searching for God means four Ds and two Fs."

I shrugged my shoulders and limped my head to show that I didn't feel like talking anymore. I was ready to retreat to my room, where I could feel like the only person in the world.

"What have you found in your search?" he asked.

"Nothing."

"You don't believe in God?"

"I don't know."

"Doubt is good, Ray."

"Yeah," I said. "I know."

He flipped the progress report between his fingers. "God is everywhere. It's hard to know that, but it's true. He's in school too. He's in homework, in tests, quizzes, and essays. Working at life is searching for God."

His eyes locked on mine. Dad was a psychiatrist, and sometimes he'd look at me the way I imagined he looked at his clients—like he was gazing down a well after tossing a coin, hoping for a miraculous splash of light when the penny hit water down in the darkness.

"You understand?"

I nodded.

"It takes time," he said.

"Okay."

"If looking for God is that important to you, you could start coming to church with me again."

"Okay."

"Would you like to do that?"

"Sure," I said.

"You don't have to."

"I want to," I said. I did want to, but somehow the words weren't coming out right. I couldn't make them sound sincere. "I'll go with you."

"In the meantime, we have work to do. And this"—he flapped the progress report in front of me—"this won't do."

He rose and stepped toward the door, dropping the report on the table as he passed. He stopped at the threshold, pressing his palms against either side of the doorway. I could tell that he was waiting for me to say something. He gave me the look parents give you when they want you to know that if you have anything to ask them—anything at all—now's the time to do it. But it's always at those moments when you can't think of a single question, isn't it? You know they're in there somewhere—a whole list of them that you've studied over and over, waiting for the time when you can finally start firing away. But then the moment comes and you forget your lines, and all you can do is say something pointless, something that barely even means anything at all. Something like "Sorry, Dad," which is what I said as he stood there leaning against the wall, before he finally tapped his knuckles twice against the doorway's paneling and disappeared.

The next day during gym class, Nick shoved me down a hill. We were running laps around the soccer field, which was bordered by steeply sloping woods on one side. I was struggling—on lap six of eight, drenched in sweat, heaving breaths, barely able to keep my arms up at my sides. Coach Fritz was at the far end of the field by the bleachers, facing the opposite direction from us, one hand on his hip and the other twirling a whistle around his finger. Last year, if you had been standing at the top of those bleachers at the right time of day, facing New York, the towers might have appeared as hazy forms above trees. But not anymore.

It happened quickly. I heard a sound behind me like a stampede of elephants. Then, in what seemed like a single motion, my shorts were tugged down to my ankles, and before I even had time to trip over them, something—fist? foot? head?—speared me in the back. I plunged down the muddy hill to my left, pantsless, breathless, grasping at roots and branches until I smacked into the brambles of a thorn-bush. The thorns stuck me all over. I heard a high-pitched cawing of laughter from above while I thrashed out of the thorns, snared pieces of skin stretching and then breaking and bleeding as I pulled away. I hoped nobody would come down to help me and then, when nobody came, wished someone had and hated myself for feeling like that.

From far off, Coach Fritz's whistle piped out a single, meaningless note.

I pulled up my shorts. Eyed the hill. I'd fallen a long way in a short amount of time. In the other direction, thirty yards down the hill, a car pulled into the school's parking lot.

I don't know why in the world I thought that would be a good time to meditate, but I wasn't about to climb up the stupid hill and subject myself to another thirty minutes of humiliation, and I couldn't very well go roam the halls when I was supposed to be in class. So I situated myself, legs crossed, beneath a mossy, rotting oak tree stump. I tried to wipe the blood and mud from my legs, but all I did was mix the two together into a dark-colored, slippery mess. Each little wound felt like someone was holding a lit match to my skin.

I realized it probably didn't matter if I ever climbed back up the hill or not. If I had landed wrong and snapped my neck . . . if I'd hit my head just the right way . . . if I disappeared completely, would anyone even notice?

I closed my eyes and tried to detach myself from the world—from the cold and wetness and pain. And to my complete astonishment, this time, for the first time ever . . . it worked.

Suddenly, I wasn't where I was or who I was. I left my body behind, and the pain too. It felt like I'd peeled off some outer layer of myself that I didn't need anymore, like a molting snake. I saw water—clear, cold water through which some form of me was sinking. And there was a voice. A strange echo telling me to sink. To sink to the bottom and through the bottom and through the bottom of the bottom. The voice told me things. It said that if there was no God, then there was no joy or love or hope. That the world as it had been presented to me was a lie. That the only difference between life and death was pain. That life hurt—too much—and that death didn't hurt—not even a little. Death was the best way. The easiest path. I listened and sank into a bottomless darkness, but I wasn't scared. I loved the voice and knew who it was and, like in one of those dreams where the one big thing you've always wanted is suddenly yours and you wonder why you could never figure out how to get a grip on this thing that's all of a sudden so easy to latch on to in the dream, I promised myself that I'd hold on to the voice when I stopped sinking. It was mine now. He had spoken to me.

Then the voice went quiet and something ripped me through the water by the ankles. I screamed and gasped for air, losing my hold on the voice, and I came back into the real world.

It was dark. Not night, just darker than it had been before I'd tumbled down the hill. And it was raining. I was cold.

There was a voice.

"Yo."

I blinked raindrops from my eyes and squinted through the darkness at a person. A man. No, a boy. A student. I clicked off key details: shirt, tie, official St. John of the Cross navy blue blazer, mud on the cuffs of his khakis. He must have seen me through the trees and walked up from the parking lot.

"You okay?" he asked. He looked at me the way parents look at a baby who's trying to tell them something without words.

I nodded. The rain fell hard, and I saw that I was resting in a puddle of mud. He gave me his hand and pulled me up.

"Got a name?"

"Ray," I said.

He wiped rain from above his eyes and grinned at me.

"Freshman?"

Again I nodded.

"I'm Cullen."

"Cullen Hickson," I said.

"Heard of me?" He smiled a little, proud of this fact.

I pointed to the cast on his arm. "My sister was in the car."

His eyes twitched in recognition.

"She said you jumped in front of the car."

"She said that?"

"Yeah."

"Why would anyone jump in front of a moving car?"

"Beats me," I said. "Maybe you thought it'd be fun."

I blinked rain from my eyes. Cullen didn't say anything for a while. His eyes passed over the cuts on my arms and legs, and then he glanced up the hill toward the soccer field.

He looked like he was about to say one thing, but then thought better of it and said something else.

"Better hit those showers, Ray O'Dell." He glanced at his watch. "Late bell in three minutes."

He patted me once on the shoulder and then took off, leaping downhill through the woods toward the lot, kicking up mud with his big boots as he went.

Cullen

A STUNTMAN'S HANDBOOK, available for loan at the Rosewood Public Library, was written by Jimmy Marvel, a man who proclaims himself to be the "Godfather of Hollywood Stuntmen." Chapter 12, titled "How to Get Hit by a Car," is brief and to the point. The whole of it takes up one and a half pages and amounts to four principles: (1) Ensure the car is going less than twenty-five miles per hour. (2) Jump in the air at the moment of collision. (3) Aim first for the hood, then the windshield. (4) At all costs, and in any way possible, protect your head.

I'd trailed the girls home often enough to know that, in order to make the turn at the corner, Meghan slowed the car to between twenty-three and twenty-eight miles per hour in front of my house. All that was left after that was to pick the day. There was no practicing for a thing like this. I just had to leap and hope for the best.

Jimmy also uses that brief section to insist that his readers not romanticize the life of a stuntman. The best guarantee of safety, he implores, is to not be so shortsighted as to get struck by a moving car in the first place. Plenty of people, after all, lead long, satisfactory lives without ever being hit by a car or jumping off a building or being lit on fire. It takes a special sort of devotee to chaos and disorder to *want* to perform such feats. The Godfather also predicts at least three broken bones on the first crash attempt. I suffered a broken wrist and, though the leather jacket safeguarded my arms and upper body, some seriously excruciating road rash across my legs and face.

So, by the Godfather's standards, I was already ahead of the curve.

Brielle

AN AMBULANCE took me to the hospital as a precaution. A rainstorm was gushing between my ears, while around me sat my mother, father, and Cullen, his broken wrist wrapped in a splint. The scene after the accident was chaos: the porch, my parents, Meghan's parents, every EMT in town, neighbors— all recounting what they'd seen. Cullen talked to me relentlessly for the first half of the ride. I don't remember much of what he said, but I remember the vibration of his voice hammering against the back of my eyelids. At one point I told him, "Please. Shut up. Please."

My mother held my hand, and every time I closed my eyes Dad would tug on my earlobe and whisper, "Stay awake, Beaker."

That was a Wednesday. I missed the next two days of school with a concussion.

In both fifth and sixth grades, I won the Perfect Attendance Award, even though in sixth grade I had to share it with Leigh Stambler and at the time was dismayed that a student couldn't have *more* than perfect attendance. But at least back then if I did miss school, they sent homework home for me. In high school, missing class meant that when I returned, I'd be scrambling to catch up to everyone else. I hated being behind. I wasn't a genius or anything. I knew I'd lose points here and there that a handful of smarter girls wouldn't lose. The one thing I could control, though, was to never, ever miss a single assignment.

When I wasn't vomiting during this unwelcome two-day hiatus, I spent a lot of time sinking into my bed, watching muted black-and-white movies (sound was too much, colors too much) and generally feeling as though my brain had been pureed. On Sunday morning, Mom crept into my room.

"Are you up, Bri?"

I was awake, but the morning was gray, and I had no plans to get out of bed anytime soon.

"There's someone here for you," she said.

I blinked at her, computing. She scratched at her hair, which was a beautiful deep red shade that neither Ray nor I had inherited.

"That boy from the ambulance. The one with the mustache." Mom put a finger to her upper lip and grinned.

I pulled myself into the folds of sheets, a pouting princess in exile. "My head hurts."

"He's brought flowers." Mom kept grinning. Apparently

she thought it all very sweet. Mom had mostly dismal days, but sometimes there were good ones—days when maybe her pills were working better or when her cloud lifted away for the briefest period of time. Most days, her depression brought the whole house down. It soaked into our clothes and made us all a little slower, a little dimmer. But some days she'd brighten, and on those days it was difficult not to want to please her. Not to do anything she asked of you if you thought it would keep her lit up in that rare way for just a little while longer. So, amid the abating drizzle that swished about in my head, I fixed myself up until I was presentable and ready to receive my visitor, with the intention of saying hello, thanking him for stopping by, and sending him on his way.

His intention, conversely, was that the two of us go for a walk. He said he thought I was one of those girls who liked Jane Austen, and that the girls in those books were always walking everywhere. I thought maybe he was making fun of me and assured him the living room would be fine. Under normal circumstances, I might have been nervous. Or afraid. Here was this boy, wearing brick-like black boots and ripped jeans—through which poked his bowling-ball knees— reeking of cigarettes and gasoline, pushing slimy black hair out of his eyes with the cast on his left hand and holding a bouquet of lilies in his right. It was like he'd stepped out of a movie and was either wholly ignorant or refused to acknowledge that he didn't fit in with everyone else—the way they dressed and spoke and behaved. Under normal circumstances, I might have been intimidated. I might have realized I'd forgotten to put on deodorant, or thought to wear long pants. As it was, I was lost beneath the hum of a fading concussion, working up a nice funk under my arms, and wearing a short khaki skirt on the first of November.

"Have you read *Pride and Prejudice?*" I asked him.

"It is a truth universally acknowledged," he quoted, "that a single man in possession of good fortune must be in want of a wife."

He laughed and rolled his eyes at himself, wiping sweat from his forehead. It was hard to tell if he was actually nervous or if it was simply part of the performance.

"You like it, though?" he said. "The book, I mean?"

"I do."

"See?" he said. "I knew it."

"How could you tell?"

"It's a good thing, though. It's better than, like, Harry Potter."

"I like Harry Potter too."

"Right," he said. "That's cool. Bad example. But anyway . . ." He offered the nervous laugh again and didn't finish his thought. I noticed the flowers in his hands were shaking in their plastic wrapping.

"Look," he said. "I live just on the other side of the woods. Walk me halfway. Then you come back and I'll keep going. Half a walk. That's all I'm asking."

I shut my eyes as a wave of pain rippled through my head. When I opened them, he was still looking at me.

"Did you read the whole book?" I asked. "Or just memorize the first line?"

He smirked and didn't say anything.

"Let me get a jacket," I told him.

We walked through the woods that stretched for a mile or so beside two puddled baseball fields where the summery bustle had recently fallen quiet to the onset of autumn. The air was crisp but not so cold that my absentminded choice of a skirt posed a problem, though the path was so wet that my ankles were soon dripping with mud.

Cullen talked and talked. He recounted the entire plot of *Pride and Prejudice*, maybe hoping to convince me that he had read it but more likely, I suspected, because he could sense I was in poor shape to sustain a conversation. I followed little as he recited the story, but his voice sounded fine—deep and rhythmic, like one of those stand-up jazz basses—and it soothed the lingering ache in my head.

We stopped at a short bridge that stretched over a stagnant, oil-puddled brook. Through the thinning trees we could spy the clearing of the town's dump and the white cinder-block patches of a utility garage. Farther on, behind the dump and beyond the garages where we couldn't see, was a police firing range, and without a word about it, Cullen stopped talking to hear the pop and reverb of policemen firing their pistols at imaginary bad guys.

"My brother used to play in this brook," I told him. "One day my dad marched back here and dragged him home. Now I see why. It's disgusting."

"You have a brother?"

"Ray."

"Ray O'Dell!" he said.

"You know him?"

"Our paths have crossed." He grinned slightly, then spit absently into the muck below. "Anyway, it's not so bad. Just rearranged."

I was curious, but the pain had lazied my brain substantially, so I didn't ask. Cullen continued as though I had asked. This was one thing I liked about him.

"There are only ninety-two natural elements in the world. Everything you see, touch, smell, you know, whatever, it's all made of these same ninety-two elements. And probably even fewer, because, really, how many things do you know that have, like, fucking polonium in them, right? Anyway, it's all the same stuff, but rearranged. So like a flower, or your hair, or this cigarette, or the mud on your sneakers—it's all the same ingredients. This brook, it's got nothing in it that's not part of the same ninety-two elements."

Above us, November's trees knocked in the wind—a dark, brambly web of branches. "You can make a lot of things with ninety-two things," I said.

Cullen watched the sludge below, knocking his cast against the railing.

"Does it hurt?" I asked.

"The wrist? Not anymore."

"What were you doing out there? In the middle of the road?"

"Me? I was one step from the curb. What were you two doing swerving toward me?"

"No . . ."

"Yeah! I don't know how that girl's so good at field hockey. You ask me, her hand-eye coordination is for shit."

I inspected his eyes. "I don't like missing school."

"I went out to get some air," he said. "Took one step off the curb. Bam."

"One step?"

"One little step."

"Okay then."

"Don't believe me?"

"I'm not sure yet," I said. "But I have another question."

"Okay."

"What about today?"

"What about it?"

"Why are you here, Cullen?"

He picked at a splinter in the bridge's railing. The wood was damp and growing blue-white fungi.

"You crashed into me. I felt indebted to you."

"Like you owe me?" I said. "For crashing into you?"

"Not owe. More like . . . I'm tied to you. You can't just walk away from something like that. The universe has linked us together."

"What about Meghan Ngyuen? You're not linked to her?"

"She's not as pretty as you."

"She's your own age. And she's beautiful!"

"Brielle," he said. "You're not listening to me. Forget about Meghan."

He had his eyes fixed on mine. I didn't look away. I wanted to, but I didn't. His forehead sloped over his eyes so that they sunk deep into his face, but way back there, hidden in the shadows of his brow, the eyes shone a serious, brilliant blue. Aside from my parents and grandparents, nobody had ever called me pretty. I was a sophomore in high school and had kissed four boys in my life. When Cullen's mouth, glinting with a moist sparkle, tilted toward mine, I wet my lips quickly, and we kissed.

In the distance, a flurry of police guns cracked and echoed.

Cullen

I SAW RAY in the library one morning before first bell. He was wearing headphones, bent over a computer screen. Funny-looking kid. Not ugly or anything like that, more like . . . he reminded me of the mouse from *An American Tail*. Fievel Mousekewitz. Brownish-blond—almost gray—hair, big eyes, and a short, upturned nose that, even if he weren't skinny as hell and even if his face weren't as smooth as a twelve-year-old girl's, would make him look forever like a little kid. He'd pulled his seat absurdly close to the computer screen, shoulders hunched like he didn't want anyone to see what he was doing. When I walked over, I saw why.

He was watching videos of people jumping out of the burning towers on September 11.

At first I didn't say anything. He didn't seem to know I was there, so I stood behind him and watched. Last year, from Mrs. Montagna's classroom on the third floor of the school, which stood on the side of a green hill in South Orange, I'd watched the towers come down. We saw it happen before we turned on the news. It only took one of us staring out the window at the right moment—easy enough considering there was nothing to do *but* stare out the damn window and wonder what was going on in that wild city out there across the river. Peter Grimaldi pointed out the smoke. Mrs. Montagna tried to keep her lesson going, but when she saw what we saw, she quit talking and stared with the rest of us. We put the news on the classroom TV. While they were showing the first tower blow smoke like some rusty tailpipe, the second plane glided into the other tower and exploded. Until that point, we'd been in a confused daze, trying to figure out what the hell was going on. But when the news showed a fireball blast out of the second tower, the room erupted into chaos. There was a lot of shouting and swearing. The kids who had cell phones pulled them out. Others raced to the pay phones. Mrs. Montagna couldn't stop them—some guys had parents in those buildings. I kept glancing out the window and back to the TV and back out the window.

And then they fell. First one tower. Then the next.

I remembered later that week and throughout the following months seeing a video on the news of a guy jumping out of one of the towers, but nothing like what Ray was watching in the library. He watched one clip after another of people falling. Dozens of jumpers. Maybe hundreds.

"Fuck," I said aloud.

Ray spun his chair around to see me. His eyes were red, but not from crying. He looked more tired than sad.

The video kept playing. People crawled out of the building like bees from a honeycomb. And they fell fast. It wasn't like they floated down like wayward leaves. The bodies looked heavy and dropped through the air like bullets.

I tried to talk again, but my throat was tight. Ray took off the headphones.

"The hell, man?" I choked out.

"What?"

"The hell you watching that for?"

He shrugged. "It happened."

He turned back to the screen. A guy had stuck his coat on the end of a mop and was waving it out the window. My stomach turned. He thought someone could help him. Why wouldn't he? How could he know? Eventually the heat or maybe the smoke was too much and he climbed out the window, trying to navigate down to the next floor. One hand slipped. He hung for a moment, and then the other hand went. This part had been edited into slow motion. This guy did, in fact, fall slowly. Arms and legs splayed out, he spun to the ground like a paper star.

"What's that supposed to mean?" I spun the chair around so he faced me. *"It happened."*

"So, I mean . . . don't you think you should see it?"

"Just because it happened? The hell's the matter with you?"

He rubbed a hand into his eye. The bell for first period

rang. "I don't know," he said, yanking his backpack free from under the chair. He had a trembling energy that he tried to hold in—something deep down inside that he was trying to hide.

I noticed a bruise creeping up from his collar—ugly and swollen, purple with spots of yellow. His hand went right to the welt when he saw me look at it.

"You a fighter?"

"Just some kid in my class."

"What happened?"

"Before gym. We fought once. Look, I gotta go."

He tried to step around me, but I didn't let him.

"You fight back?"

"Of course," he said. A terrible liar. His whole body shrunk under the weight of it. "Why wouldn't I fight back?"

"Who's the kid?"

"Nick O'Dwyer."

"Yeah? Big dude. You land anything?"

"Maybe, I don't know. It was all a blur, I guess."

"Guy's kind of a dick, huh?"

Ray looked at me, his eyes lit up. "Yeah," he said. "I hate him." He said this second part with strength in his voice— the first thing he'd said that I knew he felt certain about.

He tried to move past me again. This time I stepped aside, and he hurried into the hall.

Earlier that week, once Bri was well enough to return to school, I'd surprised her at the field after practice, but she blew me off. I wasn't so naïve to think that one innocent kiss in the woods between our houses would seal the deal, but I was still pretty stunned she'd tossed me aside so briskly. I'd watched her come out of the locker room with those same two blond girls from the dance. She glanced once in my direction but didn't acknowledge me, so I called out to her.

The three of them hesitated, eyeing me from across the lot. I waved. The two girls looked at Bri, waiting for her next move. One of them laughed.

"Need a ride home?" I ventured.

The one girl laughed again, and then the three of them walked off. Bri said nothing. Not even "No." Not even "Why would I want a ride from you?" Just . . . nothing.

But I wasn't pissed. In fact, after processing the initial blow, I was grateful. Because what I wanted, above all else, was to know Brielle. And this was a lucky little glimpse into an essential truth: Brielle O'Dell was embarrassed of me. Brielle O'Dell actually gave a damn what all those needle-nosed girls thought about her. She believed she was just like the rest of them.

But I knew better. I knew she had a strange, glimmering star exploding inside her. And I knew now how to get close enough to prove it to her.

I chased Ray into the hall.

"Hey!"

He glanced back once and scurried away.

"Ray O'Dell!" I jogged up next to him.

"I can't be late."

"What're you up to later?"

"I have to go to class."

"After school, I mean."

"Oh. I don't know. Nothing?"

All around us guys hurried to class, stomping, running, shouting, slamming lockers. I leaned in close to Ray.

"Want to steal a car?" I whispered.

Confused, but intrigued, he remained silent. I nodded at him. The second bell—the late bell—clanged out. Ray fidgeted, tugging on the straps of his backpack, tightening it.

"Senior parking lot. Mine's the Buick. Five minutes after last bell. Look at me."

He lifted his head.

"Do not be late."

Ray

I WAS STANDING on the front steps of the school watching a long line of yellow buses inch down the driveway, waiting for mine to arrive. I didn't think Cullen was serious, but even still I had no intention of following through on whatever after-school activities this weirdo loner senior had in mind for me, whether they involved stealing a car or not. While I was standing there, though, he found me. He waltzed by on his way to the parking lot, tossing a glance my way, tapping the watch on his wrist.

Amir Shadid was standing next to me, waiting for his own bus, and he gave me a funny look. "What was that about?"

I shook my head and didn't say anything. Amir was short—shorter than me, even—and he had to move to the top step to see over the bushes that bordered the stairs. He watched Cullen go.

"You know that guy?" he said.

"I guess. I don't know."

"What's the watch thing about?"

My bus pulled up, brakes grunting as it stopped. The wonky accordion door folded open, and guys shuffled up the stairs. I took a step to fall in line with them and said—again, not even seriously, not at all like this was even remotely a serious possibility—"He asked me if I wanted to steal a car with him today."

Amir was in a lot of the same classes as me—honor classes, advanced-level classes. We were the only two fresh-men in the sophomore math class. We saw each other a lot, but it wasn't like we were good friends or anything. It's easy to think if I'd made it onto the bus that day things wouldn't have turned out like they did. But sometimes I think they would have turned out even worse.

He grabbed my arm and pulled me away and said, "What?"

"Yeah," I said. "He was probably just fucking with me. I don't even get how, though. He's a weird guy."

I stepped again toward the bus, but again Amir pulled me away, this time more forcefully, saying, "Come here."

"I gotta get this bus," I told him.

"Forget the bus."

"Amir!" I twisted my arm free. "What the hell? I need to go."

"What if he was serious?"

"He wasn't."

"But what if he was? What exactly did he say?"

"I told you. He said, 'Do you want to steal a car?' And to meet him in the senior lot after school."

"Oh sick," Amir said. "That's so sick!"

The bus inched forward. The driver muttered, "You coming?"

Amir stared at me, bursting, so excited.

I turned away from him and faced the bus. I didn't step forward. But even as I watched the bus doors clap shut and the bus pull away without me, and even as I paced across the parking lot with Amir, who was ecstatic now, bopping his head to some beat I couldn't hear . . . even then I wasn't thinking about what a rush it would be to steal a car or, more accurately, to *try* to steal a car and, as I was sure would happen, definitely fail at it. What I was thinking was much simpler than all that, and it amounted to the obvious fact that hanging out with Amir Shadid and maybe Cullen Hickson too seemed infinitely more promising than yet again taking that stupid bus home, where I would sit in my room for hours on end trying, and failing, to figure out what it meant to be alive.

So five minutes later I was riding shotgun in Cullen's Buick that belonged to his grandmother and that was so big it seemed more like a boat than a car. We pulled into the empty parking lot of the Rosewood community pool, where the bottom of the deep end was covered with soggy autumn leaves and where, on the other side of the woods, a highway that could take you west to the mountains or east to New York City droned like a big machine.

We left the car at the pool parking lot, twelve blocks from the center of town. I followed Cullen and Amir through side streets and back alleys, the three of us pausing behind a dumpster in the alley next to Franny's Pizza. Amir looked like someone who carried a great treasure he'd been charged with protecting—like he'd somehow been waiting and preparing his whole life for this moment. Cullen eyed the road— Main Street on a Friday afternoon, busy with shoppers and strollers. I watched a team of twelve-year-old soccer players come out of Franny's, bouncing their way through the parking lot, all happy with dirt, sun, pizza, and Coca-Cola. I recognized the guy with them as one of my own former coaches. He waved a lazy, coach-like signal my way. Cullen watched him watching me. I was supposed to be sticking by Cullen's side and not getting spotted by anyone.

From his jacket, with a casted hand, Cullen pulled a portable electric drill and a pair of needle-nose pliers. He'd told us during the ride that the guy he worked for at the gas station showed him how you could drill a half inch into a keyhole to destroy the lock pins and then turn the ignition without needing a key. It made enough sense to me, but then I wasn't really thinking about whether or not it would work. I was thinking, now that this unreal feat had suddenly turned very real, about God. That I maybe could find Him by getting as far away from Him as possible. *Wickedness*

is what St. Augustine called it. Because maybe you didn't
know the boundaries of your world until you smashed clear
through them.

Cullen, a whole head taller than both Amir and me,
gazed down at us two freshmen, scratching the mustache
above his lip. He handed us black ski masks and gloves. I
lost my breath for a moment and tried to hide the shaking of
my hands while I pulled on the gloves.

"What about you?" I asked

"Didn't plan on three of us." Cullen pushed a flop of
greasy hair out of his eyes and looked at Amir, the late addition. Cullen had objected to him tagging along, but I'd said
I'd walk if Amir couldn't come—somehow Amir's enthusiasm
fueled my own, his confidence shrank my doubt. I knew I
wouldn't go through with this without him.

"Doesn't matter," Cullen said. "I don't need them."

He peered through the alley toward Main Street. "Okay?"
he said.

Amir nodded. I nodded. Cullen pointed to an old pow-
der blue Oldsmobile parked across the street, standing out
among the much newer SUVs and luxury sedans, every
other one adorned with a "God Bless America" or "Never
Forget 9/11" sticker.

I followed them through the alley, into downtown
Rosewood, dodging slow-rolling cars that were hunting for
parking spots, across to the south side of the street. Cullen
pulled a pinched-together coat hanger from the inside pocket
of his jacket, but just as he did Amir picked up a fist-sized

piece of loose asphalt from the gutter and, sprinting toward the car, letting out a wild, yelping war cry, hurled the rock right through the driver's side window.

The glass shattered. So loud.

Cullen screamed, "What the fuck?"

There was no car alarm, but everyone was looking at us.

Amir shouted, "Let's go!" and raced around to the passenger side.

Cullen lurched in through the broken window, unlocked the door, and dove into the car. The drill sang as he sunk it into the ignition hole. It felt like whole minutes passed—those long kinds of minutes like when you're watching the clock at the end of the school day. Cullen shoved the pliers into the ignition and, with a grimace, turned something in there that made the engine come alive.

I was still standing on the street behind Cullen. I couldn't move. Cullen screamed at me, "Get in the fucking car!" which finally I did, and I slammed the door, and Cullen gunned the thing, tearing off through the center of town, shouting at me, "Holy shit, Ray, what the hell was that? Who the fuck is this kid?"

Amir was smiling, yanking his seat belt on, having the time of his life. "Amir!" he shouted. "My name's Amir!"

I don't remember the first time I met him. It seemed like before we even said one word to each other, he was always just around. Like the natural tilt of the universe had rolled us into the same dusty, forgotten corner, and so it only made sense that eventually we'd end up friends. There was one time, though, in theology with Father Joe, when he made me laugh like crazy.

Father Joe was one of those great teachers you meet sometimes who speaks to you like you're a real person. Just about everyone could get a word in during his class—even I ventured to jump into the conversations every so often. He was always encouraging us to talk out our questions about faith and catechism and all that, and so one day Sal DelViccio asked Father Joe if masturbation was really a sin, and do priests masturbate, and, if it *was* a sin, and if priests *did* masturbate, did that mean priests were all on the road to Hell with the rest of us?

We waited to see what would happen next. Father Joe ran a palm across his brow, which was covered in freckles. "Well," he started, "think of it like this: Imagine God puts you on the earth with a million dollars. Each sin you commit costs a certain amount, and if you spend the whole million, you won't get into heaven. So, murder, that's a big one. That's probably the whole million. Stealing, let's say that's ten thousand. Lying, maybe a thousand. Yanking your own chain . . . in the grand scheme of things, probably be about a nickel."

We all laughed. Father Joe turned back to the board to continue with his lesson, and the class settled down. I, however, dug out my algebra II calculator and started doing the calculations. Next to me, Amir leaned over to see what I was up to. When I showed him the tally, he smiled like a little kid about to do something he knows he's not supposed to do and raised his hand.

I whispered at him, "Don't!"

Father Joe turned around, saw Amir's hand, and called on him. *No way*, I thought. *There's no way he says it.* Amir was a Saudi Arabian kid with a funny-looking bowl haircut who some kids called Toadstool, but who others had started calling Osama. It was such a stupid insult—not even the most basic attempt at being clever—but it was so easily accessible to everyone that it pretty much made it impossible for Amir to do or say anything without being subjected to immediate, crushing ridicule by anyone in earshot. So no way did I expect him to speak up right then.

In a way, I was right. Amir didn't say what I thought he was going to say. Nothing about the number on my calculator or what it signified.

What he said was: "Ray has something he wants to tell you."

I lost my breath. It felt like my heart had stopped and that if I were made to speak in that moment it would never start up again. The entire class had turned around and was gawking at Amir and me.

"No," I managed to say. "No I don't."

Father Joe's eyes found me. He looked at me gently, curiously—like he was trying to tell me that no matter what Amir wanted me to say, I could say it. Somehow Father Joe reacted to everything in that same way—nothing ever surprised him. It was a big part of why we liked him.

"What's up, Ray?"

Amir held back a grin, motioning for me to speak. I noticed for the first time that he had a pale scar cutting across his eyebrow.

"Well," I said. "I was just thinking that if, uh, masturbation costs a nickel, and assuming you never committed another sin . . . that means you could . . . masturbate . . . twenty million times before going to Hell."

Amir couldn't hold it in anymore. He burst out laughing. And I did too.

We dared to look at Father Joe.

"Something like that," he said.

Amir giggled. "That's pretty messed up, Father Joe."

"Yeah, well . . ." Father Joe shrugged. "Just make sure you keep count. Years go by . . . things like that can add up quicker than you think."

Amir and I laughed and laughed. I mean . . . it was really funny. And if we'd been different kids—if we were good at sports, or had girlfriends, or were maybe a little bit bigger, or just somehow different in a way we would never really be able to understand—no doubt the rest of the class would have been laughing with us. But instead, all that happened was Matty Gearhart, the kid who sat in front of us, who had long hair and dirty fingernails and was always penning tattoos on the underside of his wrists during class, mumbled— low enough so Father Joe couldn't hear, but loud enough for everyone else to hear—"Circle jerks cost extra, homos."

And, of course, that's when the rest of the class erupted in laughter.

It wouldn't be long before Amir was my favorite person I knew. But today he was the kid who'd just chucked a freaking rock through the window of a beat-up car that we'd stolen right in front of dozens of people.

We sped out of Rosewood, into South Orange and Maplewood, where the blocks stretched into long avenues that snaked through hilly woods. Patches of trees smeared by like a finger painting in Thanksgiving colors. I heard the whine of faraway sirens.

"You guys hear that?" I asked.

Cullen nodded.

"We need to get off the road, right?"

Again he nodded. But he didn't slow down. Did not pull over.

Amir bounced in his seat, still bopping his head to that beat, turning to look at me, his eyes more alive than I'd ever seen in anyone, and just then, mostly subconsciously, I started to bop my head too. I started to understand why he'd insisted on going through with this adventure.

Cullen navigated one curve, anticipating the next, never overcorrecting. He was really, really good. We screamed past a lumbering box truck. Swerved away from oncoming traffic. Fishtailed, recovered, straightened, sped on. I clutched the headrest of the seat in front of me, squeezing so hard my knuckles would be swollen and sore for a whole day afterward. Cullen checked the mirror. I flipped around to see, in the distance, the tumbling lights of a cop car. We wheeled around the next curve, and the lights disappeared briefly, then came back.

Cullen gunned the car up a short hill. At the crest, the wheels lifted off the pavement and then thumped back down. We sped downhill. Amir pointed. "There. Go there!"

Ahead, on the right, a turnoff into the woods. We sped toward it. Amir eyed Cullen.

"Ease up," Amir said.

"I got it."

"Dude!"

Cullen grinned. Instead of slowing down, he sped up. He didn't look at Amir—his eyes were steady, unblinking— but I knew this was for Amir. To one-up him for the rock through the window.

"Come on, man!" I shouted.

"Ease up!" Amir told him.

But he didn't ease up. We came at the turnoff at full speed.

"Oh shit, hold on!" Amir said.

At the last possible moment, Cullen cut the wheel. He almost made it, too. But the car skidded and screamed, and we just missed the turnoff, throwing up dirt and mud, spinning into the forest, Cullen wrestling the wheel, for the first time all day unable to control the car. The wheels swung us left and he cut the wheel right, and that's when there was that briefest hiccup of whirling, silent space, and time, and the next thing that changed was the sound. Glass cracking and steel exploding, the car bouncing like a pinball against trees. And then it was quiet again. And it smelled like metal and ash.

The door had collapsed into my arm, which didn't hurt yet, but it would when I finally had time to feel it.

"Go!" Cullen shouted. "Go, go, go!"

I climbed through the smashed window, stumbled briefly in the muck of leaves, then took off after Cullen and Amir, who were already sprinting through the trees, running for their lives.

Sirens sang behind us. A voice shouted at us through a megaphone—no recognizable words, just a threatening, angry noise. We ran. Didn't turn back. There was no telling how close they were, assuming they could even see us. At a time like that, you don't turn to look. If you're running, they're close enough; how close exactly is beside the point. So you keep running so fast and for so long that you think you might die from running.

But you don't die. From running or from anything else. You get away. You follow Cullen Hickson through the woods, splashing across brooks, startling deer, dodging trees, leaping roots. Follow Cullen because Cullen knows. When Cullen stops, you stop. When he's safe, you're safe.

We came to a Little League field and picnic area. Far off in the distance there was a gazebo. This was Eagle Rock Reservation. Couples walked hand in hand down a wood-chip trail. Families peeked in and out of the gazebo. People lounged in the grass reading books, soaking up the last of the October sun.

Cullen took off his jacket, and we did the same, along with our ski masks. We chucked them all in a dumpster at the far end of the parking lot near the restrooms, and Cullen said, "Walk. Down the trail. Slow but quick."

Three cops stepped out of the woods from where we'd come, fifty yards down the hill.

I started laughing. Couldn't help it. It was all so funny in a way I couldn't explain. Amir bumped his shoulder against mine. He was laughing too.

"Easy, guys," Cullen said.

Cullen cracked a grin and winked at me as we stepped into a restroom just as two police cruisers glided down the paved road to our left—a pair of fat sharks.

The bathroom smelled like mud and bleach. Cullen peeked out the door. I looked to Amir, who tried and failed to see out the door past Cullen. Amir turned back, pacing the floor, clutching one hand in the other, trying to stop them from shaking, finally looking at me. We started laughing again.

Cullen waved us over. He tapped his foot on the linoleum, like he was trying to find just the right rhythm of the moment, to get in perfect synch with the universe so this could unfold in our favor. He held the door ajar and pointed outside.

The cops were fifty yards down the hill. They lingered in the parking lot and spoke to a young couple pushing a stroller, then walked along the bottom of the hill, looking to the ball field. They stopped to question a guy reading the newspaper in a beach chair, and when they did, Cullen said, "Go."

We slipped out of the restroom and ran up the hill behind us, into the woods, climbing through mud and moss and dead trees to the top of the hill and then dropping down to a stream, sliding on our butts, kicking sticks and scrub out of our way. During all of this, I felt good. Full of fear, but a new kind of fear—not the kind that makes you hide. The kind that makes you breathe and shout and go. We swung a left at the stream, sloshing through it, and headed west where the sun was trying to shine through a gray haze.

We ran and ran and ran.

Brielle

I NEEDED A STUDY BREAK. I was in my room, practicing a speech I had to give in French class the next day—an assignment everyone else had completed while I was absent. Normally such short oral exams could not be made up even if you were sick, but Mme. Barret had made an exception after I pleaded with her for a half hour after school that I couldn't afford to lose even one point. I was pacing my bedroom, reciting the speech, and my mind drifted. I thought about college. I already had my list of favorites: Amherst, Cornell, Northwestern, Dartmouth, Stanford. I liked to picture our family cars adorned with a sticker from one of these schools: Dad's SUV pulling out of the driveway in the morning; Mom's sedan rolling through the center of town; all four of us stepping out of a car and walking into a busy restaurant together, everyone watching and noting the unmistakable mark of success on the back windshield. *Amherst, Cornell, Northwestern, Dartmouth, Stanford.*

I snapped out of this daydream and realized it was time for a break. From the big window at the top of the stairs, I saw a car pull up to our house and Ray step out. I didn't think much of it at first—couldn't have known he'd just come from some lunatic, illegal escapade. I figured he'd missed the bus for whatever reason and had gotten a ride home. But then something clicked—not just any car. Cullen's car.

I met Ray at the front door. His shirt was untucked, and his hair was a sweaty mess on his head. His khakis, tie, and blazer were covered in mud.

"Ray," I said. "You okay?"

He nodded, trying to move past me without further inquiry.

"You're a mess," I told him.

"It's fine." He marched up the stairs.

"What about your blazer? You can't wear it to school like that tomorrow."

"It's fine," he called from upstairs before shutting his bedroom door.

The Buick idled at the end of the driveway. I could only make out Cullen's silhouette, but I could see he was peering at the house. Then the car turned off, and he stepped out.

I raced into the living room and shuffled into a pair of slippers. Mom sat under a blanket on the couch watching some horrible entertainment news show. Dad was fixing himself an early dinner in the kitchen before leaving to see his Thursday-night clients. I scurried into the hall and out the front door, catching Cullen just as he was about to ring the doorbell.

What happened next was something I did not plan. Something that, even as I was doing it, I wasn't sure I wanted to do. But I was in short sleeves, it was a cold night, and I didn't want to stand outside and defend myself or apologize or try to say all the things I wanted to say to him before my dad came rushing out the door chowing down on a grilled cheese sandwich, finding me once again with the boy with the broken wrist. As long as my grades were good and I checked off some random extracurriculars like field hockey, my life tended to evade serious inquiry from Dad, who was otherwise burdened with Mom's illness. There was no reason to offer him any clues that my world remained anything else than fully predictable. So before Cullen could even get a word in, I told him, "Go around back." And when he looked at me, confused, possibly angry, I said it again, and then I hurried back inside.

In my bedroom, I peeked through the slats in my blinds and saw Cullen standing in the backyard, our dog, Lincoln— who has five legs and no vocal cords—running laps around him. Cullen wiped hair out of his eyes and bent to scratch behind Lincoln's ear. I looked over my room and wished I could change everything about it: the bright yellow carpet; the pink-and-white flowered wallpaper; the bed with its wispy canopy, hung from four oak posts. Beneath the canopy, a society of stuffed animals was piled at the head of the bed. Pink bears, blue lions, orange monkeys—a great multicolored zoo. Everything as soft and clean as could be. A little girl's room.

I looked at myself in the mirror and thought about the girls at school. *I should change my clothes*, I thought. *I should paint my toenails and lose ten pounds. Dye my hair blond. Or maybe not. Maybe dye it blue and pierce my tongue. Shave my eyebrows. Cut my ear off. Light myself on fire.*

Oh God, I thought. *What is wrong with me?*

I opened the window. Cullen looked up, and I told him to climb.

He squinted at me. "Huh?"

"Climb up!" I told him.

The cast made for an awkward scramble, but he made his way onto the railing that encircled the deck and then onto the sloping roof below my window, which he scampered up, finally reaching for my hand at the window and diving in, tumbling upside down to the carpet with dripping, muddy boots that I caught in midair. He gazed at me from the ground while I unlaced the boots and balanced them outside on the roof, just below my window.

He stood. Took a breath. Looked around the room.

"I'm due for a remodeling," I said, talking too fast. "It's stupid."

"Your dog," he said.

"Lincoln. Five legs. No vocal cords. We rescued him from a freak show on the boardwalk down the shore. The guy—asshole—cut Lincoln's vocal cords when he was a

puppy so that he wouldn't bark and disturb the other animals. Two-headed monkeys and stuff like that. My dad
paid three hundred dollars to take him home. It was his
idea."

"Whose idea was it to go to the freak show?"

I tried to hold back a grin. "Mine."

Again he looked around the room.

"I'm sorry," I said.

"It's fine. You should see my room."

"I ignored you, I mean. I'm sorry."

"Why did you?"

Because I had no choice, I wanted to tell him. But before
the words made it out, I realized how limp they would
sound. How meaningless they'd be to him. But it was the
truth. Or at least it felt like the truth.

When I'd returned to school after the accident, everyone
had already known Cullen had ridden to the hospital with
me and that he'd come to my house with a dozen lilies. Who
knows how they knew? Maybe Mom—who actually managed to make it to the grocery store last week—had run into
someone and mentioned it. Moms had talked, and daughters
had talked, and then the whole school was talking. At lunch,
Katie and Scarlett slurped down yogurt and only yogurt, asking me to please tell them that I hadn't given Cullen Hickson
a blowjob in the woods behind my house.

"Who said that?" I slumped my shoulders, hoping to melt
into my chair. Suddenly the whole world was watching me.

"Bri," Katie said, almost like an apology, like she was sorry I didn't already know what was so plainly obvious to her. "*Everyone* is saying that."

Scarlett was nodding her head, her dripping spoon bobbing and poking at me. "Everyone."

"Whatever. It's not true."

"Doesn't matter," Scarlett said, and in one moment I wanted both to slap her and plead for help. Because she was right. It didn't matter. One month ago *everyone* was saying that Francine Garcia was having an affair with Mr. Foster, the youngest, most popular teacher on campus, because they'd seen her get into his car after school. Francine fought back against the rumors by insisting that Mr. Foster had just gotten engaged to her older cousin. But by then it was too late for even the most reasonable explanation to have any impact. Francine would forever be looked at as the girl who slept with her history teacher.

Again, I said, "Whatever."

"I can't believe he was in your house," Scarlett went on. "Does it, like, still stink in there?"

"What is wrong with that guy?" Katie shook her head sharply, like Cullen was actually inside it and she was trying to jiggle him out.

"I don't know," I told her.

And that, as much as it was a dismissal of my feelings for Cullen, was also the truth. I didn't know what was wrong with him. In fact, I suspected the opposite—that something was wrong with everyone else and something was irresistibly and astoundingly *right* about Cullen Hickson.

I'd tried to talk to Mom about it. She'd seemed unusually energized since the car accident—shocked out of her listlessness. It wasn't entirely unusual for her to be an engaged member of our family every so often. Last year, for instance, while Dad was away in New York every day and night providing grief counseling for victims, family members, and first responders, Mom stepped up big-time. She made dinners. She checked homework. She took me, on my sixteenth birthday, to get my driver's permit, and she let me drive home, talking the whole time about how she couldn't believe how grown up I was.

But it never lasted. Something would always beat back the brightness. Sometimes we knew what caused it—like when I was eleven, for instance, and she had a miscarriage with what would have been her third child, and she slipped into what seemed like a years-long, hopeless trance. But other times, we couldn't trace the cause, if there even was one. One day, suddenly, maybe she'd be a little less alive, a little less conversational. Maybe she'd ask someone else (i.e., *me*) to make dinner because she was too tired. And the next day, maybe she wouldn't get out of her bathrobe until just before sundown. And the day after that . . . she'd be somewhere very far away. She'd hardly talk or move or give any signs of being anything other than a zombie. And there was no telling how long it would be before we got her back, if we got her back at all.

Encouraged by her recent spark of vitality, however—the way she cared for me while I was hurt, her amusement at Cullen calling for me, and her curiosity about the walk we'd taken in the woods—one night I dared to seek some motherly advice. She was lounging on her bed watching television. Every small action—or non-action—was a clue into her state. She was on top of the covers, not under them. She wore jeans and a sweater, not pajamas. Her makeup looked nice. Her hair, recently washed and styled, glimmered red. All promising signs. And yet . . . the way the remote hung limply in her hand. The glazed eyes. How she hadn't looked at me when I entered the room or acknowledged me when I sat on the bed.

"What're you watching?" I asked.

She shook her head. "Just flipping. There's never anything on. I don't know why I bother."

"Hey, can I ask you a question?" Trying to keep it light. High energy.

"Of course."

"I'm thinking of quitting field hockey."

"Oh," she said. "How come, honey?"

Concern in her voice. Something close to nurturing. But no eye contact. No invitation to move closer.

It's so stupid, I thought. *It's so incredibly stupid that I feel this way.* This phenomenal urge to crawl across the bed, dig under the covers, and curl up in the warmth of her. *You're sixteen*, I told myself. *Get over it.*

But then, unable to stop myself, I told her about Katie.

How smart she was, and how Scarlett wasn't so bad once you got to know her. I told her about that awful practice, how I didn't really like *any* sports, let alone this one that I played so poorly.

"Nobody even comforted me," I said. "Not even, like, a pat on the back as I was walking off the field. Isn't that how sports are supposed to work? You support your teammates, right? If I'm being honest . . . I'm not even sure if Katie really likes me."

There was something in her eyes as she listened. How were you supposed to tell the difference between sympathy and fatigue? I thought about the car accident—a crisis. That's what had woken her up—that I'd needed her. Badly.

So I kept going.

"And this guy, Cullen. You remember him? With the mustache?"

She nodded, a stray piece of hair springing gently above her eyes.

"I like him, but he . . . scares me."

I watched her, waiting, hoping. The television light reflected on her face.

"I kissed him," I said.

Her hand went to the remote balanced on her thigh. She scratched at one of its buttons. She seemed to be slowly, subtly sinking into the bed, disappearing into its folds. As though the things I was saying to her were literal burdens, weighing her down, drowning her.

"Mom?"

She looked at me again.

"Do you have any thoughts about any of this?"

"Oh." She sat up in the bed. She inhaled deeply and summoned some last measure of strength to say, "You know what, honey? Whenever I think about you, I always admire how smart you are. And mature."

I waited. She did not elaborate. She sat there looking at me with pleading eyes, silently begging me to assure her that what she'd said was enough.

"Yeah," I said.

"I love you, sweetie. You know that?"

"Yeah," I said. "Okay, Mom."

So one week later, in my bedroom, when Cullen asked me why I'd been such a jerk to him after practice, I still had no answers for him. The right choice? The whole problem was that there *was* no right choice. That every potential path stretching out before me suddenly seemed definitively, unequivocally *not right*. I felt like I'd lost all bearings on what I was doing and why I was doing it.

So I lied.

"I'm not embarrassed of you," I told him.

"No?"

"No! It's . . . my parents." Lies.

"Your mom made you get out of bed with a concussion to meet me."

"I know." I shuffled across the carpet to the bed, pushing the canopy apart, not looking at him. "But . . . there's my dad."

Lies upon lies upon lies.

"I remember him," Cullen said. "From the ambulance."

"I just need to think about how to introduce the idea of you."

"You are embarrassed of me."

"No!" I gripped his wrist—a slim, bony wrist that contradicted how big the rest of him seemed—and pulled him onto the bed next to me. "No, it's not that at all. He's very . . . religious. Conservative. I'm not sure what he'll say or do or . . ."

I went silent, again not looking at him.

"Okay," he said.

"Okay what?"

"Okay, so we don't tell them. None of their business anyway, right?"

"Really?" I asked. "You don't mind?"

"It might get tougher to climb that roof when it's frozen over," he said. "But what the hell?"

His finger moved over the inside of my arm, and I could see in his eyes that he meant to kiss me. My stomach flipped over itself, and our lips met.

He shoved the mound of stuffed animals onto the floor and sunk his arm under my back, and I held him back with a hand to his chest. "But like not even my friends. Nobody can know."

"Okay."

We kissed again. Rain started falling outside. I moved my fingers under his shirt. His skin was hot all over.

His hand went, rather clumsily, to my breast.

"And we're not going to have sex," I said.

"Ever?"

"Yet."

The rain came through the open window. I closed my eyes and pushed myself against him.

Ray

DAD WAS RIGHT—it was pretty pointless to claim I was searching for God if I wasn't even going to church. Which is how I found myself one Sunday morning wearing an itchy sweater that smelled like my dank closet, sitting next to Dad in the front row, watching Father Francis hold up a thin, circular piece of bread and quote Jesus: "Take this, all of you, and eat of it, for this is my body, which will be given up for you."

The church was dark from the wine-colored light coming through its stained glass windows, and the place smelled like old people—heavy perfume with a touch of mothballs. We rose, we sat, we rose again. People sang—not me, but Dad did, barely. He tucked his chin to his chest, mumbling words from the hymnal in a voice only he could hear. At Communion, we shuffled in line up to the altar, where, placing the piece of bread in my hand, Father Francis said, "The body of Christ," and I responded, "Amen," and walked back to my seat, where, while chewing down the chalky thing, I closed my eyes, trying to feel something, waiting for Him to speak to me.

After mass, people mingled on the steps of the church. Dad seemed to know everyone—priests, parents of the altar boys, the guys who bring the donation baskets around, men and women of all ages whom I'd never seen before or, if I had, didn't remember. I stood beside him, shoulders hunched, head down, every so often yanking my hands out of my pockets to shake someone's hand. These people adored my dad. Couldn't get enough of him.

When Bri and I were little, all four of us would go to church together, always stopping at Dunkin' Donuts on the way home, where we'd get one large box of Munchkins, a coffee each for Mom and Dad, and chocolate milks for Bri and me. These days Dad went to church on his own. He loved God. Always said so. He gave away a third of his salary to all sorts of local and national charities, which explained why he drove a used, boring car instead of a new, swanky one and why we only took family vacations to my grandparents' house down the shore instead of to any of the many exotic places people we knew would go. He'd entered the seminary briefly after earning a degree in theology from Rutgers, but then he met my mother, knew she was the only person he loved more than God, and abandoned his holy,

celibate path. Mom was different then. Or so I assumed, anyway. She must have been, right? To have diverted Dad's path
so permanently like that?

Earlier that morning, while I was in the shower trying to
wake myself up, I'd committed myself to asking Dad about
God after mass. Had God spoken to him? If so, what did
He say? What did it sound like? Feel like? On what grounds
did he enter that seminary, planning to devote his life to an
invisible man in the sky? What made him so sure?

But by the time we were driving home, I realized it
wouldn't do me any good to ask. Because whatever church
did for all these people, it didn't do for me. Not even close.
Standing there with a bunch of blank-faced worshippers
reciting lines like "I confess one baptism for the forgiveness of sins, and I look forward to the resurrection of the
dead and the life of the world to come . . ." What was the
point of that? They all droned along, on autopilot. *These people*, I thought, *have absolutely no clue what they're saying!*
"Resurrection of the dead"? They're not even registering this
stuff as words—just a pattern of sounds they've memorized,
having delivered it once a week, year after year, decade after
decade. So stupid. So pointless. I suddenly couldn't imagine
a place where you were *less* likely to encounter God than in
church. And so I couldn't imagine someone less qualified to
ask about Him than Dad.

We were stopped at a traffic light. Dad motioned a half
block ahead to the Dunkin' Donuts.

"Hey," he said. "Should we stop?"

"I'm okay," I said.

"You sure? Bring back Munchkins for Mom and Bri?"

"If you want," I said. "I'm not hungry."

Dad stared ahead, saying nothing, chewing on his bottom lip. I had other things on my mind. The idea, I was starting to realize, was to divorce yourself from the known world. Because God wasn't visible in this realm. If Heaven was real, then the only way to really meet God . . . was to die. And if Heaven *wasn't* real, then the same premise held true: The only way to know for sure was death.

And why not, I thought. Why not take the quickest route, if the alternative was staying here, with all these people and their dreadful, pointless recitations and their cold, cavernous, Godless churches? What was the point of even being alive?

I shook off this thought as quickly as it had come in. Like inching too close to the edge of a cliff and then, when the wind blows strong and you feel your stomach tumble upside down, stepping back to where it's safe.

The car came to a stop, and Dad opened his door. He had, in fact, stopped at Dunkin' Donuts. I sat in the idling car and watched him hurry inside to the counter, where he pointed out his Munchkin choices, even though nobody at home was going to eat them.

I remembered the feeling of being in that stolen car.

I needed to feel that again.

I could sit in the woods and close my eyes all I wanted, but that was only going to take me so far. I needed the type of pure, undiluted enlightenment that could not be argued with. It wasn't an undertaking I could orchestrate on my own. I needed a guide. Someone to help me rip a blazing hole in the margins of my visible world and then, when I hesitated at the sight of whatever awaited me on the other side, to shove me through.

Cullen

A WEEK AFTER we'd lifted the Oldsmobile, Ray rode his bike to the gas station where I worked.

"I want to do it again," he announced.

I was pumping twenty dollars of regular into a Ford Explorer. Ray straddled his bike, wiping a line of sweat from his brow. It was chilly out, but he'd ridden a long way to see me.

"Yeah?"

"Yeah."

"Why?"

He looked away and shrugged—the kid was always shrugging. I flipped the tank door shut, replaced the nozzle, and collected the cash from the driver. Ray followed me inside the office, out of the cold.

I flicked on a space heater, sat at my boss's desk, and kicked my feet up. Ray stood near the door.

"Why not?" he said. "You scared?"

I laughed at his attempt to be hard and then felt bad about it. Ray wasn't a kid you could laugh at. Too many people had laughed at him in not entirely friendly ways before, so when you laughed at him he'd tug his shoulders in and study the floor, rubbing his eyebrows.

"Have you ever meditated?" he said.

"Huh?"

"When we were running from those cops—it was just like meditating. Only better. A thousand times better. I wasn't thinking about anything. I wasn't in control of my body. And I felt something. I found something."

I didn't know the first thing about meditating, but I knew what he meant. The car thing was fun as hell, and I'd been dreaming of doing it for a while now—since I'd become something of an expert at breaking and entering after quitting all organized sports my freshman year of high school. Sports were something my parents—not just Dad, but Mom too—had pushed me into because (1) I was bigger than most kids my age, which meant sports were something I might be good at, and (2) sports were supposed to keep easily distracted kids like me out of trouble. Whether or not it was true that I would have been good, I'll never know—I never bothered to try hard enough to test my skills against all the hard-nosed asshole athletes of my grade—but my parents got the second part right anyway, about staying out of trouble. Because as soon as Mom and Dad were gone and I was left with only Nana, I walked away from all that order and control and started walking into people's empty houses, uninvited.

After school I'd check in with Nana—put together a snack of cheese and crackers for her and watch an hour of daytime court shows. Nana couldn't get enough of *Judge Judy*. When she'd eventually drift off in her La-Z-Boy, I'd hook her up to the oxygen tank and wander all over the neighborhood, letting myself into houses. At first, I did it only to prove I could. Easy enough. Most neighbors were astoundingly trusting of each other, leaving back doors open, failing to lock first-floor windows, storing spare keys in all sorts of dumb places like under the welcome mat or in a fake rock that came not even remotely close to looking like a real rock. The farther away from my neighborhood I walked, the taller the houses got and the more security obstacles I faced. I started wrapping Nana's nighttime pills in bacon for edgy German shepherds. I short-circuited alarm systems when I could and, when I couldn't, raced like crazy through the drawers of offices and kitchens to find that little scrap of paper with the security code scribbled on it. The first time this worked I couldn't believe it: a torn corner of loose-leaf pinned in plain sight on a corkboard, right next to the fridge. And those alarms give you longer than you'd think. And if I didn't get the code in time, I'd race like hell out the back door, flipping over fences from one yard to the next, escaping capture from the private security guys I never stayed around long enough to see.

I never stole anything. Just looked. Examined the porn

collection buried in Dad's closet, the bag of weed flattened under Son's mattress, the bottle of Ritalin stuffed to the toe end of Daughter's sneakers. I read diaries, inspected music collections, mentally recorded bra sizes, always on the lookout for the most shocking size in the neighborhood (Mrs. Garr, 1432 Grandview Drive, 38FF—no joke). This is how most of my afternoons were spent freshman and sophomore year.

I don't know who owned the Oldsmobile, but it was parked downtown just about every day—old car, manual locks, no alarm: an easy target.

Still, though, I'm not sure I would have ever gone through with it if Ray hadn't come along. Being with him—and Amir too—made it feel like more than simple joyriding. I eyed Ray now and thought about how to push further, how to keep feeding into his impression of me, and the feeling it gave me.

"I'm not scared, Ray. You just don't get the same feeling by doing the same thing again."

"So what then? Something else."

"Something else," I said, as though I already knew exactly what that something was.

"Like what?"

"Let me ask you something first." Buying time. Thinking about what kind of stupid shit we could get into next. "Why?"

He stared outside at the empty gas station. "Have you ever . . . I mean, don't you ever get disappointed with the way things are? With all the things we can dream up, all the fantasies . . . but in reality, it's just . . ." He looked off, trying to find the word but not finding it. "I don't think I can find what I'm looking for with the way things are. I don't want my current life anymore."

"Well, I can think of one surefire quick fix for that."

It was a joke. Stupid joke. But Ray didn't laugh. He went quiet. He appeared, to my surprise, to be sincerely considering the idea of ending his life, perhaps not for the first time.

"I'll pay you," he said.

"Pay me?"

"For your time."

"Ray . . ." I lifted my feet off the desk and sat forward to look at him.

He pulled a stack of cash from his pocket. "This is all I have right now. But I'll get more."

"You're gonna pay me to hang out with you? Is this how you think people get friends?"

"Just take it," he said.

"I don't want it."

"Look," he said. He moved closer to the desk. Getting angry. "If you're going to do what I want you to do, you have to take money for it. Because this isn't about being friends. This is me asking for something and you giving it to me. And in order for it to work the way I need it to work, you can't ever feel like you want to go easy on me or let me off the hook."

He breathed heavily, anxious.

"Three hundred dollars," I said.

"Fine."

The heater buzzed at my feet. Outside, the garage bell dinged—a car pulled up to the pump. For as long as I could remember, most of my exploits tended to tear things down, not build them up. Every instinct I ever had seemed, by most people's standards, definitively wrong. But now here was Ray O'Dell . . .

"You know the QuickChek down the road from school?"

"In East Orange," he said.

"Christmas Eve at midnight. No Amir this time. Just you and me."

"What? We rob it?"

I nodded. Ray tried to nod coolly like this idea did not, in fact, totally terrify him. And he almost—not quite, but almost—pulled it off.

I pocketed the cash he had tossed on the desk and moved toward the door. I had one foot outside when Ray said, "So we'll need a gun."

I locked eyes with him and found myself trying to pull off the same move he had just attempted—nodding like this idea had obviously already occurred to me.

Like it did not totally terrify me.

Brielle

THE NIGHT CULLEN CLIMBED into my room—the night I let him take my shirt off, and my pants off, and let him kiss me, and touch me in that warm and yielding part of me until a volcano of heat trembled frightfully inside me so that my skin threatened to boil and melt, at which point I grabbed his wrist and told him sheepishly that I couldn't take anymore—I forgot to ask what he'd been doing with my brother.

Moments after Cullen escaped out of my window, I was sitting at the dinner table trying to calm the flutter of my heart and dissipate the flushing in my face while Dad stood at the stove cooking pasta. Two minutes later, Ray stumbled down for dinner, energized and distracted. He'd washed his face and changed into sweatpants and an old New York Knicks T-shirt that was worn away at the shoulders, but he'd missed a big stripe of dirt down the side of his neck.

He sat at the table. Dad dropped a spoonful of pasta onto his plate, walked over to my side of the table, served me a plateful of noodles, paused to observe Ray, and then slipped into full therapist mode.

"Ray?" he said. Quiet. Gentle. He placed his serving spoon in a bubbling pot of marinara sauce on the stove.

"Ray?"

Ray wiped a hand across his brow, looking at our father from a distant place—a place, it seemed, from which he did not care to return. His hair was a dreadful mess—long and dirty and reaching wildly out from his head like a robin's nest abandoned for winter. He couldn't yet grow a beard, but there was a mousy fuzz encroaching on his upper lip that needed tending to, as did the acne blooming on either side of his nose. It was as if, convinced that he was invisible or at the very least wishing himself so, he no longer saw a purpose in hygiene and basic upkeep. Or rather—and this version concerned me more—convinced that he was ugly, that he was a wicked and contemptible presence, he had taken deliberate measures to align his outer appearance with this troubling understanding of himself.

"Ray," Dad said. "How are you feeling?"

Ray nodded. "Fine."

Dad's eyes drifted to the place at the table he'd set for Mom. He looked again at Ray and then at the clock and sighed. "I'll be right back."

"Dad?" I said. "Can we start?"

"Just wait." He marched across the room. "Two seconds." And then he hurried upstairs.

Ray tapped a fingernail on the table. Steam rose from our plates. Mom and Dad's bedroom was directly above the kitchen. We heard the creaking of Dad's steps and then the vibrations of his voice through the ceiling.

"Hey," I said.

Ray didn't look up.

"Hey."

"What?"

I poked at my pasta with a fork—a brief moment of hesitation. "What were you doing with Cullen Hickson?"

"None of your business."

"How do you know him?"

"How do you?"

"He's my friend. We're the same age." I shrugged. "Almost, anyway."

Ray nodded, kept tapping the nail against the table. From upstairs the incomprehensible rumble of Dad's voice grew louder.

"So?" I asked. "What were you doing with him today?"

No answer. More creaking from upstairs. Dad's vibrations.

I sighed. Shook my head. "Everything doesn't have to be so tragic, you know? You can talk to me, if you want. I'm not . . ." I trailed off, staring at Ray, waiting for him to save me from having to continue. To see me. Engage with me.

"Okay," I said. "You win. Forget it."

He ran a hand through his hair, which flattened against his head before springing and rebounding back into shape. "He's just helping me with something."

"Helping you?"

"Yeah."

"Like a school thing?"

"It's hard to explain. He's not like other people. He . . . I don't know."

"He what?"

"It sounds stupid."

"Try me."

"He notices me."

I nodded. And then feigned surprise. "Oh my God!"

"What?"

"I think . . . yes! I can't believe it! I think you just had an actual conversation with me. Could that be right?"

He managed a reluctant smile. It didn't last long, though. In the next instant came more noise from upstairs. First Dad, in one big explosive shout: "KAREN!"

And then, finally, came Mom's voice—angry, shrill, pained.

Then silence. Ray and I stared at our food. More creaking from the ceiling. Then the stairs—two pairs of feet coming down.

"Hey," I said.

Ray looked up. I motioned to his neck. "Missed a spot."

He swept his fingers along the condensation on his water glass and rubbed at the streak of dirt.

Dad entered the room, Mom behind him. She took her

seat at the table. Her face was pale, eyes swollen with sleep. Dad served her a plate of noodles, then spooned some for himself. He sat, crossed himself, and began grace: "Bless us, O Lord, and these, thy gifts . . ."

I quickly crossed myself to keep up. Ray didn't bother. Nor Mom.

When grace was over, Dad picked up his fork, and we ate. Ray was never a big eater—like Mom, he always seemed exhausted by the prospect of consuming and digesting food—but tonight he went at his pasta like he was a hungry orphan we'd just taken in off the street. Dad watched him. He took a few mouthfuls for himself and then continued where he'd left off before he'd disappeared upstairs.

"Ray," Dad said.

Mom sighed and shook her head. She knew what was coming and couldn't stand to face it.

Dad eyed Mom, saying nothing, but seeming like he wanted to say, *Karen, please, help me get through this.*

Mom patted a gentle hand on Ray's forearm. "You're happy. Right, sweetie?"

Ray smiled—a fake one that Mom couldn't be troubled to see through. "Great, Mom," he said. "I'm great."

Mom glanced at Dad with a told-you-so look.

Dad pressed on. "Well, look. This isn't an attack. Things have been a little different with you lately, and we want to know what's going on."

Ray waited, appearing to think there was more to it than that.

"How are things at school?"

"Great." Ray stopped eating briefly to look at Dad and then shoved in another mouthful of pasta. "School's great."

"It's not easy," Dad went on. "Starting at a new place."

Ray nodded, kept eating.

"What's with the mud?"

"Huh?"

Dad pointed to the streak on Ray's neck, which he hadn't fully scrubbed off.

"I was—" He paused, wiping at the dirt, eyeing Mom. She looked worried, like if Ray gave the wrong answer here she might crumble to dust. "I was with my friends. After school. Touch football."

"Friends?" Mom asked.

"Yeah." He put on another big grin for her. "Some guys from school."

Mom stood slowly, moving like she was in a dream. She stopped behind Ray and wrapped two arms around him.

"I think that's so great, honey," she said. "I think that's a wonderful thing for you to do."

She squeezed tightly, closing her eyes. Ray shrank away from her, like her touch burned him. The more he cowered, the more firmly she clung. Dad watched this with his lips pressed tight, his plan thwarted. I took a bite of my pasta, which had grown rubbery and cold.

The next time I saw Cullen, I skipped practice and he and I drove out to Jockey Hollow Park, the site of a Revolutionary

War camp two miles from Washington's headquarters in Morristown that was now largely the destination of second-grade class trips and retired couples. We stepped into a dank cabin that was a replica of soldiers' quarters and watched a spider construct a perfect web in one of the room's corners. It was dark. Cullen looked at me, and I looked at him, and I had a feeling like tumbling upside down, and we kissed. My hand in his hair. His on the back of my neck. Down my chest. Unbuttoning my jeans. I caught his fingers there and opened my eyes.

"Look," I said.

The spider was on the move, retreating to the center of its web, where it settled and waited, an electric bull's-eye.

Cullen smiled, reached out, and plucked the spider off its web like it was a tack in the wall. I tried to look like I wasn't petrified. The spider crawled over his fingers while he moved one hand in front of the other so the spider never reached the end.

"Wanna see?"

I shook my head no.

"You sure?"

"What if he bites?"

"He won't."

He took a step toward me, the spider running madly over his hands, all creepy legs with a big brown spotted bowl on its back. "Here," he said.

"No."

He pinched it between his fingers and held it toward me.

"Here!"

"No! Cullen, stop!"

"Ah!" He flinched and dropped the spider, breathing through his teeth. "Ah . . . shit."

"He bit you?"

He nodded, clutching his hand.

"Does it hurt?" I asked him.

"Shit," he said. "Yeah."

"I'm sorry."

"It's fine," he said.

Already there was a swollen red mark on the inside of his index finger.

He stepped out of the cabin into the sun. The replica quarters stood at the crest of a small hill, below which stretched a field of religiously mowed grass. Cullen trekked across the damp lawn, and I went after him, the ground growing softer and swampier with our every step into the basin of the sloping grounds. I thought about what kind of person would pick up a spider like that. Without anticipating the very obvious outcome.

The sun peeked above the tree line, offering the airy field perhaps the only patch of light in the wooded area. Cullen slowed, allowing me to catch up to him.

A phone buzzed in his pocket. He answered and talked while we moved through the muddy grass, offering mostly one-syllable responses: "Yup. Nope. Cool. Got it." Then he said, "I'm out with that girl. Brielle. Yeah. Got it."

When he hung up, we walked for a time in silence, while I worked up the courage to say what I wanted to say.

"Who was that?" I asked.

"Roman. Guy from school."

"And you told him about us?"

"He's harmless. Doesn't even know who you are."

"Right, but . . ."

Cullen stopped walking, blowing warm breath into his hands. "But what?"

"I thought we decided . . ."

He exhaled loudly, as though we'd had this argument many times over and here it came again. Only this was the first time I'd brought it up.

"Right," he said. "Our secret arrangement."

The sun delivered a golden halo to his hair, and he squinted through it, staring, I could see, at my breasts. I wore a tweed coat and pulled its flanks over my chest.

"Why did you want to come here today?" he asked.

"This was your idea."

"But why today? I wanted to come on the weekend. You said you'd skip practice. Come today."

"I thought it'd be fun. Adventurous."

"Have you ever skipped anything before? Ever?" He observed me, computing.

I turned away. Walked away. He jogged a few paces, sloshing through the wet lawn to catch up to me as we approached his car. I pulled my arms closer across my chest.

The day was growing darker, it seemed, and Cullen's eyes fell farther into the shadow of his mountainous face.

"Monday," he said. "When everyone that matters to you is at practice—not on a Sunday, when there's the slightest, most remote possibility that one of those girls might see us."

"Maybe I just didn't want to go to practice today, okay?"

"Maybe. Or maybe it was never about your dad. The whole secret thing."

All I could do was look away, at the ground, to the sky, anywhere but at him.

He opened the car door but didn't step in yet. "Just say it, Brielle. Once you say it, we can go from there. We can fix it. But until you admit it, and say it out loud, it's always going to be there."

"Say what?"

"You. Are. Embarrassed. Of. Me."

I looked again at the sky. Smelled smoke from some unseen chimney of a nearby house.

"Say it!" he said.

"What were you doing with my brother the other day?"

"When?"

"You know," I said. "That night. When you and I . . ."

"Just hanging out. He needed a ride home."

"You're lying," I said.

He eyed me for a moment and then laughed. "That makes two of us, then."

He got in the car, started it up, and waited for me. The last thing in the world I wanted was to step in that car with him, but I didn't have a choice. Dad almost budged once when I laid out the familiar teenage argument that owning a cell phone would actually make it *easier* for him to keep track of me, but in the end he maintained that cell phones were unnecessary costs. That dropping fifty cents into a pay phone every once in a while would do just fine. That just because the rest of the world was moving at a certain pace didn't mean we had to adjust our own. If I'd had a cell phone that day, maybe I would have called someone. Was it too much to ask for Mom to muster the energy to come retrieve her daughter, miles away from home and all alone? *Tell us if you need help.* That was one of Dad's favorite mantras. *No matter what. We just want you to be safe.* But who knows where the nearest pay phone was, and I didn't have any quarters, and there was no guarantee Mom would answer the house phone anyway, and interrupting Dad at work would be making a much bigger deal out of this than it was.

So I got in the car.

Cullen and I didn't talk the whole way home. For a while I was astounded at how quickly this connection between us had fallen apart, but I soon found comfort in the notion that Cullen was a dumb idea. Another future deadbeat. I had all the friends I needed—pretty girls with papery blond hair and cute-colored pens that they used to fill up notebooks with lists of all the boys they'd kissed and all the boys they hadn't kissed yet but wanted to kiss before high school was over. And in the very back of the notebooks were the very short lists of boys they would go all the way with. Guys who grabbed at spiders even when they knew they'd be bit were not on any of these lists. Only boys with curly brown hair in their eyes and roll-neck sweaters and stellar SAT scores. *Amherst, Cornell, Northwestern, Dartmouth, Stanford.*

So let him sit there not talking to me, I thought. *Let him work at the Shell station forever. Let Cullen Hickson live his shitty life.*

Ray

THERE WAS A REPRODUCTION of Caravaggio's *Crucifixion of St. Peter* in my theology textbook—a used paperback copy called *Ecclesiology and Moral Theology*. In the painting, St. Peter is upside down on a cross while three other guys haul the cross off the ground. Peter's lifting his head, looking off all crazy. He's got a clean white cloth over his groin that fits him like a diaper, but he's not a child. Peter is the rock. He asked for inverted crucifixion because he thought he was unworthy of the same fate as Jesus. He must have known that the images, idols, and statues of Jesus would show up all over the place, and he wanted his own death to be separate from that. It makes sense, if you think about it. Like having something really good or really bad happen to you on a day when a famous person dies. Here you are with this great story, but all anyone wants to talk about is how Kurt Cobain shot himself in a greenhouse.

I was thinking about St. Peter in my bedroom one night while balancing upside down on a ratty old pillow wrapped in a yellowing *Star Wars* case. The idea was not so much to clear my head but to focus on balancing by way of two points: one where my head touched the pillow and one at the mystical center three inches below my belly button. My thoughts kicked and squirmed. I was fighting to capture a sense of control that was always just out of reach, flitting by like a gnat that, no matter how dumb and lazy, always seemed to escape my clapping hands.

But then two things happened: first, a knock at the door, and then that same door was thrown open. I looked, and there was Dad, staring up at me from the bottom of my upside-down world. When he came in, I found a brief moment of total focus. My legs pinned together, and my middle stiffened, and my breathing steadied. I didn't fall. This, I knew, was Zen—one of those intuitive moments that you can't make happen and that you can't get back once they're gone. I thought, *This must be what being dead is like—totally blank and at ease.*

"Can you come downstairs," Dad said. It wasn't exactly a question.

"I'm supposed to stay like this for five more minutes."

"Ray . . ."

"Dad, I will, can you just . . ."

But he cut me off. "The police are here, Ray. Downstairs."

They were two large men I didn't know but who looked like guys I might have seen around town: big guys with arms like Popeye and eyes with dark scoops like mussels underneath. Mostly the cops in our town were the guys who'd spent their childhoods making trouble in Rosewood and who now spent their adulthood on the other side of the fight. If you could even call it a fight. In our town, it was more of a scuffle, really. Or at least that's how it used to be. After the towers fell, suddenly every cop was G.I. Joe and every wayward kid a terrorist.

I sat across from them at the kitchen table, my father next to me. It was two hours before dinner. For much of the meeting, only one cop spoke. The other guy wrote in a little flip-pad and hardly even looked at me.

The speaking officer shook my hand, introduced himself as Officer Esposito, asked me to sit, and assured me that this wouldn't take much time—that as long as I hadn't done anything wrong, I didn't have anything to worry about. "You know Frank Marconne?"

"Coach Marconne," my father put in.

The cop glanced at Dad and said, "Chuck, it's easier if he does it himself."

My dad nodded and put his palms up in apology. Nobody had ever called my dad Chuck before.

Esposito told me that Coach Marconne had seen me downtown last Friday.

"Last Friday?" I pretended to think about it. "Yeah, I guess so. Maybe."

"Who were you with?"

"I don't know," I said. I said it too quickly, and Esposito's partner looked up for an instant, then back to his pad.

"You don't know who you were with?"

"I was . . . by myself."

"Ray," my father cut in, but again Esposito called him "Chuck," and Dad went quiet.

"Frank says he saw you and Cullen Hickson and some Arab kid hanging around the alley behind Franny's on Friday."

Esposito paused. I felt my leg bobbing manically beneath the table.

"Were you with Cullen Hickson last Friday?"

"No," I told him.

He nodded, thinking, not believing me. "Been reading the paper lately?"

I shook my head no.

"Know anything about a stolen Oldsmobile?"

I shook my head no.

"Didn't read about the chase up through Eagle Rock?"

Again I offered the shake—trying desperately to keep it a tight, firm, honest refusal, but feeling my head jittering nervously atop my uncooperative neck. I could never make my body do any of the things I wanted it to do.

"So you didn't see Cullen Hickson downtown last Friday?"

"No, I mean, I guess, yeah. I saw him."

"You just told me . . ."

"I wasn't *with* him, I meant. But I saw him. By the pizza

place. When I saw Mr. Marconne." My words rattled around in my throat.

"He was with an Arab kid?"

"I don't know," I said. "Maybe."

"Hm-mm." The two cops glanced at each other so quickly I wasn't sure if it really happened. "And what time was that?"

"I don't remember."

"Did you stay with him all day?"

"No. I just ran into him. He's older than me. I barely know him."

"What did you do after you saw him?"

"Came home. Walked home."

"And what time was that?"

"I don't remember."

"Maybe around two?"

"That sounds right, I guess. I just walked home."

Esposito looked to my father. "So he was here around two thirty." This part, oddly, didn't sound like a question as much as a suggestion.

My father nodded, not saying anything.

"And you didn't see where Hickson went after that?"

"I don't really even know him."

Finally the partner spoke up, reading from his pad: "You witnessed Cullen Hickson near Main Street on Friday, October 4, at two o'clock in the afternoon. That's correct?"

A sound emerged from me that was no discernible word, a smudge of a thought, and then, resetting, I tried again. "Yeah," I told him.

"Yes," Esposito corrected.

"Yeah," I said. "I mean . . . yes."

There was a silent pause. The officers leaned back in their chairs, seeming to communicate through some sort of telepathy. Then they both stood.

They each gripped my hand in a devastating shake and then did the same to my father. Dad walked them to the front door, where Esposito thanked him for his time and apologized for interrupting our Sunday night. He said in so many words that there was nothing to worry about. That I was a good kid. But that Dad should get a handle on the company I was keeping. Especially now, I heard him say. Especially these days. From my seat in the kitchen I couldn't make out the words Dad mumbled in reply.

Dad came back to the kitchen, and there was a minute of him standing at the sink in silence. Then finally he said, "You have homework to do."

"Why did that guy call you Chuck?"

"That's what they used to call me in high school."

"He went to St. John's?"

Dad nodded. "His uncle is NYPD. I know the Espositos very well. Were you with this Hickson kid last weekend?"

I thought about all the clients who saw my dad as someone to confide in. A person they told things to. Things they would never admit to anyone else in a million years. What did they see in him that I couldn't see?

"No," I lied. "He's Bri's friend. I only met him like once."

"Brielle?"

It wasn't exactly a nice move, shifting the lens onto her like that, but I didn't think about it too much. That's just what brothers and sisters do. "She's been hanging out with him, I guess."

"Did he steal a car?

"How would I know?"

Dad eyed the linoleum at his feet. "You don't get many breaks in life. Could have been any number of cops to show up tonight."

"I know."

"I hope you do."

"Will you tell Mom?" I asked.

"Of course," Dad said. "Why wouldn't I?"

"I don't know."

"She's not feeling well right now, Ray. You know that."

"Okay."

What I wanted to say was *I know*. Of course I knew she wasn't feeling well, and that's exactly the reason I didn't want Dad to tell her. Because if she heard about it, she'd want to get close to me and hug me and comfort me, and I couldn't stand much more of that. It was like she was trying to squeeze me into being happy. And she wasn't even doing it for *me*. She had so closely attached her own well-being to mine, convincing herself that if I was okay—with all the hugs and hair caresses and "I love you, honey"s she could muster—then the same would be true for her. So whenever she asked me how school was, or how I was feeling, or if I had a good day, I'd always tell her, "Everything's great, Mom.

Just great." I'd smile. I'd be happy. And she'd smile, exhaling quietly, convinced.

But two cops arriving at our house to confront me about a stolen car was obviously the exact opposite of "great."

I hung around the kitchen for another moment thinking about all this, wondering what Dad would say if I unloaded it on him, but when I looked up he was going through the mail, so I left.

The next morning at school, I ripped the *Crucifixion of St. Peter* out of my theology book and taped to the inside door of my locker. I was staring at St. Peter's upside down face, wondering what Cullen might do if he knew what I'd told the cops, when Amir stopped at my locker and nodded at the painting.

"What is that?" he asked.

I explained, and he stared at it some more, nodding a little. "Why is it there?"

I couldn't really explain why I liked the painting. All I knew was that I wanted it to be in a place where I could look at it many times a day. Because looking at it felt good in a way that I didn't care about figuring out. So what I said to Amir was "Probably for the same reason you wanted to steal that car."

Amir's head twitched one way and then the other, and he looked at me real seriously. "Shut up about that," he said.

"Right. Sorry."

"It's okay. I get what you mean."

I was relieved to hear him say this, but the feeling fled as soon as Nick O'Dwyer showed up and, in the span of maybe thirty seconds, looked at the photo, said that "Osama" and I worshipped the devil, called me "Ray-Gay," which was his new brilliant nickname for me, then corkscrewed a finger into a bruise on my neck that he'd caused a few days ago. When he did, Amir slapped his hand away. Nick pushed Amir against the locker, and Amir pushed back, saying, "What the fuck is your problem?" My face went hot because I wasn't sure what I was supposed to do—call for help? Throw a punch? Run away? Nick was much bigger than Amir and would have easily kicked his ass if given the chance, but as it was, they pushed each other only a few times before Mr. Fanning stepped out of his classroom and stepped between them.

"All right, cut it out and get to class," he said.

"I'm just trying to get to my locker," Nick protested. "Shadid was trying to plant a bomb in there."

"Get what you need and get to class, Mr. O'Dwyer."

Nick fiddled with his lock. Amir and I walked away. Mr. Fanning called to us as we went: "And please tuck your shirt back in, Mr. Shadid."

When we made it to the stairwell, Amir glanced back at Nick and muttered, "I hate that fucking asshole."

I watched him in awe. How the hell did he just fight back like that? What in the world made him think it would work out in his favor? He tucked in his shirt and adjusted the blazer, which was at least two sizes too big—a hand-me-down from his brother Malik, whose name was scribbled on the inside pocket—and made Amir look even smaller than he actually was.

"Anyway," he said. "What're you doing after school?"

"Oh," I said. "Actually I'm hanging out with Cullen again."

He nodded and, like I'd invited him along—or like he didn't care whether I'd invited him or not—said, "Cool. See you then."

I met Cullen in the parking lot after school, dressed in sweats and sneakers like he asked me to be. He sat on the hood of his Buick, eyes in a book. He still wore his school uniform, but the shirt—a wrinkled black button-down that he wore every single day—had been untucked, and the tie—also wrinkled, also black, also worn every single day—had been loosened around the neck in a way that made him look really cool—just like the first day I'd met him in the woods. I stood next to him, waiting. Fumbled my hands over themselves. He stroked his mustache with the back of his ugly, greasy thumb.

"Say something," he said.

"What?"

He snapped the book shut. "Don't stand there waiting for people to see you, all meek and whatever. Walk up and say something. Hopefully something smart, but really any fucking thing will do. Say, 'Hey, Cullen.' Say, 'Hello.' Say, 'What up, homes?' Say, 'Hey, asshole, what the fuck are you doing? I told you I never wanted to see your face in this place again.' Got it?"

"Got it."

"You been talking to somebody?"

Amir approached from across the lot, also in his shirt and tie.

"Huh?"

It was a gray December day. I hopped in place to keep warm.

"Esposito come talk to you?"

"Who?"

"The cop."

"No," I said. Again I found myself fighting against that stupid quivering in my breath, made that much harder to control by the cold.

"I hope you lied to them better than you're lying to me."

Amir stepped in, fist-bumped Cullen, and said, "What's up, motherfucker?" It sounded silly in Amir's high voice, but somehow he sold it, refusing to search Cullen's eyes to see whether Cullen had thought it was cool or dumb, like I would've done.

"See that?" Cullen slapped me across the shoulder. "That is how one arrives."

Cullen's eyes always seemed plugged into something that lit them up, powered with a spark that might explode at any time, in any one person's direction.

"I know the cops showed." The eyes were on me now—almost but not quite twitching. "What'd you tell 'em?"

"They just asked me if I was downtown."

"And?"

"I told them yes."

"And what else?"

"That was it."

"Didn't ask about me? Or Amir?"

"My coach saw me when we were in the alley. That's all."

"He saw me too," Cullen said.

"How do you know that?"

"Least that's what Esposito told me when he showed up at my house. After he came to your house."

"Oh."

"And so he asked you if you were with me? Yeah?"

I shrugged.

"Look me in the eye, Ray."

"The guy saw you and me together. What was I supposed to do?"

"You say you never fucking met me! You have no idea what they're talking about. That you weren't downtown at all. That this coach of yours or whoever must have been mistaken. How hard is that? How does that guy even know you or me from any other of the dozen kids hanging around downtown on a Saturday?"

Guys peppered the school lot, some lounging by their cars and some peeling off to freedom. The football team walked out of the locker room in groups of two or three, sometimes a loner, all making a lazy trek up the hill to practice, helmets hanging from their fingers, laces untied, ducking into shoulder pads and shoving cups in their pants.

Cullen ran a hand across his chin. Amir wouldn't look at me or Cullen.

I reached into the pocket of my sweatpants and produced a crumpled stack of bills.

"What's that?" Cullen asked.

It was fifty of the sixty dollars I had to my name, saved from a summer spent mowing lawns. I shoved it into Cullen's hand.

He flipped through the bills. "This isn't even enough."

"I'll get more."

In one quick motion Cullen buried the money in his pocket and produced the keys to his Buick. "Be back here tomorrow."

"What about today?"

"I can't think about it now, because I'm too distracted by wanting to murder you. If I'm here tomorrow, we'll keep going with this stupid thing of yours. If not, forget it."

"Fuck that! Decide now!"

Cullen turned on me. He laughed.

"Decide now," I said again, quieter this time.

Cullen looked to Amir, who nodded at him. Again he ran his hand over his face, never able to think clearly without some visible sign of it. "I'm not the fall guy here, Ray."

"I know."

"You can't just immediately put the blame on me the minute things go bad."

"I know!"

"Because it'll work and I'll be fucked. People will believe you. Not me. And I know you know exactly what I mean. You know or you wouldn't have said what you said to those cops."

I didn't say anything. Amir was chewing on his nails. I could feel Cullen's eyes on me, but I didn't dare look at him.

"Look, are we gonna do something cool today or not?" Amir tightened the straps of his backpack. "If not, I gotta catch the bus."

Cullen spit into the leaves and cleared his throat. A long moment passed while he stewed, trying to decide what to do. Finally, he announced, very formally, like he was speaking to a large audience, "Listen up. Today is the first day of Ray O'Dell's training. The game is this: cops and robbers. Just like when we were little: I run, you chase me. It's not over until you catch me, no matter what happens. Ready, go."

And then, just like that, he dropped into a dead sprint across the lot, shouldering me out of the way as he went. Amir turned to me for the briefest moment—shock, thrill, fear, daring—and off we went.

We darted through the rows of cars, down the steep hill of the driveway at the south end of the lot and into the streets of South Orange, after Cullen. The cold air bit at my throat. Cullen plodded along in his black shoes, and Amir raced behind him, his short legs wheeling along beneath him, the back of his blazer flying up behind him like a cape.

We ran out to South Orange Avenue—a two-lane road that wound to the top of South Mountain Reservation. It was no place for runners. Cars whipped their way up and down the hill, negotiating one curve after another, switching lanes like crazy, sometimes dipping into the shoulder just to get their bearings before steering back onto the main road.

Amid all of this, we ran uphill. Cullen's pace was steady, but mine was a mess of dry heaves and flailing arms. There was no hope of catching him. I tripped along the last inch of pavement before the grass. Cars screamed through the wind. Some honked. I was already so winded that I feared I would lose my balance and tumble into the road. I worried that maybe this was Cullen's plan all along. That he was pissed enough about the cop stuff to do something like that.

Someone hurled a McDonald's soda cup at us. Cullen swiped at it with his cast, knocking it to the pavement so it splashed on my ankles. He kept running, head down, but Amir was pissed. He picked up the cup and ran into the road to hurl it at the car, which of course was already hundreds of feet away. Amir shouted, "Motherfuckers!" and held up two middle fingers, stepping back onto the shoulder just as another car sped uphill and whipped past him.

Just before the top of the hill, we steered away from the road. Amir and I followed Cullen blindly into the woods—no trail, no markings. We clomped through mud and stone. We dodged trees—bare trunks with patches of moss at their bottoms. Sticks snapped and cut at my ankles. Cullen was too fast. Too strong. I grabbed the damp branch of an oak tree, caught in a fit of coughing.

"Don't stop," came Cullen's voice. He moved through the forest—a dark figure taking superhuman leaps through the bush.

I stumbled forward, anxious not to lose him, coughed again, and then finally I couldn't take it anymore and stopped to vomit—a disgusting, burning release onto a bed of long-dead leaves.

"Don't stop," came the voice.

I wiped my chin on my sleeve and kept moving through the dry heaves, trying not to lose Amir and Cullen among the trees. They were mostly silhouettes now, ghosts dancing through the forest. I spat as I went after them. It wasn't at all like the running we'd done with the cops at our heels. Nothing to laugh about today.

I caught up to them at the base of a tall rock face, which, to my complete distress, Cullen started to climb, just as Amir was about to catch him. Cullen grinned at me while clinging to the rock, a few feet off the ground. "Don't stop!"

I pushed my hands into my thighs, my knees gave out, and then I was sitting in the dirt, watching Cullen move up the rock. I bent over and closed my eyes. I spat into the leaves. I couldn't go any farther.

"Hey."

It was Amir's voice this time, soft and high-pitched. He'd turned back, and he now stood above me, offering a hand, which I weakly swatted away.

"Come on," he said. "We have to get him."

He took my hand and pulled me up. We jogged to the

base of the rock, which felt so cold I didn't even want to touch it. My legs shook like crazy as I climbed, pausing to find good holds in the stone, one last push upward, and then another, and then one more, following Amir. At the top I tossed myself onto the plateau, facedown, wanting to die. I breathed. It was all I could do. One breath, and then another, and then another. Each one a miracle.

"He's trapped," Amir said.

I flipped myself over. Looked at the flat rock—Cullen was indeed trapped. Three sides of the rock dropped straight back to the ground, and the fourth was a steep, slippery slope of mud and roots that was impossible to climb. Cullen stood against this wall. He nodded behind Amir and me and said, "Check it out."

Amir and I turned around. In front of us, sweeping all the way downhill, was the entire world—trees, fences, houses, yards, churches, highways, streetlights. And beyond the trees, beyond the hill, beyond forever, was the skyline. It was faded from this distance and soft around its edges, flickering like a bunch of weak candles, but there it was—no mistaking it. From left to right: George Washington Bridge, Empire State Building, Wall Street. In spring, twin searchlights had shone in tribute, but by December they were gone, and now you couldn't tell where the towers were supposed to be.

I heard a shuffling before Amir shouted, "Oh shit!" and I turned just in time to find Cullen sprinting straight at me, about to leap off the rock face. "Stop him!" Amir screamed. And without thinking about it, I dove for Cullen.

His shoulder speared me in the chest. I wrapped my arms around him as we soared off the rock. We fell quickly. The ground met us with an excruciating, full-body punch.

Cullen rolled away from me, half-moaning and half-laughing. "Aww," he said. "Aww, shit."

I took a moment to catch my breath, then rose and wiped myself off. My shoulder throbbed, and my head felt woozy. Amir shouted from the top of the rock, "Game over, motherfucker!"

Cullen lifted a hand toward me, and I helped him up. He shook his head, smiling. "Come on. I want to see that view again."

He limped toward the rock face, and up we climbed.

The three of us sat with our muddy khakis hanging off the edge of the rock. Amir and Cullen recounted their favorite moments of the chase, laughing in disbelief that any of that had truly just happened, but soon we all grew quiet and just watched the skyline, thinking our own thoughts, breathing our own air.

Eventually, Cullen said, "So. How about teaching us how to meditate?"

"Oh," I said. "Really? It's easy."

I crossed my legs and straightened my back. Somehow my muscles cooperated. Held me upright and steady. *This*, I thought, *I can do. This I've practiced*.

"Straighten your back," I told them. "And hold it."

Amir and Cullen sat up like I was doing.

"Now you close your eyes and focus on breathing. In through the nose, out through the mouth. Sometimes it helps if you have a mantra."

"You have one?" Amir asked.

"Yeah."

I looked at Amir and then at Cullen and then out at the skyline. Wind knocked the tops of the trees together. Somewhere a stream of cars was whirring. The mantra always felt real heavy for me in the moment, but saying it out loud was different.

"Well?" Cullen said.

"Bloodfire."

Amir nodded, looking out into the darkness, not at me. "Cool. Why that?"

"I don't know," I said.

"You don't know the reason behind your own mantra?" Cullen said. "Isn't that the whole point?"

"It's hard to explain. I don't know what it means. I don't even know where it came from. But when I say it, it helps me focus. Bloodfire."

What I didn't tell them was that I didn't only say it—I saw it too. I'd inhale and visualize a lake of boiling blood—a lake so big you couldn't see the other side and with the sun shining on it so intensely that the red was as bright as a melted crayon—then exhale and ignite the whole thing with my mind and watch the flames sweep across the bloody surface.

Cullen and Amir sat cross-legged, and we all tried it.

Usually I closed my eyes, but tonight I kept them on the skyline. *Bloodfire. Bloodfire.* The buildings appeared shaky from this distance, glowing orange like they were on fire. Those "Never Forget 9/11" stickers were so dumb, when you thought about it. Because the truth is that everyone forgets so quickly, even if they don't realize it. We watched videos of the buildings going down over and over. We had a few days off from school. The president talked. There was a war in some faraway place. But for the most part, everyone had gone on with their lives by now. Work resumed, school started up again, and on and on.

It was the same thing with those kids in Columbine a few years ago. They killed fifteen people—one teacher, twelve students, and themselves. And we all mourned. We all talked about how horrible it was. CNN showed a funeral for one of the girls—just about the saddest thing you could possibly show on television. And while the families and the people who lived there weren't likely to forget anytime soon, everyone else in the country got wrapped up in their own lives again. Focused on their own families, their own kids. The news stopped talking about it. The kids in school who had delighted in joking about which freaks were most likely to shoot up the class moved on to new stupid jokes. Whenever there was a national tragedy, no matter how many times people said, "Never forget," it seemed like what everyone was most interested in doing was, in fact, forgetting.

But not me. I thought about those kids all the time: Rachel Scott, who played the lead in the school play; Kyle

Velasquez, who had a stroke as a baby that left him mentally disabled; Steve Curnow, who liked soccer. They were all dead now. Same went for the people in the towers. That's why I was watching those videos that morning Cullen found me in the library. That's why I wanted to be here, in the woods with Cullen and Amir, doing what we were doing, thinking: *Bloodfire. Bloodfire.* Because all around us was horror and death and the worst kinds of pain. It was so hypocritical to pretend to care for like a week, or even a month, and then go back to ignoring it all.

I listened to the three of us breathing. There was a light inside me that most people—people like parents and teachers and priests—didn't want to see. It was an explosive light, powered by the burning of all the things I was pissed off about, and Cullen was the one who showed me what to do with it.

I balanced on the rock, felt its cold come through my sweatpants, straightened my back, held my head steady, closed my eyes, breathed my mantra—*Bloodfire . . . Bloodfire . . . Bloodfire*—and watched as I lit that lake up again and again and again.

Cullen

THE DEAN OF MEN—a bald guy in a wrinkled suit who was also the JV track coach—took me out of last period to greet two police officers in his office. One of the cops—Esposito, the same guy who'd come to see me and Ray—was twiddling a pair of cuffs while staring at a painting on the wall of St. Michael stomping on a demon. The questioning that followed at the police station wasn't at all like I thought it would be—like it is in the movies, where the detectives shake the guy down and toss around threats and lies to get a confession—but it still required a basic amount of restraint.

The whole thing lasted all of ten minutes. I was lying on a bench in a bulletproof, glass-enclosed cube—some sort of holding cell before I'd be transferred to the real deal—when one of the guards escorted me into a gray room at the end of a gray hallway. Esposito sat across from me with a manila folder. He flipped through a mess of documents and photos—the guy had huge, dirty hands and a face that was all jowls and permanent five o'clock shadow—and said, looking at a photo of the totaled car, "Banged up that Chevy pretty good, huh?"

He almost had me, I have to admit. He grinned at how I caught my words just before I corrected him.

"Oh, that's an Oldsmobile. That's right. Heard you did a pretty nice piece of driving. For a while, anyway."

He eyed me, then scribbled something down. I demanded to see a goddamn lawyer, hoping to sound like I'd done it before.

His grin came back again. "You're in school, right?"

I nodded.

He read from his folder. "No priors. No gangs. We'll expedite your case to the judge so he can get you home to your guardian. You want a lawyer, we can probably have one here by this time tomorrow, if you'd rather spend the night."

"Okay," I said. "The first one."

"I'm not required to tell you this, but since you're seventeen, you can have a parent or guardian here with you, if you want."

I shook my head. "I'm good."

"Suit yourself."

He rose and rocked a fist against the door, which was opened by another officer in blue. "Don't get me wrong," he told me, as I shuffled past him. "Most definitely, Mr. Hickson, you will need a goddamn lawyer."

* * *

Six hours later I stood before the judge who, noting my age and—just like the detective had predicted—the court's desire to return school-aged first offenders to their homes, set my bail at $5,000. I asked the jail guard if I could make two phone calls.

He looked at me with absolutely no expression. "Never seen a movie, asshole?" he said. "One call."

I dialed Nana. I knew it would take her a while to get to the phone, so I hung up after three rings, just before the machine would kick in, and called back.

"Hi, Nana."

"Daryl," she said.

"It's Cullen, Nana."

"Daryl, where are you?"

"Nana, it's Cullen, your grandson."

Daryl was my father. Seven years ago, he and Mom had taken a trip to High Point State Park in northern Jersey, which offered bikers a winding strip of blue-and-green heaven. Dad took one corner too fast and spilled himself and Mom into the path of an oncoming minivan. Mom was dead at the scene. Dad passed out with a nasty head wound but first handed the EMT a sheriff's card with his cousin's name on it. Cousin Sal was a sergeant in Nutley who sped to the scene just in time to bury the suspicion that alcohol was involved in the wreck, which it most definitely was. Once he was out of the hospital, Dad lasted twelve weeks under the strain of the guilt before he took enough of his newly prescribed painkillers to dial his heart down to zero. I was ten years old. Since then it had been me and Nana.

"Nana," I said. "Did you eat dinner?"

"Not hungry," she said.

I could hear the television in the background. Some old sitcom on Nick at Nite—*Cheers*, maybe.

"There's a sandwich in the fridge."

"Tired of those."

"I'll be home late tonight. I need you to eat a sandwich."

There was a long silence. Canned laughter from the television. Nana's gravelly breathing.

"Nana, please, will you eat?"

"Fine," she said.

"Right now?"

"Fine."

"I'll be home later. I love you."

"Yeah, yeah," she said and hung up.

I pushed the hook down, keeping the receiver near my ear. I was hoping the guard had caught enough of my conversation with Nana to reconsider his stance.

"One more?" I ventured.

He nodded—or rather, he moved his head the absolute least amount a person could move his head in order to indicate a nod—so I called my buddy Roman. After a few minutes of begging him to cough up the required 10 percent of my bail, Roman finally agreed to dig into his pot-selling stash and come get me.

Roman was a tall, gawky kid with big, twitchy eyes and

two overgrown, rat-like front teeth. He never looked you in the eye and was always rubbing the back of his neck like he couldn't figure out what to do with his hands. Nobody trusted him, and very few guys would even talk to him. People didn't fuck with him, though, because he was tough as hell. I saw him fight his older brother once. The brother smashed Roman's head into a radiator, and Roman paused for a moment, shoved a shaky fist into the wound, and mashed his teeth together before exploding his brother's nose with a furious elbow. I liked Roman. Hanging out with him was like trying to stay on your feet during an earthquake.

Roman wasn't the kind of guy to give up large sums of money quietly, and he bitched at me the whole ride back to school, where, at nine P.M., my car was the last one in the lot. He insisted that we drive back to my place so he could be paid, but it'd been a long, lonely, shitty day, and I was facing the prospect of an upcoming court date and a maximum five years in county. Promising Roman that I'd get him back, I climbed into my car and tore away with his figure silhouetted in my headlights, his arms extended in appeal.

At home, Nana was in bed. I checked the fridge for the missing sandwich and, satisfied that she'd eaten, climbed upstairs. I peeked into her room to make sure she'd put her oxygen mask on, which she had. In my room, I sat on my old, sagging, dusty mattress. It was too early to sleep. I had some homework, but that was never at the top of my to-do list, least of all tonight. I wandered back downstairs, hearing the steps creak under my feet, suddenly overwhelmed with the feeling that the house was too big and empty and quiet. I couldn't stand to be there anymore.

I slipped out the back door and walked through the woods to the O'Dell yard, where I stood staring at the hot white light glowing from Brielle's window. The five-legged dog appeared across the yard, galloping toward me, barking with no sound. He halted, bared his teeth, and growled his sad-as-hell mute growl.

I crouched and offered my palm. He circled me once, then approached.

"What do you think, Lincoln?" I let the mutt lick my hand, and he muzzled his head against my leg. "Think she likes me?"

I stepped up onto the banister of the porch and then shoved my hand once more into the muck and grime of the gutter. I crawled on all fours across the gravelly surface of the roof. The sound of a screen door squeaked, and I froze. A man stepped out of the house next door, spotlighted by a motion-sensored lamp on his deck, where he crouched beneath a purring gas grill to kill the flames. My foot slipped and sent a drizzle of gravel down the roof. Not startled, but curious, the man studied me on his neighbor's roof.

I waved. "Howdy, neighbor."

His hand rose into the air—a slow, confused wave—and then he drifted back into his house.

"Jesus Christ," I whispered. "What are you doing, Cullen?"

I scrambled up the rest of the way to Bri's window and tapped on the pane.

The neighbor's back door squeaked open again, and a

head poked out—a woman this time, phone held to her ear. I waited until she ducked back inside and then knocked again on the window.

The curtain peeked open, and a face appeared that wasn't Brielle's at all but her mother's. She, of course, screamed like hell. I flinched from the shock and lost my footing, skating down the slippery roof on my ass, scratching at the shingles with my fingernails. At the end of the roof I stomped my foot in the gutter, but the rest of me kept coming and my foot popped out, so I wheeled to my belly, which scraped against the grating surface as I slid right off the roof. I hooked myself into the gutter with one and then another hand, hanging there four feet above the deck. When I dropped, I stumbled briefly, then rose just in time to stand eye to eye with Charles O'Dell as he opened the sliding glass door with a look of curiosity stamped on his pale and very cleanly shaven face.

Brielle

Dad was standing in the yellow light of the kitchen, an unpaid bill in one hand and a cold pork chop in the other, when the phone rang. "Gina," he said into the phone. "You want to talk to Karen?"

Gina Russell lived next door. Dad peeked out the window as he listened to her. I sat at the computer desk in the living room. I was meant to be reviewing material for tomorrow's test on Greek civilization, but in typical Bri fashion, I'd read and memorized all the material on democracy, senators, and city-states a full week in advance, so instead I was on the computer messaging with Katie. This was my most comfortable form of socializing—wearing sweatpants, leaving my lifeless hair in a lifeless ponytail, and, most importantly, having the chance to think about what I wanted to say before typing it out. Katie was complaining to me that she was on the phone with Scarlett, who apparently couldn't sustain a full minute of conversation without singing along with the NSYNC CD playing in her room.

That music is so insipid, I typed.

Thank u! Katie wrote back. **INSIPID! That's exactly the word.**

Even as I was delighting in having won this nod of approval from Katie, I was simultaneously missing Cullen and despising myself for feeling so. My thoughts flipped from longing to shame and then back again in what I feared to be an endless loop—one I would simply have to learn to live with the way some people learn to live with chronic illnesses.

Scarlett's awesome tho, Katie typed. **Love that girl.**

A scream from upstairs—Mom. And then a scraping sound, like someone had taken a rake to the roof. Dad was off the phone and moving into the living room, stepping toward the sliding door to follow up on what must have been one troubling neighborly report. He didn't look afraid. Didn't look angry, or worried, or even brave. He was a man opening a door. Calm and composed as always.

There, in the threshold, appeared Cullen—standing on the deck, as tall as Dad and almost as broad-shouldered. They met each other's eyes for a brief, silent moment. I clicked the computer screen to black. My insides quivered.

"Good evening, sir," Cullen said. "Have you heard the Good News?"

Dad shifted where he stood and said nothing.

"Sorry," Cullen said. "A joke."

"Can I help you with something?" Again a slight readjustment of Dad's stance, slightly off-balance but knocking back Cullen's volleys, holding serve. He was the adult here.

"Oh, umm, I wanted to ask if I could talk to Brielle." Cullen snuck his eyes over Dad's shoulder and found me. Fresh cold air crept into the house and nipped at my toes.

"You wanted to see my daughter, so you climbed up on my roof."

"Yes."

"You climbed on the roof with the intent of crawling into her window."

"Yes."

"Frightening the neighbors and my wife in the process."

"Sorry about that."

"And then you fell off the roof."

"More or less, yes."

"Are you all right?"

"Physically speaking? Yes."

"You're Cullen, right?"

Cullen nodded.

"Cullen Hickson," Dad said.

Cullen ran a hand over his chin and tilted his head down. The way Dad said his name like that—as though the name itself was guilty. Guiltier than Cullen would ever actually be, no matter what kind of terrible misfortune he brought upon himself or his friends.

Mom held her hands against her chest at the doorway to the living room. I watched Cullen smear his hair away from his eyes.

"Bri," Dad said. "Do you want to see Cullen?"

I looked again at Mom at the far end of the room. She scratched her nail against the wood paneling of the wall. I thought about how, in the upstairs closet with our winter coats and boxes of old shoes, there was a photo album of a vacation we'd all taken to the Outer Banks in North Carolina. Ray and I were very little—he was still a baby; I was maybe three or four. I don't remember much of the trip, but I remember one moment. Somewhere in the middle of the book there's a picture of Mom and me. She's standing at the surf holding me up by my hands. My arms are stretched above my head—so thin and extended they look like they might tear at the shoulder—and my feet dangle a foot above the sand and water. A thigh-high wave has just splashed into Mom, and the picture captures her face in a perfect, frozen moment of pure elation. Her smile seems to take up the whole picture. And even with the wave almost knocking her over, she looks beautiful in a brilliant, sky blue bathing suit, her hair gleaming crimson in the beachy light. I'm laughing so hard, my eyes closed behind a pair of goggles, mouth wide, crooked teeth shining.

From my seat at the computer, I looked at Mom across the room and couldn't remember another moment like the one in North Carolina. Probably they happened, but I couldn't place them. I wondered if I actually even remembered that day at the beach. Maybe I just manufactured a version of it in my mind based on the picture. If the picture didn't exist, maybe I'd never have believed the potential for re-creating that smile still survived somewhere within Mom. But I did believe. She could get better. Would get better.

Still, it wasn't going to happen right now. Right now all she did was continue to scratch her nail against the wood paneling of the wall. Her eyes met mine, and in them I searched for my next move and found not an answer but only anticipation. Found her as curious to see what I'd do as I was, intent to let me navigate the maddening tangle of my existence on my own.

Dad, meanwhile, was waiting for an answer. I couldn't stand his question, though. *Did I want to see Cullen?* You tell me, Dad. Do I? Is it safe? Will he hurt me?

"Yes," I said. "I'd like to see him."

Cullen hesitated at the door, thinking perhaps, like I was, that I'd be sent out to meet him rather than the other way around. Finally, he scrubbed his boots on the mat and stepped inside, where Dad motioned him toward a rocking chair in the corner.

I rose from the computer and moved to the couch. Cullen and I both grinned, nervous. Dad sat beside me, eyes on Cullen.

"Dad," I said. "Can he and I talk alone real quick?"

He was shaking his head before I even started the question. "We can all talk," he said. Casual now. Happy. Polite. Welcome to group therapy, everyone.

"Here, Karen," he said, shifting close to me to make room on the couch.

Mom had already taken what she undoubtedly hoped were unnoticed steps into the hallway. Her whole body resisted joining us. Her face was tight, almost panicked, while one shoulder leaned into the other room like someone was pulling her away.

"There's room," Dad insisted, patting the open square of cushion next to him. Mom shuffled into the room and, in her own small act of rebellion, landed on the far couch, sighing as she sat, as though the action had worn her down completely. Dad let his gaze hold on her for a disappointed moment, and then he turned to Cullen.

He asked Cullen how old he was. Where he went to school. How he and I knew each other.

"You know," Cullen told him. "Just from around."

He asked about Cullen's parents, and we all had to sit there while Cullen told us about a horrendous motorcycle accident and how he had lived with his grandmother half his life. It wasn't a hard story for him to tell. It was clear he'd told it many times before. But it was not an easy story to listen to, and none of us knew how to respond. Dad tried, of course.

"That's very difficult," he said. "I'm sorry that happened to you."

"Happened to them," Cullen said. "Not me."

"No," Dad told him. "I'm not so sure I agree with you there."

Cullen shrugged. "It was a long time ago."

There was an awful pause where it seemed the conversation had died for good until Dad said, "And you know my son too? Ray?"

Cullen shook his head no, looking confused. A comfortable liar.

"Well, I'm not one to cast blame before the facts are in. But there were some police officers here the other night asking about Ray. And a stolen car. And they mentioned your name."

"Dad . . ."

"Seems like whenever I'm within ten blocks of a crime, someone comes knocking on my door," Cullen said. "Always been that way."

Dad nodded, pressing his lips together.

Throughout all this I was watching Cullen, but it wasn't until now that he looked at me. He'd been hunched on the rocker, avoiding eye contact. Eyeing the carpet, the ceiling, the blank television. Waiting, just like me, for this to be over. But Cullen looked at me now, and I at him, and we saw that strange something in each other's eyes that meant we were both done with this dreary business of parents and could wait no longer to retreat to the place where it was only me and him.

"As I mentioned," Dad was saying, "we don't like to judge in this house. And so, Cullen, Karen and I . . ."

Dad turned to Mom, who jerked her head up and nodded, as though she'd been following the conversation all along.

"We want you to know you're welcome to come by anytime you want. Our door is always open."

"Thank you," Cullen said and rose to shake my father's hand.

"The front door," my father clarified. "The one with the doorbell."

"Right." Cullen drooped his shoulders, and his hand went back to his hair. "Sorry about that."

I was granted permission to walk Cullen out. In the hallway he and I stood at the door, whispering. I could feel the air between us trembling.

"Cullen . . ."

"You can be embarrassed of me," he cut in. "I don't mind. I get it. I'd be embarrassed of me too. You deserve one of those dudes who plays lacrosse and will write you letters every day when he goes to college. I get it."

"I missed you." The admission dropped right out of me. No chance of holding on to it.

His face brightened. "You did?"

"I didn't realize . . . I thought it wasn't as real . . . me and you, I mean. But it *is* real, isn't it? Don't you think so?"

"I missed you too."

"I mean, I *really* missed you."

"I know. Me too."

I noticed his wrist for the first time.

"Your cast," I said.

Proudly, he held up the bare arm. Wiggled his fingers. "Healed."

I glanced back to the living room. "I have to go."

"Next Saturday," Cullen said. "Come to my house. I'll make breakfast for you and Nana."

He took my hand in his—a rough palm and cold as a rock. We stared at each other from our tiny distance.

We never had breakfast. I said we would before opening the door and watching him jog away—always moving fast, wherever he went—but we never did. I hiked through the woods that separated his house from mine on a gray Saturday morning, a chilly walk that left me winded and bewildered. From across the street, I stared at Cullen's house—two stories of yellow siding faded pale, browned screen windows, and no shutters save for one hanging crooked from a stubborn nail. A two-foot-tall statue of the Virgin Mary stood, untouched, next to what was once a stoop and a wrought-iron railing but that was now, since the accident, a heap of blasted asphalt and warped metal. Mary's original white was lost beneath a green-gray film of dust, soot, and mold. She gazed down at the dirt and the crumbled asphalt pieces littered across the flowerbed, holding her hands out in a gesture of either welcome or surrender.

I imagined the house's interior, where Cullen's grandmother would sit in a recliner that swallowed her gray figure and where a tiny Jesus no doubt hung from a tiny cross on the wall and where all the curtains were probably drawn and no light shone but for the burning blaze of the television, which blared at an earsplitting volume. A metal TV tray and olive carpet. Lace and linoleum and the lingering smell of turkey dinners stretching back decades.

It wasn't the scene itself that kept me from entering. I imagined the home as easily and, it turned out, as accurately as I did because of its resemblance to my own grandmother's house—to all of our grandmothers' houses. It was Cullen's connection to the scene that unnerved me. The house was very much real—more so than I'd considered him to be. Cullen was one of those characters you assume has no home, no family, no day-to-day existence—the type of person who simply seems to exist unto himself, spontaneously conceived in a grease stain struck by a lightning bolt from the stars. But here was his home, one more dilapidated square amid rows and rows of others.

A panic lit up inside me and, jaw clenched at the thought of his glimpsing my cowardice through one of those grimy windows, I hurried back toward the woods. It was as though I'd been waiting my whole life for a specific door to open and then, when it finally had, I kept faltering at the threshold, unable to plunge through and accept the mutated wonder of some extraordinary new world.

It did not take much longer for me to finally take the leap. The following week I was hunched over the school lunch table, nibbling at a peanut butter and jelly sandwich while social crises whirred about me. From a few words here and there and the overall tone of the screams and yelps from those gathered around her, I surmised that Katie liked a boy or a boy liked Katie and someone had told Scarlett something about the boy or something was in fact said by the boy himself that was either exciting or revolting.

Histrionics, I thought. *That's a good vocab word for you, Katie. Histrionics.*

Thinking about Cullen did not elicit cries of glee nor compel me to conspire with friends to call his house and hang up for hours on end. Rather, the notion of him dropped me into a storm of aching—so much ecstasy it made me hurt.

"Oh my God, look." Scarlett thrust her head into the center of the chattering faces and pointed to the red door in the corner of the lunchroom, perpetually propped open in the winter months to combat the intensity of the lunchroom's stubborn radiator.

There stood Cullen.

Katie grabbed my arm and sighed. "Oh, Brielle. Please tell me. *Why* is he looking at you like that?"

More heads turned. By that time, we'd all heard about the totaled Oldsmobile and Cullen's arrest. The entire lunchroom of girls planted disbelieving eyes on him—a mustached man in the corner, resistant even to the infantilizing effect of a tie-and-blazer uniform that left so many boys—like Ray, for one—swimming beneath shoulder pads and extra fabric meant to last through four years of growth spurts.

He waved me over.

The girls at my table watched me. I shifted where I sat, not looking at anyone, wishing them all away. Across the room, Meghan Ngyuen chewed her lunch and straightened her hair, looking anywhere but at me or Cullen; she wouldn't be troubled to acknowledge the existence of the guy who'd wrecked her car, threatened her safety, thrown into jeopardy—for ten horrifying seconds—her athletic scholarship to the University of Virginia.

Katie whispered something to Scarlett, who giggled. *How many other times?* I thought. How often had they conspired like this? Laughed at me? What did they say when I wasn't around? I thought about Katie rolling her eyes at me in response to Scarlett that first day. I thought of her complaining about Scarlett to me while at the very same moment talking to Scarlett on the phone. Katie Kinney, I suddenly thought, was not a real person. She was paper-thin. A mirage. A one-note actress.

The lunchroom monitor, Mr. Richards—a young English teacher fond of bowties and Homer—stepped into the room, spotted Cullen at the far corner, and ambled over to him.

"I just want to talk to Brielle real quick," Cullen told him.

A soft, daring girl's voice from nowhere: "Careful not to suck his dick this time, Bri."

Guffawing laughter. Blurting yelps and spittle. Who knows who says these things? They boil up, spontaneously and inevitably, from the anonymous depths of high school halls. Everyone says them and no one says them.

I understood then that it didn't matter what I did or didn't do. My time at that lunch table had been a farce. We all knew it, if not right from the start then soon thereafter. I'd been granted admission through some bureaucratic error that had misidentified me as someone I was not. Blunders like these happen all the time at new schools as we sift through the mess of new faces to decipher who belongs in which group. After the first few months, such matters tend to sort themselves out without injury. My own case had taken a bit longer than expected: one year and three months. But finally, inevitably, my moment had arrived.

I wiped my mouth with a napkin and marched toward the door. Mr. Richards stooped at Cullen's side, informing him that he was not permitted on school grounds until the last bell, Cullen telling him, "I know, I know, but . . ."

When I arrived, Cullen was turning to me to ask, "Can we talk outside for a second?" but on "for," I grabbed the lapel of his blazer, arched up on my toes, and kissed him—a long, warm kiss with a lot of tongue and a bit of mustache.

The commotion of the cafeteria and the warnings from Mr. Richards remained sunk beneath the swooshing sound in my head until after Mr. Richards had separated me from Cullen with a hand on my shoulder, and then I rewound the event in my head and deciphered all the glee and horror in the roar of reactions.

Cullen was escorted off school grounds. I stepped into the bitter cold and watched him march across the parking lot. When Mr. Richards returned, shoulders drawn tight against the cold, he explained that there'd be no detention but that I'd be wise to reflect on my decision-making. I nodded, and he stepped inside. Winter blew up my skirt. Cullen's car started up across the lot with a soft purring. I leaned up against the brick wall of the school and shivered as the wind bit at my eyes and ears. But I didn't mind the cold. I liked it.

Ray

AMIR AND I ate lunch at a table near the front of the cafeteria, right by the door. If you entered in a rush, hungry, steering toward the food counter, you'd probably walk right by without noticing us. And that, obviously, was the point. Once other kids like us caught on to our strategy—pale kids, pimpled kids, weird kids, nerdy kids, quiet kids—they joined us at our table, but we didn't really talk or hang out much with those other guys. Especially once we started this thing with Cullen—once we had a good reason for talking to each other and only each other.

One day we were sitting at our secret-not-so-secret table and a lacrosse player waltzed by, plucked Colin Yeager's Powerade off the table, opened it, drank down the entire thing in a few enormous gulps, and plopped the empty bottle back down, smiling. "Just fucking with you, man."

Yeager smiled weakly, nodding—like, yeah, of course, no problem, we're great friends. I thought Amir might step in to say something, but it wasn't worth it—a forgettable enough moment, but it reminded me of a question I'd been meaning to ask him.

"You remember that day you and Nick almost fought at my locker?"

Amir nodded, chewing on his sandwich—the same beautiful, towering sandwich of fresh, crisp vegetables his mother prepared for him every morning.

"How can you be like that?" I asked.

"Like what?"

"I mean, he would've kicked your ass. You know that, right?"

He shrugged. "Maybe. You never know."

"Well, okay, but . . . unless you're secretly a master of some deadly martial art, he's got, like, forty pounds on you. I don't get how you can be like that."

"You know something?" Amir dropped his sandwich and wiped his hands on a napkin. "In middle school, I was afraid of everything. *Everything*. If somebody drank my Powerade, I would've sat there just like Yeager—like some lobotomized cow."

Yeager turned and gaped at Amir like . . . well, like a lobotomized cow.

"And when I started at St. John's, I just, like, stopped being that way. I don't know how I did it. But I decided, you know what? Fuck it. What's the worst that could happen? I get hurt? Embarrassed? Who cares about any of that? I just decided I was going to live."

"It's that easy," I said.

"No," he said. "Definitely not easy. But it's better than the alternative. I mean, look at me. It's not like people are ever gonna stop picking on me, right? So if I'm going to get hurt anyway, I'm doing it on my own terms. I'm not about to let some dickhead like O'Dwyer do it for me."

I went back to my own sandwich—a measly ham-and-cheese melt bought from the food counter for four dollars.

"I know you know what I'm talking about," Amir said.

"What do you mean?"

"Whatever you're up to with Cullen."

I looked at him, frozen. Somehow I thought he would never ask. He seemed content enough to run around with us without asking what the endgame was.

"It's cool," Amir said. "You don't have to tell me."

I eyed the rest of the kids at the lunch table and shook my head. "Not here."

Amir nodded. He took a big bite of his sandwich, washed it down with a gulp of water, and smiled at me.

"What?" I said.

"So let's leave."

"The lunchroom? Sure, I'm almost done."

"The game is cops and robbers," he said.

"What?"

"Just like when we were little. I run—"

"Amir, no."

"You chase. It's not over until you catch me—"

"We have class!"

"No matter what happens. Ready, go!"

His chair squawked against the linoleum as he bolted from his seat and raced out of the cafeteria. A dozen or so people turned his way but then went back to their lunches, uninterested. I felt the seconds ticking away. Stay or go. Stay or go. Stay or go. "Oh Jesus," I said.

I raced out of the cafeteria to the end of the hallway and looked one way, then the other, where I saw the top of Amir's head right before he disappeared down the stairs. I ran toward him just as Mrs. Montagna, the Spanish teacher, stepped out of her classroom. I slowed to a brisk walk.

"*Despacio*," she called down the hall, smiling as she strolled toward the lunchroom.

I leaped down two flights of stairs. The first-floor hallway was mostly empty, save for one or two students milling outside the main office. I cracked open a door to the outside, where Amir stood in the middle of the parking lot, waiting to see if I would follow him. As soon as he spotted me, he turned and fled. I took one last peek down the hall for any spying teachers and then burst through the door, out into the blue-skied, chilly winter day.

We ran for what seemed like forever. Across city streets, through alleys, down residential blocks, over fences and through backyards, into the woods, through the woods for at least a mile, up hills, over fallen trees, across swampy gulches, until we came to a sound wall bordering Route 280.

I expected him to double back through the woods, or at least skirt along the wall for a while. Instead, he climbed a tree, reached out for the wall, wriggled himself to its top edge, and balanced on it for a wild moment before looking back at me. "Amir, wait!" I shouted.

Then he jumped.

I pulled myself up the same tree and leveraged my middle atop the narrow, coarse wall, which scraped painfully across my stomach. I expected to look down and see Amir lying with two broken ankles on the shoulder of the highway. Instead, I found him staring up at me from a strip of overgrown weeds, waiting.

"Amir!" I shouted to him. "What the hell!"

He yelled something I couldn't hear.

"What?!"

"Tell me now!"

"We're going to rob a convenience store!" I shouted it, but not loudly enough. The rush of the freeway hushed it out.

"What?"

I shouted again, but again he couldn't hear me. He threw up his arms in confusion.

The sound wall was shorter than most. Fifteen feet, maybe. I closed my eyes and breathed. Searched for and pinpointed the wrath inside me. *Bloodfire. Bloodfire.* This was the only way—out of this world, into another.

I opened my eyes, let the pulse of highway sing the background music to my mantra. *Bloodfire. Bloodfire.*

And I jumped.

When I picked myself up out of the weeds, Amir stood ten feet away, watching me, still edgy, ready to run. The freeway roared. Wind from passing cars pushed angrily against us. I wiped dirt and grass from my palms.

"We're going to rob a convenience store," I said.

He smiled. "With a gun?"

I nodded. Someone laid on their horn, the sound compressing and then stretching out again as the car sailed away, gone forever.

"Why?" Amir shouted against the chaos.

"What do you mean, why?"

"I mean, *why?*"

"You know why!"

"No I don't!"

"Amir, Jesus, can we talk about this another time?"

"Just tell me why!"

"I'm looking for God, okay? I'm just . . . looking for God."

"Really?"

"Yeah. Do you believe in God?"

"No," he said.

"Don't you want to?"

He shook his head. "No."

"Okay, well . . ." I looked all around me—at the cars and the steel railing and the brown weeds and the sky, trying to think against the noise. It felt like the earth was shaking—like we were inside a giant's snow-globe. "Can we go back to school now?"

"Game's not over," he yelled.

"I got you!"

"Gotta tag me."

"Fuck, come on. Are we ten years old? I'm right here!"

He laughed. "Gotta tag me!"

I reached out for him, and he stepped toward the highway, and again I shouted, "Amir, wait!" but again it was too late. There he went. Scurrying across eastbound Route 280. A car honked. And another. Tires screeched. Amir ran wildly, dodging, juking, almost tripping, arms flailing. Finally reaching the midway point, straddling the median, he turned back to me. That look of his: serious but thrilled. Excited but angry. I backed away from the road—as far as I could get, pressing myself up against the sound wall, hands trembling, legs shaking, head buzzing—and watched him. He lifted the other leg and turned away from me. Eyed traffic for a full minute or more, waiting, waiting, waiting, and then . . . into the mayhem, one lane to the next, all the way across to the other side.

Brielle

AFTER SCHOOL, in a light frozen rain, the school bus swept along a slippery road that took us sailing past Cullen's Shell station. At the next red light, on a whim, I flung open the bus's back door, sat on my butt while an emergency bell blasted and the driver howled a slew of warnings, and kicked off, dropping into the road.

My shoes skidded across the wintry street while I smashed the heavy yellow door shut and half-ran, half-skated to the sidewalk. The bus's front door folded open. I feared the bus driver might come chasing after me, but the traffic light flipped to green and, in a huff, the bus rumbled along.

I arrived at the Shell station soggy, with chattering teeth and icy toes, to find Cullen lounging in the office with Roman, a gangly guy who moved like an oversized insect and who gazed on me with jittery eyes as though he wanted to scuttle up my back and chew my head off. Grunge music bellowed from an old cassette player—something from a decade ago when angst and mournful righteousness still had a place in popular culture. Cullen pocketed a sloppy pile of cash on the desk. A space heater burned dust at my feet.

Cullen motioned to Roman. "Brielle, Roman. Roman, Brielle."

"Hey," I said.

Roman let out a laugh like a pair of worn-out brakes and nodded his head at me. His eyes were glassy and clouded like marbles.

"Is he stoned?" I asked.

"Ask him."

I turned to Roman, who shrugged and laughed. "Heeeeeells yeah," he said.

Cullen asked Roman to wait outside, assuring him that they'd be on the road in a few minutes, and when he went, Cullen stood and flipped the blinds closed on the door. He smirked at me, and we played a game of looking and not looking at each other.

"I skipped breakfast," I said.

"You are forgiven."

"Did you get in trouble from Mr. Richards?"

"Just asked me to leave. You?"

I shook my head no.

"Seems like a decent guy."

"Yeah," I said, and Cullen dared an imperceptible step toward me, and then another. "He's really . . ." And his hand was on my hip. ". . . a good . . ." And we kissed. ". . . teacher." And we kissed again. His hand was in my hair, on my neck, creeping down my spine. Our arms locked. There was that volcanic moment when our midsections met, and he pushed himself stiff and warm against me, and the dangly little bell of the front door sang out, the blinds whooshing, and then, astoundingly, I was staring at my brother.

Ray said, "Oh," as he tripped away from us. I stepped back from Cullen, who turned and caught the door before it closed.

"What's up, Ray?" Cullen said.

Ray faced Cullen and, after some clumsy fumbling and without looking at me, told him, "Oh, well, Roman just talked to the guy. Says we have to go now and, um, that we can't be late."

"Got it."

Ray stepped outside into the weather. Cullen let the door ease shut again. The music faded, and the tape clicked off. Cullen said, "I gotta go do this thing."

"What is my brother doing here?"

"It's kinda hard to explain."

"Is he . . . are you selling him drugs?"

"No."

"Selling *with* him? I don't understand . . ."

"No. Nothing like that," he said.

"Are you going to steal another car?"

"No."

"What then?"

"It's not a big deal! Don't worry about it."

"I want to come," I said.

"No," he said, shaking his head. "Not a good idea."

Wind flung a gust of icy pellets against the office window. I met Cullen's eyes and didn't look away.

"I want to," I told him, almost whispering. "I want to see."

He hooked his forefingers in the straps of my backpack, and I let myself be tugged toward him. We kissed. We kissed, and it was wet and firm and hot and lasted forever.

Later, I was stuck on thoughts of this kiss and all the things I thought might follow it while crammed in the tiny backseat of Roman's pickup truck with my brother, all of us on our way to Elizabeth. I still wore my school uniform—a navy skirt thick as burlap, navy stockings, and a navy sweater and white blouse underneath my burgundy tweed jacket. Roman drove and snuck peeks at my legs in the rearview despite the wool stockings and even though Cullen glared at him and cleared his throat every time he glanced.

We sped over a set of long-unused railroad tracks and slowed in front of an abandoned redbrick chemical plant ornamented with broken and boarded windows and a pile of blankets clumped in the doorway, under which an unseen form hid from the winter chill. Roman gazed across the street at an apartment complex that appeared only slightly less run-down than the warehouse.

Somewhere the sun was setting; everything was colored pale. I watched Ray, but he wouldn't look at me. He dug his hands into his coat pockets, fixed his eyes on the street, and marched behind Roman, whom we all followed across the empty, quiet street.

Cullen took my elbow in his hand. "You have makeup? In your bag?"

I nodded.

"Put it on. A lot of it. More than you would ever wear."

I dug through my purse and hurriedly smeared a thick stain of lipstick across my lips and too much blush over my cheeks, while Roman tapped the button for 8C over and over, getting no answer, hopping in place from the cold, one hand in his pants, eyes looking up and down the street in search of what I did not know.

Cullen approved of the paint job. "You're a crazy-ass bitch," he told me.

"Okay."

"You don't have to say anything. Don't have to say one word if you don't want to. Just remember it deep down, and they'll believe it as surely as you do: You're a crazy-ass bitch."

I nodded, shivering where I stood and hoping to God nobody would answer from 8C, but of course eventually a voice replied—a static-filled, incomprehensible combustion of malice from upstairs to which Roman retorted with "Yo, it's Roman, kid! Let me up."

The door buzzed. Roman danced over and yanked it with his free hand. Ray still would not look at me, and while we waited for the elevator in a grim lobby that was not any warmer than it had been outside, I understood why. Today,

Ray could not be Ray and I could not be Brielle—at least not as far as the two of us understood what it meant to be those two people. Which meant being soft and safe. Which meant no television while studying. Vocab quizzes and calculus. Attending mass before opening presents on Christmas morning. Mowing the lawn and scrubbing dishes. *Amherst, Cornell, Northwestern, Dartmouth, Stanford.* Those O'Dell children would never last here. Those O'Dell children might have waited for the elevator for who knows how long if Roman had not understood very early on that the thing didn't work and had not worked for quite some time, if ever. So Ray stared at the floor—remained fixed on it almost exclusively from the time we got out of the car until we hurried back into it. Ray wasn't Ray, and Bri wasn't Bri. Only I don't know who Ray told himself he was that day. How he convinced himself to disown Ray O'Dell and who he tried to become instead. Because the moment I realized that I wouldn't look at him and that he wouldn't look at me, all that I held on to was that *I* knew what *I* would have to be in order to survive.

I would be whatever Cullen wanted me to be.

Ray

CULLEN NEVER SAID ANYTHING to me about being arrested, but obviously I knew it had happened. The day after our first run, I waited at his car after school, sore all over but ready to do it again. It was a long time before he stepped out of the front doors of the school. When he finally did, his hands were pinned behind him and two police officers were taking him across the lot to their car.

I supposed he was still mad or disappointed that I'd given up his name, but he never said anything else about it. The day after his arrest he was back at his car after school waiting for me. When I arrived he told me about the plan to buy a gun in Elizabeth.

"Okay," I said. "Perfect."

I imagined myself storming into some place and terrifying the guy working there so much that he pissed his pants and then running out with a pile of cash. I was sure the feeling I would get from that was the feeling I'd been after all along. That the whole thing would be about as Zen as you could get. One of those moments of total, otherworldly purity that most people only dream about. Death on earth.

Cullen was looking at me like he didn't really believe I was on board.

"You sure about this?"

"Of course. This is what we agreed on, right?"

"Yup. But we can always do a fake if you want to back out."

I'd never held a gun in my hand or even seen a real one in person, but it was clear that the real thing was the way to go, especially if the moment was to feel the way I wanted it to feel.

"You can get a real one?"

Cullen nodded. "Need cash, though. On top of what you still owe me."

"Okay," I said. "No problem."

Except this part was a problem, a small one, at least for the time being. I'd already spent all my lawn-mowing money, and it wasn't like I could get a job after school—being with Cullen was my job. Learning how to run was my job, and studying maps was my job, and screaming at Cullen from inside his grandmother's garage while he played the role of convenience store clerk was my job. I would try to bring up enough of the bad stuff inside me to make Cullen flinch during these sessions, but mostly all he did was stand there with a blank look on his face, unfazed by my yelling and jumping around, and then afterward he'd tell me that I was getting better but to keep working. I knew the gun would help, but he warned that I shouldn't rely on that too much when the moment came.

On the night before we bought the gun, I snuck into my parents' bedroom while Dad was with clients and Mom was asleep in bed. Bri was sitting at her desk in her room, and she leaned back to see me in the hallway.

"What are you doing?" she asked.

"None of your business."

I stepped into the bedroom like I was in a rush and like I wasn't doing anything wrong. I knew what I was looking for and where to find it. A few years ago, Tim Mason had told me he'd found a stack of *Playboys* in his father's closet, and so we'd gone looking through my own father's stuff one afternoon but had only found one single black-and-white picture of a naked woman stuffed at the bottom of his underwear drawer. The picture was wrinkled, and the black surprise of hair at the woman's middle against all that white was wild. Tim asked if he could borrow the picture for the night. I told him no, but he only relented when we found a shoe box full of cash on the top shelf of Dad's closet and I gave Tim a twenty-dollar bill in exchange for his not taking the photo.

And so this night I moved a little stool over to Dad's closet, which creaked when I opened it and made Mom stir in bed. The room was lit only by the hallway light, and Mom was just a small shape beneath blanket folds and pillow mounds. The room was damp and smelled like bad breath. It was eight P.M.; she'd been in bed all day.

"Ray," she said. "Everything okay?"

"Great, Mom," I said. "Just getting something for Dad."

"Anything you need, sweetie."

I looked at her for a moment, trying to see where her eyes were, but I couldn't find them. She twisted a little in the bed and then sighed quietly. I thought about asking her if she was feeling okay or if she needed anything or if she thought she would get better anytime soon, but of course I didn't. I knew she wouldn't answer. She'd tell me she was feeling a little tired or a little sick and that everything was going to be okay.

I pushed the little stool into the closet and reached up onto the top shelf to find the shoe box, out of which I took enough for the gun and to pay Cullen the rest of his fee. When I walked out of the room and into the light of the hallway, Bri was standing there looking at me. I walked to my room without saying anything and shut the door.

Who knows what the shoe box was for? Dad had all kinds of money that he never spent on things the rest of us wanted, like cell phones and big televisions. Maybe Dad had read St. Augustine in seminary school and also decided to turn his back on the "things of this world" that delighted him. Maybe the box was a way of avoiding the temptation to spend this money. Whatever the case, I didn't question why the shoe box was in the closet any more than I questioned my decision to take a big stack of money out of it and give that money to Cullen so that he would keep teaching me how to be a different person.

Two weeks later I stood in a freezing apartment building in Elizabeth with Cullen and Roman, hoping to buy a gun from a guy that Roman said he was boys with, and my sister was there too. I was surprised to find her with Cullen at the gas station earlier in the day but tried not to think too much of it. Even when I was little—before my friends knew why they liked my sister or what they wanted to do with her—kids I knew were always staring at Bri in funny ways, asking me questions like did she want to hang out with us or did I ever see her coming out of the shower and stuff like that. I started to think that some of these kids came over to my house to see Bri rather than hang out with me, but once I noticed this I decided to quit worrying about it. People have all sorts of reasons for doing what they do. You could go crazy trying to figure them out.

In any case, Bri was standing there next to me in that freezing apartment building in Elizabeth when Roman shoved the door of apartment 8C over a crappy carpet without knocking. Inside the apartment, a man was screaming. Had been screaming. And when the door opened, another guy started screaming too. "Shut the fucking door!" A baby cried, and a woman screamed too. "Shut the fucking door!" they all said.

The place smelled bad. Like some sort of chemical.

"Shut the fucking door!"

Roman pulled me by my arm so that I was in the room whether I liked it or not, and when he pushed the door shut over the swollen carpet I focused through the screams and smells to see a black guy holding a glowing ember of a metal rod to the bare arm of a white guy, and in the corner a pale redheaded woman was sitting on a blanket, and a diapered baby was propped against the wall, crying and crying.

The black guy placed a small block of wood in the other guy's mouth, and the white guy nodded, and then the black guy pressed the burning piece of metal into his partner's arm, and the one guy squealed like an animal through the wood in his teeth while his friend with the metal smiled an ugly smile. The baby cried and cried and wouldn't ever stop.

None of us newcomers said anything. Doing so seemed like a bad idea. I'd been struggling through Hume's *Dialogues* and was fixed on the idea of the unmoved mover, which was Plato's idea that some force must have flipped the switch to set the cycle of the world—one unending system of causes and effects—into motion and that this force, the unmoved mover, was supposed to be God. Father Joe had lent me his copy of Hume after I'd invaded his office one afternoon to discuss how impossible the prospect of God was starting to seem and how totally desperate this was making me. But even Father Joe, with his undone collar, perpetual five o'clock shadow, Radiohead creeping from the stereo, even he, like all people of God I'd met, couldn't explain what the calling had felt like or how he had come to know God. What he did was give me a book and invite me back to discuss it, which gave me a little bit of hope at the time, even if the book ended up confusing me even more. Because even if God *was* the unmoved mover, what good did that do for any of us now? So long after the fact?

Cullen had stepped into my own world and set it into motion. What had moved him, I don't know. It wasn't his parents, who'd been gone for I don't know how long. But something did it. And something had moved that something, and on and on. Cullen was our unmoved mover, and at each key point we waited for him to send his signals from up on high. So we all stood there at the door of apartment 8C, waiting to see what we were supposed to do next.

When the glowing iron dropped from the white guy's arm, he—a short, square-headed bunch of muscle with a pockmarked face—spit out the block and snatched a glass tube from the table, ignited one end with a lighter that hummed like a blowtorch, sucked in deep, and blew out an almost invisible blue smoke. He handed the pipe to his partner, who did the same. I thought maybe they'd forgotten we were there. The room filled with that chemical smell again.

"Terry." The girl in the corner scratched at her oily hair. "Terry, who are all these kids?"

The white guy turned to see us.

Cullen nudged Roman, who stepped forward. "Ter. It's me." Roman bent over and looked into the guy's blank face. "Roman."

"What the fuck"—the guy's throat spasmed, and he swallowed down gulps of air—"do you want?"

"Uh, I wanted . . ."

"Who let you in?"

"You did, man. You, uh, you buzzed . . ."

Terry rose, taking the pipe from his friend. "I did?" he said. His eyes seemed to come alive all of a sudden, back from the dead. "You knocked, and I said, 'Who is it?' and you said, 'It's Roman,' and I opened the door and welcomed you into my home and told you to bring all these goofy-ass kids with you? Is that what happened?"

"Terry . . ."

"Is that what just happened, Roman?"

"But you buzzed us up."

"Is that what happened, yes or no? You knocked, and I answered, and let you in. Yes or no?"

"No, man. That's not what happened."

Terry sniffed and wiped his nose with his fist. The blister on his arm was in the shape of an *E*. He looked us over, lingering on Bri, then reached out and touched her face— poked at it with his middle finger, dimpling her cheeks, then moving down to her neck, and then her breasts, just poking like a kid nudging a dead body with a stick. I stared at the ground. He poked her chest again and again, and I stepped toward him, but Cullen gripped my wrist and shifted in front of me. Terry glanced at us, barely distracted, his eyes blank again, dead, and Bri took his finger and put it in his own mouth. He grinned—a dumb, drooly smile with his middle finger hanging from his teeth—and then handed the pipe to Bri.

Bri stared at the pipe. Cullen dug his grip into my forearm. Terry glared at me. "Easy," he said.

I thought about how Amir wouldn't just stand here and let this happen. I pictured ripping the guy's esophagus out. Gripping and pulling it through his skin. If I'd already had a gun in that moment I probably would've shot the guy and not thought twice about it. My sister held the pipe in her hand and looked at me, and I looked away from her. Suddenly I couldn't understand that this was where we'd come and this was what we were doing.

"Just show me you cool," Terry said. "That's all. You can pay?"

Cullen produced a wad of cash from his pocket.

"Perfect, man. So, just show me you cool. That you not just a bunch of assholes who broke into my shit and don't even knock." He pointed to the pipe, wobbling where he stood, then turned to his friend on the couch. "Fuck," he said, fingering the blistering scar on his arm. "Shit kills."

The guy on the couch nodded. The baby was crying again.

Cullen took the pipe and the lighter from Brielle and smoked from the pipe—sucked a puff of smoke that gathered inside the glass like a tornado and then shot from the chamber into his mouth. He coughed it back up again.

Terry laughed and shook Cullen's shoulder.

"Okay?" Cullen said.

Terry watched Bri. He wobbled on his heels and reached his finger out again, but she snatched it before it touched her.

She raised her eyes to meet Terry's, and when I looked over to see this I wasn't as angry as I'd just been. Instead, I was surprised to find that this wasn't my sister at all. Something had changed in her face. Her eyes squinted and her jaw tightened, and she gazed at this guy with his tattooed neck and the tiny beads of blood oozing from his arm and a head twisted with crack or meth or whatever it was in the pipe that made all that blue smoke. She looked at him with the look of a girl who not only belonged in the room but somehow seemed to own it. She didn't say anything, but everyone saw it and got real quiet. Her body shifted a little, and her chest rose, and she took Terry's finger, placed it between her teeth, and bit down, softly at first so that Terry's eyes blinked and his knees twitched, but then harder and harder until Terry folded and blurted out a screaming laugh, his body bent and hanging by a fingernail from Bri's teeth, groaning, one hand on his crotch, until she let him drop and he curled up on the floor, squirming around like a cut-in-half worm.

The redhead rose from the corner and was screaming at Bri, "Fucking bitch! Fucking stupid bitch!" The guy from the couch intercepted her and pushed her back into her corner, saying over and over: "Calm. Calm." But even then, the Bri who eyed the girl wasn't any Bri I'd ever seen before. She glared at the girl like she wasn't afraid of anything.

Brielle

THE O'DELLS do not exactly thrive on confrontation. Only once do I remember a true familial altercation—at my grandmother's house down the shore, soon after my grandfather had died, during a period in which I'd once overheard Grandma telling my mother, her daughter, that she'd been crying herself to sleep every night for the past month and a half. The trips had grown into caretaking missions—checking in with Grandma, cooking a small dinner for her, some vacuuming, some laundry. Maybe we went to the beach and maybe we didn't. And in this new world, Ray and I—no longer adorably scrappy and photogenic youngsters but now gawky and surly teenagers—faded into the background. Maybe it was that fading that let my aunt and my grandmother forget themselves one night and burst into a shouting match that shook the walls of my grandmother's seaside cottage and culminated in my aunt—my mother's drunk, red-cheeked, red-haired sister—hurling a beer bottle at my grandmother that just missed her head and smashed into the wall behind her.

Mom and Dad quickly escorted us away from the fracas that had shaken our world, where family meant everyone getting along at all costs. Where there was no bellowing and no swearing, and if there were any real issues they were, as far as my brother and I knew, resolved quietly and mysteriously behind closed doors by grown-ups. But there on a warm July night in Lavallette, New Jersey, with the salt of the ocean sneaking through the screened porch and a pot of crabs boiling on the old yellow stove, suddenly the veil had dropped, and behind it lay a trembling and violent rage that shook me to the core so much that I stamped my head to my mother's shoulder and pushed my palm over my other ear to plug the gap and halt the flood of growing up coming on too fast. Mom hurried us out of the house, loaded us in the car, and Dad drove us away—an hour and a half back to Rosewood—hoping to let the moment dissolve before the memory congealed into permanence for Ray and me. At some point on the way home, Ray started crying and we pulled over so Mom could sit in the backseat with him. I had to move to the front. I remember wondering why Mom couldn't just sit in the middle, between the two of us, but I never said anything. I just curled up against the window in the front seat and felt so alone, trying to forget what I'd seen that night.

It was a similar feeling that overtook me that day in

Elizabeth. Those same thoughts: *Get out of here, Bri. Make this stop. Stop the screaming and forget it now, because you are not safe here. If you stay much longer, this will be inside you for good.*

But I didn't leave. We were huddled close together—Cullen's arm touched my shoulder, and I focused on feeling him there. I was passable as long as Cullen was here, and there he was, I could feel him. His world. His story. And in his story, I was meant to be the type of girl who wouldn't gasp and weep and fumble for the door but instead would do something bitter or cruel or perverted or whatever it was that I did when I took that guy's finger in my teeth and clamped down harder and harder with a sick, simmering anger, staring at the girl coming at me from the corner—a sparkling fire of bone and freckles and big lost eyes flaring at me—telling her with just one look: Back. The fuck. Off.

And it worked.

They took the money and gave us a gun.

Cullen pocketed the pistol inside his coat, patting it while his hands twitched, his mouth seeming to chew on his tongue, nodding at Terry and his partner, who now held a glowing metal rod over a hot plate by the window. Terry grinned at me when we left, sucking on his finger, eyes twinkling with perversion.

In the truck, on the way back, Cullen rocked in the front passenger seat. Shoulders hunched, fingers clawing at his neck, he couldn't stop moving, chewing, looking all over, and talking because of the stuff Terry had made him smoke.

"I'm fucked up," he was saying, cracking his neck. "God, I'm fucked up." He whipped his head back and forth and popped his eyes wide, letting the icy wind from an open window whip his face. "Shit, God. How long does this last?"

Roman shrugged. "One time I smoked a dime bag laced with PCP. Lit me up for a *while*."

"Everyone-always-says-that." Cullen's words ran together as one. "That they smoked some shit laced with whatever. Whatever, man. I can't even . . ."

"I did, though. For real."

"Whatever, man. I never seen anybody feel like I do from smoking a blunt, Ro."

I dared my hand onto his shoulder, and he shrugged it off. Ray pulled his jacket in tight against the wind from Cullen's window.

"What's it feel like?" Ray asked.

"A lightning storm. Like . . . like my veins . . . my veins are electrical sockets and my brain is, like, squeezing out through my eyes."

Roman reached over and popped open the glove compartment while he steered. "Grab that."

Cullen produced a leather eyeglass case and took a small joint from it.

"Calm you down," Roman told him.

Cullen flipped through the glove compartment and found a lighter. A trembling hand fixed the thin, twisted thing between his lips, and with a flick and a spark it flamed from one end. He pulled on it, eyes closed, breathing in until he couldn't fit one bit more, and then one last pull on top of that, all of which he spit out in a spastic fit of choking.

He passed it back to Ray with his chest still convulsing. Ray took it between his fingers, considered it, and then passed it to me without inhaling. A gray urban world flickered by. Irvington or Orange or Brick Church. I didn't even know. Just rails and houses and something of a sky—all smoky and dimmed beneath a dreary blue winter light.

I held the joint. Cullen fixed his stare at the dashboard, stuck in his pose like a bird I saw once on our backyard fence post. It was so stiff and motionless I thought it was dead, but Dad told me it was "stunned." Lincoln must have scared him, he told me. Scared him stiff. Stunned, not dead, was Cullen, looking at the dashboard and not at me.

I put the joint to my lips and breathed in.

"Like you're going underwater," Cullen mumbled. "A big breath like you're going under."

I tried again, and this time I felt it. Suffered the smoke pushing into me then fleeing. Cullen picked the joint from my fingers while I coughed so much I thought I might die.

"Feel better?" Roman said.

Cullen shook his head no. Dank smoke settled into the old upholstery. The truck rattled out of ironbound streets and into the suburbs, where the season's first Christmas lights sparkled from handsome houses like thousands and thousands of tiny stars in the dull twilight. Cullen chewed on his tongue and turned the gun over in his hands, feeling its weight.

The pot swallowed me up into myself like a starburst. Left me windless and cold and fluttery. Aware of my heart and its insistence. Its relentlessness. I didn't like it, and I was left wondering what in the world made me think I would. I reached out to Ray and took his hand in mine, but he quickly pulled it away. My breathing tripped, and suddenly I was crying. But then I had the thought that maybe I'd been crying all along, and it was only now that I noticed it.

Cullen

IT WAS METH. I'm sure of it. Felt like my blood was on fire for like forty-five minutes, and then it was gone and I was burned out. Bone dry. Next day at school I fell asleep in the library before the first bell. My car was in the shop getting new shocks, so I'd hopped on the school bus with all the freshmen and sophomores that morning, which delivered me thirty minutes early. I'd curled up in a cubby at the far end of the library before class, and when I woke it was the middle of third period and nobody knew I was there. I felt so shitty that I just left. Walked home. Took me three hours to cover the ten miles home, but it was better than the alternative—staggering into the dean of men's office and trying to explain why I was so wiped out that I'd slept through almost the entire morning. Why my eyes were shot with blood and why my breath reeked like death no matter how many times I brushed my teeth. I stopped at White Castle on the way home and ate a six-pack of burgers before hurling them up in the filthy bathroom. When I got home, Nana was halfway through *Days of Our Lives*.

I collapsed on the couch next to her. She waited until the first commercial break to turn to me, confused.

"What're you doing home?" She spoke in a perpetual whisper, courtesy of six decades' worth of Marlboro Reds.

"I'm sick," I told her.

She leaned over, the chair creaking, to peek out at the driveway, where the car was missing. "How'd you get here?"

"Walked."

She watched the show. I tried to sleep but couldn't—my brain felt like someone was stretching it end to end and it was about to come apart in the middle. Many minutes passed. Another commercial break.

"Walked?" she said.

"Yeah."

"Let me see your face."

I leaned my head halfway off the couch.

"You're sick?" she said.

I nodded. She inspected my face. And then smiled.

"What?" I said.

"Just like your dad."

"I'm sick!" I insisted.

"Your dad always assumed I was some kinda dummy too. What'd you get into last night?"

"Nothing."

"*Nothing*," she said, smiling, nodding. "Mm-hm."

The show came back on. I remembered that I hadn't made a sandwich for her that morning, feeling as terrible as I did and rushing to catch the dumb yellow school bus three blocks away. It took just about all of my strength to make it to the kitchen now, where I slapped three pieces of turkey and one piece of Swiss on a roll and cut an apple into eight slices.

"I'm not hungry," she said, when I returned with the food.

I plopped it on the TV tray next to her La-Z-Boy. "Yeah, yeah."

I was so exhausted, about to tilt over like a rotten tree onto the couch, when Nana said, "There's a beer in the bottom drawer of the garage fridge."

"Huh?"

"Drink it," she said, not taking her eyes off the show. "It'll help you sleep."

"You sure?" I asked.

She nodded. Watched the show.

"*Nothing*," she said again, smirking, chuckling softly. "Mm-hm."

I had to hand it to her. At eighty-three, she couldn't remember to make—nor sometimes even eat—her own food, and she needed an oxygen tank to help her breathe, and even right now, as she looked at me, a bewildered, watery gaze in her eyes, I couldn't be sure if she knew for certain—as she had just moments ago—that I was her grandson and not her son . . . but she always knew when I was lying. She couldn't have known exactly what kind of seriously off-the-wall stuff I'd gotten into yesterday, but still, she knew enough. And I was thankful for that, actually.

As I left in search of my garage-fridge beer, I saw her pick up the sandwich and take a bite.

The next day was Saturday. Bri, Amir, Ray, and I took the pistol down to the Pine Barrens in south Jersey, where nobody would hear us firing it. We brought along a box of bullets that I bought from a local sporting goods spot, twenty-four empty beer bottles that we lifted from a curbside recycling container, and lunch—hot dogs, rolls, and two cans of beans.

After about an hour south on the Parkway we headed west toward Harrisville and then into the part of southern, rural Jersey where nobody lived. We followed back roads and dirt roads and finally off-roading paths through miles of woods. There wasn't another soul within earshot. I jammed the old car off roots and boulders and cracked through icy mud pits, happy for those new shocks. Amir and Ray sprung and rebounded across the backseat like a couple of hysterical little pimple-faced pinballs, while Bri yelped in the passenger seat, digging into my arm, trying to stop laughing for long enough to beg me to slow down. We settled the car in a muddy mixture of sand and scrub on the shore of a half-frozen pond outlined by rows of dead trees.

We set the bottles on a pine log and aimed the Glock from a sandy clearing twenty yards away. After an hour and not a single broken bottle, we moved closer, and the shots started hitting home.

I built a small fire and stood over it with Bri to roast the dogs, which we'd speared with mossy twigs. Bri crouched across from me to focus on her cooking. Behind her in the distance, Ray stood beside Amir, whose shots struck one bottle after another—the explosion of gun and glass one big shattering echo that never stopped. Ray flinched with each new shot, but Amir stood his ground, his shoulders taking the recoil as sturdily as his squat figure would allow.

Bri wore an argyle scarf that covered her mouth and nose, so her eyes were just about all you could see of her face, and they were those perfect eyes of hers—big, brown, wet eyes. Her hair too—brown all down her shoulders, and her hands in red gloves but also perfect, thin, and girlish beneath the wool. All of her there through the smoke, heat rising from the campfire. She turned her eyes from the fire to me in a way that suggested she'd known all along I'd been staring, and at first I looked away like an oaf, but then I met her gaze with some amount of suggestion.

"Your wiener's on fire."

I pulled my dog from the flames and blew out the charred, burning edge.

"Nice," I told her. "Nicely done."

"It was right there. An easy one." She ran a finger over the underside of her thumb.

"What'd you think of the gun?"

"Fun. Scary, but fun."

She'd taken a turn after me and suffered a small burn

under her thumb but until that point had hit some pretty good shots and seemed to be happy about it.

"What are you going to do with it?"

"Have to ask Ray about that."

"I'm asking you."

"Nothing bad."

"But nothing good."

"It's just a prop, really. We're not even going to fire it."

"So why not get a prop? Why drive down here and go through all this trouble learning how to use it?"

I dropped the dog into a bun and squirted mustard on it. "Because," I told her. "What else were we going to do today?"

When Amir and Ray had exhausted themselves with the pistol, they joined us around the fire. I cracked open the beans and shoved them in the coals, building the flames up to a respectable height with the pathetic supply of twigs available. A ton of pine grew in the sandy soil down here, but it was all rubbery and oozing with sap and most of it didn't want to burn. Ray and Amir volunteered to bring back some real logs from the other side of the lake, where there seemed to be an entire warehouse of dead wood. Bri and I watched them march away through the brush in their winter getups—oversized hand-me-down coats and hats and boots, like two little orphans clomping along through the great outdoors.

From the car I grabbed two wool blankets I'd bought from the army surplus store. We laid one before the fire, and she sat between my legs and leaned back into me. We sat there, watched the fire, and didn't talk. Winter birds piped in trees. The wind came in across the water. We shuffled closer to the fire and huddled under the second blanket.

I had the thought in that moment that I didn't want to hurt anybody. If I were a different sort of person, I might have taken this as an excuse to call off the whole thing. But the thought went away as quickly as it came in. I could've held on to it if I really wanted to, but I let it go and didn't think about it anymore after that.

I rubbed a hand across Bri's side and dared to move it up to her breast—mostly a soft mound of clothing—and she shifted to kiss me. We kissed like that for a long time, not risking to go any further with her brother across the lake, and the cold preventing any real chance of baring skin. Still, I grew hard beneath my long johns, and she pushed herself against me.

Ray and Amir came back with what we all assumed was way more firewood than we'd ever need but that proved to be just the right amount, given the disaster that was about to hit us. The sun had dropped below the clouds and trees, and the general feeling was that it was time for home. But the muddy patch where I left the Buick had frozen over, and the car's tires were wedged in a foot of ice. I spent an hour chopping at the ice with a dinky little hand shovel and then a good forty-five minutes rocking the car with the boys while Bri spun the wheels deeper into what was still mud beneath the layers of frozen dirt. By the end of all this business we'd made a serious mess. Despite the bottom layer of mud, it was still the ice that locked us in. There was nothing to do but wait until the day warmed up tomorrow and melted us out. I thought about running the engine in hopes that it would melt the ground beneath it, but a car stuck in ice was better than one without gas. So we settled in for a long wait.

The night was damn cold, and we threw tree-sized branches onto the flames, which grew six feet high. We scooped off the second can of beans into leftover hot dog buns and told jokes and had a good time for a while. When Amir stepped away to take a piss, a loosened-up Ray whispered to his sister how we were going to rob a convenience store on Christmas Eve.

She didn't say anything at first. Maybe she nodded a little. Looked into the fire.

"Why are you telling me?" she asked.

"Cullen said you kept asking about it."

Bri tightened her lips and wiped a gloved hand across her nose. They were a funny brother-sister pair. Sometimes I wondered if they'd ever even talked to each other before I came along.

"I won't talk you out of it," Bri said.

"That's not why I told you."

"Do what you want. I won't talk you out of it."

Ray kicked at some leaves at his feet. He was expecting more from her, I could tell. But Brielle wasn't going to be roped into being the responsible one. The boring one. *Good for her*, I thought.

Amir skipped back toward the fire, tugging at his fly. We all stood silent in the darkness for a while before Amir asked the inevitable question. "What now?"

We took the army blankets into the back of the Buick. I dropped the gun and the bullets in the trunk and, after failing to find a sleeping bag or towel or some other source of warmth in there, grabbed a headlamp and a torn-up copy of J. G. Ballard stories. We crammed ourselves into the backseat, and I read a science fiction story aloud about a group of scientists who undergo a procedure to do away with their need for sleep. The scientists lose their hold on reality, quickly and predictably slipping into a waking nightmare. By the time I finished, the others had drifted off. I clicked off the lamp and let my head fall onto Brielle's, which had found a spot on my shoulder.

There might have been times after that night when the four of us were together like that, but I don't remember them, or if I do, I choose to ignore them. Cramped in a car, heads on shoulders on heads on shoulders, legs flung all crazy across each other's laps. You might have even thought we were happy.

Ray

SHOOTING THE GUN felt like a punch to the heart, just like I wanted it to. The guy in Elizabeth had given us a Glock 21. It looked like a cop's pistol, which probably should have made me doubly nervous about getting caught with it but which actually made me more excited to try it.

It was lighter in my hand than I thought it'd be, but it took a long time to figure out how to hold it the right way so I could actually fire it. Cullen showed me how to fix my left hand around my right wrist, which he said was too flimsy and helpless against the gun's kick. I fired one round after another, missing every time. It felt so futile to incite this terrific explosion but then have no results to show for it. No payoff. Where did the bullets go? Did they ever hit *anything*? Or did they just keep sailing until they finally ran out of momentum and dropped to the ground?

Like all of us, Amir hadn't ever shot a gun before, but he was much better at it than we were. He'd fire off a quick five or six shots, and each one of them would blast a bottle into nothingness. We laughed like crazy at how good he was.

Cullen drew a line in the leaves halfway between the bottles and me and told me to move closer. I held out the gun from this new distance and felt dumb.

"They're right there," I said. "Anybody could do it."

"Just try it," he said.

I fired off another six shots and hit two bottles. *Two.* But those two felt good. It was like the bottles were connected to something inside me and I could explode them with the slightest twitching signal sent from my brain. I felt in those brief moments something like I'd felt in the stolen car—that the junk of life was far away and couldn't touch me. But when I moved back to the original line, I was back to casting round after round of bullets into the great unknown.

"It's fine," Cullen said. "We won't load it on the day anyway."

"Why not?"

"Uh, you know . . . so we don't kill anybody."

Of course I didn't want to shoot anyone, but I was no good at lying to myself, and the gun wouldn't give me what I needed unless there were bullets in it. I needed it to be real. All of it.

"What if you need to shoot the ceiling or something?" Amir said. "To show the guy you mean business?"

Cullen looked at Amir. He spoke very slowly. "There are

a lot of reasons," he said, more to Amir than to me, "to not load the gun."

"Whatever," Amir said. "If you're gonna do something, do it all the way. That's what I think."

"Exactly," I said. "I want it loaded."

Cullen kept watching Amir, his eyes narrowing. Finally he turned to me. "Okay," he said. "Figured you might want to play it safe, Ray. But hey, if that's how you want to roll . . . I'm all in."

Later, after lunch, Amir and I were cracking our boots through icy dirt, across a muddy pond from where Brielle sat with Cullen next to a little fire. We dragged tree-sized pieces of wood behind us, stomping around the half-frozen lake, hurling much more wood than we would ever need into a giant pile. The sky was low and gray, and the forest of pines stretched to forever in every direction.

"The problem is you're in your head," Amir said.

"Huh?"

"When you're shooting. You have to stop thinking. Just see the thing and shoot. Look."

He took the pistol out of one jacket pocket and a bottle out of the other.

I glanced across the pond, where smoke twisted from the flames of our fire. Cullen and my sister appeared as one shadowed figure beside the fire.

"Does Cullen know you have that?"

"He won't care. Watch. This'll help."

Amir shoved the pistol into my hand, marched across the clearing, positioned himself against a tree trunk, and balanced the bottle on his head.

I laughed.

"See it and shoot."

"You're kidding," I told him.

He didn't say anything. He stood very still, so as to not let the bottle tip over.

"Amir," I said. "Come on, man. Stop."

"See it and shoot!" he said. "It's so simple."

"I'm not going to."

"I'll wait."

I shook my head and watched a squirrel dart up a tree. I knew what he meant. Whenever I aimed the gun, a million doubtful thoughts would swarm into my mind like a cloud of wasps. I needed to detach from myself, just like I had that day in the woods when I met Cullen. I needed Zen. I needed to connect myself through some metaphysical string to the target. I needed the kind of focus that only comes with the most intense kind of fear—the fear of shooting your best friend, for instance.

But still.

"Okay," I said. "Point made."

"Shoot the bottle, Ray."

"I won't."

"Shoot it!"

"No! Amir! Stop!"

"Shoot the fucking bottle off my head!" He was scream-ing like mad. His face went pepper red. "Do it! You coward!"

"Shut up!"

"What are you so afraid of?"

"Shut up!"

"Do it, you fucking pussy!"

"Fine!" I shouted. "Fine! Fuck you, I'll fucking shoot you. That's what you want?"

"Do it!"

I raised the gun. Clicked off the safety. Shut one eye. Aimed.

Amir's eyes were locked on mine, his face still flushed from yelling, the pale scar on his forehead turning pink. The bottle quivered slightly. I held it in sight. *It's right there*, I thought. So simple.

But I didn't do it. I couldn't. I was forever stuck. Stuck in my head, and stuck in my body, and stuck in the world. There was no way out of myself.

I lowered the gun. Amir took the bottle off his head and, disappointed, chucked it against a tree. I sat on a mossy log that was so rotted away I thought it might turn to sand when I landed on it. Amir came over and sat beside me. A long time passed before one of us talked.

"Why do we have bodies at all?" I said.

"What do you mean? What else would we have?"

"If we have souls, I mean. If we have souls, and the body carries the soul, why do we have bodies at all?"

"Because we don't have souls."

"But if we *do*, I'm saying. If we do have souls. We gather wood, because our bodies are cold. Our bodies get tired. They get hurt. And they get dirty. And they stink. And they're ugly. And they so rarely, or ever, perform the way we want them to perform. Why not just have souls, if that's the way it is? We could all just . . . be."

"Because we don't have souls."

We sat and watched the pond. Dead branches came out of the water like an army of haunted swords.

"My father believes in God," Amir said. "Prays to Him five times a day."

"But not you."

"Nah," he said. He rubbed his hands together.

"Why'd he send you to Catholic school?"

"Good school," he said. "That's all."

"You like it?"

"School? Who likes school?"

"I mean, you know . . . Amir Shadid. At a Catholic school."

Amir shrugged. "Last summer my brother told me it's easier at St. John's than at public school because at St. John's you can't forget you don't really belong. It's when you forget that you get in trouble."

"You feel like that too?"

He shrugged again. "It's only been a few months."

He stood and stepped around the edge of the pond, dunking the tips of his boots through the skin of ice.

"Okay," he said. "Say a mother bear runs out of those

woods right now. Right? And the cub is, like, over there, so we're between them. What would happen?"

"We'd be dead."

"We're all just dumbass animals, totally oblivious to the ways of the universe. We're just, like, food for each other."

"You believe that?"

"I know it. The bear doesn't know God. Why should we be different?"

"But we are different. We know about God."

"Just 'cause we can imagine Him doesn't mean anything. We can imagine plenty of things that aren't real. Dragons. Unicorns. Aliens."

"So then what's the point? Why even bother?"

"The point is don't worry about the point! You can miss out on a lot of good stuff worrying about the fucking point of it all."

My butt had caught the cold from the log. I stood and stretched, staring up into the gray sky, which was so low it looked like it had crashed to earth. Amir gathered his wood-pile. He'd been serious, I thought. He'd really wanted me to shoot that bottle.

"But for the record," he said, fussing with the mess of branches at his feet, "I think you have a nice body. Not ugly at all."

"That's not what I meant."

"I know, but I only mean our bodies aren't so bad. They're kinda nice, actually."

I hauled in my stack of branches. It was a half mile

around the lake back to Brielle and Cullen, and we dragged the sticks along the lake's shore. After a while, Amir paused and looked at me, breathing white.

"Does it make you uncomfortable? What I said?"

"No."

"I just mean it's okay to feel good about yourself sometimes."

"Yeah."

"You scared?" he said. "About Christmas Eve?"

"I don't know. Maybe."

"My dad always says if you're not nervous, you're not ready. But don't sweat it. It's gonna be so sick. I wish I was going with you."

I hugged my stack of wood to my chest and blew warm breath into my hands. Except for Bri, who was my sister, and Cullen, whom I was paying to spend time with me, Amir was my only friend. The only person to whom I'd ever really talked.

Three days later I knocked on the door to Father Joe's office during my lunch period. It was the last day of school before Christmas break, and I wanted to return the loaner copy of Hume. Father Joe opened the door. I moved to enter the office, but he put up a hand. Inside, on the leather couch, sat Nick. And he was . . . was he . . . crying? His eyes were red and swollen, and he glanced once at me and then looked away, wiping his nose.

"Give me one minute, okay, Ray?"

Father Joe moved back inside. I waited in the hall. When the door opened again, Nick stepped out, not looking at me as he marched away.

"Come on in, Ray."

I entered holding out the book like it was a shield. I didn't want to ask about Nick. I didn't want to know if he'd actually been crying or, if so, why. I'd already seen too much as it was. So I returned the book. I thanked Father Joe for lending it to me. Our conversation meandered, as it often did, to God, and I asked him about the body and the soul and humans and bears, and, even though Father Joe was trying his best, I found his answers to be pretty weak. Our talks inevitably bottomed out when I insisted that he explain his faith and he insisted that faith was the one thing he couldn't explain and never would.

"But why do you believe?" I said. "How do you know?"

"Ray," he said, and this time he stood from behind his desk and sat beside me on the couch in his office, running his hands over the cheap fabric of his pants. "There's no reason to it. You can read all the books in the world about it. And you should. And you can talk yourself in and out of God's existence over and over. And you should do that too. But, in the end, there's no reasoning with God. No logic. No proof. I believe just because I do. That's faith."

He watched me until I looked at him, and then he said again, as though he'd suddenly realized it was true, "I believe because I do."

Father Joe checked his watch, planted two hands on his knees, and pushed himself up from the couch.

"I don't think I believe," I told him.

He grabbed his clerical collar from a nearby shelf and fitted it around his neck, which was always red and irritated from a recent shave. "Maybe that's true right now. But it's not permanent."

"I don't," I said. "I don't believe."

"I know." The bell sang out, signaling next period, and he reached for the door. "Keep working at it."

He held an arm toward the door, and I stepped into the hall. The post-lunch migration herded around us, emptying into classroom doors. Father Joe stepped into the stream of students to be swept along to his next class, where he would teach about the poets and monks and geniuses and madmen and whores and prophets and kings and warriors and martyrs who had testified, lived, fought, and died in the name of God, and where he would ask kids like me what they thought about all that. And what were they supposed to say?

Theology was my last class of the day, so I wouldn't have to deal with all that for another few hours. In the meantime, though, I was due at the gym. And I wasn't wearing any shorts under my khakis. It had slipped my mind that morning, distracted as I was by our Christmas Eve plans. Instead of seeking some escape—begging a note from the nurse or claiming to have forgotten my shorts altogether—I resigned myself to retrieving the spare pair I kept in the locker room, hoping that Nick might be distracted enough by whatever he'd been discussing with Father Joe that he wouldn't insist on kicking my ass for no good reason at all. This, I found out, was a stupid way of thinking.

When I walked into the locker room, Nick wasn't there yet. Hurrying to the far corner of the room, I changed in a jerky panic, rushing the procedure, hoping to get out of there as soon as possible. When he entered, he looked right at me. He had a short, punchy face with an angry little nose and always seemed to be breathing a little too heavily, like a bull. The cheeks below his eyes were still puffy.

He dropped his backpack at his locker and danced over to me on his toes like a boxer.

"Haven't had my warm-ups in a while," he said. "Where you been, Ray-Gay?"

He started punching my arms. Softly at first—almost like we were friends and he was just playing with me. But soon the blows came more forcefully. The soft ones hurt my arm, and the hard ones hurt everything. They rocked me back and forth as the vibrations went from my chest to my head. It felt like being in that car crash over and over. For a while I just stood there, hoping it would be over soon. Usually the punching lasted only a few minutes, but this time it went on and on. Nick bobbing on his toes, dodging invisible blows, then charging in to punish my arms.

Finally, he wiped some sweat from his forehead and started back toward his locker. "Whew," he said. "Feeling good today."

I turned to my locker and said, "Crybaby," in a voice that wasn't as quiet as I wanted it to be.

"What'd you say?" He was marching back toward me, shoulders bent, fists ready.

He grabbed my shirt and pulled me close to him. He smelled like cologne and lunch meat. "What'd you say?"

"Nothing," I said.

He slapped me across the face.

"What'd you say?"

"Nothing."

He slapped me again and asked me again, and again I said, "Nothing," this time in a voice that I could barely hear because I wasn't sure if it was the right answer or not. But of course there wasn't any right answer. My face was hot from the slapping, and I was trying not to cry, struggling to remember that I wasn't a little kid, even though getting beat up like that sure makes you feel like one.

Finally, he let go of my shirt and walked away saying, "Don't fuck with me today, Ray-Gay. Feeling too good." He walked to his locker, where two of his friends were laughing, having watched the whole thing. Everyone else dressed without talking and didn't look at me.

I took off my shirt and thought about Amir with that bottle on his head.

It was a stupid word. The kind of insult an eight-year-old makes. But I knew he would know what it meant. I knew it would piss him off.

"Crybaby." I took two steps away from my locker and looked him in the eyes. "I called you a crybaby."

Nick laughed. He looked at his two friends, laughed again, wiped his mouth, and charged at me. He moved so fast I barely even saw it happen. In an instant he was on me and had thrown me into the sharp corner of an open locker, which smacked into my eye. I fell to the floor, and Nick picked me up by a limp arm, like a rag doll, and thunder-punched me in the chest. I saw an explosion of fiery red and wanted so badly to fall to the floor and not ever get up, but Nick still had me by that arm.

He dragged me to the center of the room, and the instant he let go I tried to scramble away, but again he grabbed me. This time I tried something I'd never done before, which was fighting back. I tossed a bunch of helpless fists at him, but all he did was swipe them away and hit me hard in the mouth. Then, finally, I was on the floor for good.

"Fuck," Nick said. He held the hand that had hit me at his hip, wincing while opening and closing it. "Little bitch."

I unfolded myself from the floor and walked to my locker, trying to make it look like everything was okay and like I wasn't badly hurt. I even thought that some of my punches might have landed and that maybe people thought it had been a real fight, instead of what it was.

Rather than continuing to put on my gym clothes, I changed back into my school uniform, tugging my shirt over all those new, hot bruises, trying to figure out how to tie my tie through the pain. My eye hurt like crazy, my mouth was bloody, and I didn't feel like going to any more classes. I waited downstairs until Nick and everyone else was gone, and then I snuck through the mostly empty halls, making sure no teachers saw me.

On the second floor, I found Amir sitting in the front row of his Latin class. I stood at the door, unseen by the teacher and all but a few students, staring at him until he noticed me. When he did, he gaped at me for a long time, not seeming to understand what he was looking at, and then he raised his hand and asked to go to the bathroom.

I walked down the hall and into the stairwell, waiting. Amir came in, looked at me, and put a hand on my arm.

"What happened?" he whispered.

"I don't know," I said.

We were near the corner of the stairwell. Amir stepped close and hugged me. He wrapped two small arms around my shoulders and squeezed me tight. It was all I could do to not cry.

"Come on," he said.

He took me by the hand. We snuck through the halls until we found Cullen lounging in a European history class. Again, I stood in the hall, willing him to look my way before the teacher did. Again, once he saw me, I walked, with Amir by my side this time, into the stairwell.

"Jesus, Ray," Cullen said. "What the hell?"

"Can you give him a ride home?" Amir asked.

"What happened?"

"Just—can you give him a ride?"

Cullen reached a hand out to my eye, but I flinched away.

"That O'Dwyer kid?"

I nodded.

"I have class," he said.

"You'll be right back," Amir told him. "Come on."

So Cullen drove me home. Dad was going to notice my eye and the fat lip and any other visible signs of what had happened, and I knew I'd have to explain it all eventually, to him and to teachers and counselors, but at the time all I wanted was to be by myself and not talk about it. Cullen knew that and didn't say anything on the drive, which was the best thing I could have asked for.

While Cullen drove me home, I thought about how I would miss theology class and wouldn't have to think about all those God questions if I didn't want to today. But of course, I ended up doing it anyway. The more you don't want to think about something, the more it just hangs around in your mind. When I got home and splashed water across my busted-up face, I was thinking again that God wasn't in Father Joe's prayers and parables and readings at all but instead was something you could only find for yourself through some wild undertaking. A test that could push someone like me through the fire, into the light. And if you didn't make it through, and if instead you died along the way . . . could that really be much worse than the way things were now?

Brielle

AT EIGHT P.M. on Christmas Eve, I stood before the mirror of the upstairs bathroom, applying eyeliner. I hadn't yet put on stockings, and even though it was below freezing out and even though my legs were already goose-bumped before I'd set foot outside, I decided that I would leave them bare.

Dad had fixed himself on the idea of midnight mass, and we were all in the midst of our preparations. There'd been a time, he told us, when the whole neighborhood—neighbors and their extended families—would gather for post-dinner Christmas Eve drinks and then march off to mass together in a festive parade. They were merry occasions, and they provided a sense of community that Dad was nostalgic for and whose absence he partly blamed on his children's—and probably his wife's too—wayward drift out of our familial orbit.

Ray and I had come home from our night in the Pine Barrens cold, hungry, and exhausted. I felt disembodied while talking to my parents about it, as though I were floating in the corner of the room, watching myself invent a story for their benefit like I was a character in movie. The narrative was close enough to the truth but was still, of course, a lie. We'd gone hiking, I told Dad, and lost the trail. Where? Up at Sunfish Pond. We had to sleep on the freezing wooden floor of an Appalachian Trail shelter. It was terrible. We were terrified. How did we get there? Who were we with? Scarlett's older sister, Marie, drove us in her parents' minivan. It was Marie and her boyfriend and Scarlett and me and Ray and Ray's friend Amir. Why didn't we tell them we were going? We did. I told Mom. Didn't I, Mom?

We were all in my bedroom, my father having pursued me up the stairs with this line of questioning. Mom was slumped against the threshold, eyes dark and weighty. A hand went to her hair and fiddled with a strand. "I remember," she said. "You were going out with friends. That's all you said. It's fine."

Dad tensed all over, knowing this was a pitiful move on my part—that telling Mom wasn't really telling anyone at all. "Was Cullen there?"

"No."

"You can tell me if he was."

"Just the people I said." A shiver went through me. I crawled under the covers of my bed. "I'm still cold."

Ray stood at my window, staring outside like he couldn't stand to watch all this maneuvering on our part.

"Ray?" Dad said. "Are you okay?"

Ray turned from the window but still made no eye contact. "Just tired," he said. "Like Bri said. We were freezing cold all night."

Dad's eyes went soft. *God*, I thought. *It's too easy.* So much trust in him he couldn't help it.

"Well," he said. "We're glad you're both safe."

Still, despite his limitless capacity for faith in others and for forgiveness when such faith proved to be misguided, Dad sensed we were offering an incomplete portrait of where we'd been. And so Christmas was meant to be a proper O'Dell household occasion. Midnight mass at St. Michael's, as at most parishes, now took place at the much more sober hour of ten P.M. on Christmas Eve, but Dad was nevertheless intent on the idea.

Yet, all of the social fluttering of pre-mass preparation that Dad hoped would reignite some sense of joy in our household had fallen instead into quiet, solitary primping. Ray in his room, Mom in her bathroom with her own mirror, and Dad waiting downstairs, legs crossed, dressed and prepared hours before the rest of us. The hallway beyond the bathroom door was dark and quiet—a void punctuated by Ray's closed bedroom door at the far end.

I was pulling a cardigan over my silver-blue blouse when the doorbell sounded. In another minute came the lumbering of two men up the stairs, old steps bending and wheezing beneath their climbing, and then Dad scratching on the bathroom door, motioning at the figure behind him.

"Brielle," he said. "Someone here to see you."

Cullen wore his leather jacket over a polo shirt and jeans—nice jeans, with no holes—and his customary black work boots. In his hands he held a rectangular box highlighted by clean red wrapping and a white bow. He'd parted his hair in the center, matted it down with too much gel, and tucked the loose curling ends behind his ears. Over Dad's shoulder he winked at me and wiggled his tongue.

Dad watched me escort Cullen to my room.

"Let's keep the door open, Beaker."

"Okay," I said.

Dad turned to walk downstairs but then spun back. "Maybe Cullen would like to come to mass with us."

Before I could stammer an "I don't think so," Cullen had clapped his hands together and proclaimed, "I'd love to, Mr. O'Dell."

Dad nodded. "Good then."

Once Dad retreated downstairs, I carefully clicked the door shut and turned the lock. Cullen cozied up next to me on the edge of the bed and, with a crooked grin that was half glee and half painfully endearing embarrassment, he shoved the box in my hands and wished me a merry Christmas.

The box held a crudely crafted silver necklace—gnarled pieces of metal crimped together to form a chain. From the chain hung an indelicate heart, with bent, harsh edges and cragged curves. It was strange, dark, flawed, and beautiful.

"Made it from barbed wire."

I looked at him and took his hand.

"I know a guy who makes stuff like this. I got all the materials from a junkyard, and then he helped me put it together and shape it and everything. He did most of the work."

"I love it," I said. We held hands, and I said it again: "I love it."

Cullen put a cold hand on my knee. We laughed a little before kissing. The first, like always, was a quick one. A test. Then another. Kissing him was like establishing your footing on the moon—seeing how high you can leap in low gravity without lifting away completely. Soon we were devouring each other, all breath, lips, and tongues, hands scrabbling to touch all the different parts of ourselves.

His hand shifted up my thigh and squeezed me there. He reached one hand around my back and tried to unhook my bra over my shirt and sweater but only twisted the strap, tugging on it impatiently.

I laughed.

"I can get it," he said.

"I thought you were supposed to be this suave lady-killer."

"Who said that?" He kissed me again and kept yanking at the bra strap.

"Here," I said. "I have an idea."

I stood, removed my sweater, and draped it over the lamp on my night table. It was a corny move, but the effect—a dull, baking glow—fit the mood. Without looking at Cullen's eyes, without pausing to think what this looked like from his point of view, I stepped in front of him.

"Don't laugh. Okay?"

He nodded shortly.

I took a breath, closed my eyes, unhooked my skirt, and let it drop to the floor. I opened my eyes. It turned out I was the one who laughed. Cullen was very serious. I unbuttoned the blouse and removed it. I thought for a moment that I could hear our two hearts beating—not in synch, just slightly off. First his, and then, on the half beat, mine. Their awkward rhythm pulsed through the room, pushing on the walls, feeding air to the fiery light.

I turned to the mirror next to the dresser. The sight of myself mostly unclothed and the hulking presence of Cullen on the bed sent a warm feeling to my middle. I felt dizzy. A single brown lock from his holiday-styled hair had fallen over his eyes. He sunk his chin into his palm. In the red light, his eyes had almost completely disappeared beneath his brow.

I took his hand, and he stood. We leaned imperceptibly into each other. Cullen started unbuttoning his shirt. I helped him finish, then went for his belt buckle and fly.

I kneeled to tug his pants down and tickled a hand across the back of his thighs. His legs, unlike his chest and shoulders and chin, and despite being covered in a fuzzy mess of hair, were decidedly boyish—skinny and without form. No calves. Knobby knees. Barely a butt to be found.

I stood between him and the mirror, intercepted his reflected gaze with my own, and then we were kissing again, and I reached back, about to unhook my bra, strands of his hair at my chin, my nails in his neck . . . when the inevitable knock on the door sounded out.

"Bri?" Mom's soft voice, then a failed attempt to open the locked door.

"Oh shit." Cullen raced in a slapdash circle to dress. His belt buckle clicked and clanked loudly while his feet shuffled across the carpet.

I laughed. "Yeah, Mom?"

Cullen buttoned his shirt, whispering to me, "What are you doing? Why aren't you getting dressed?"

"Bri, why is it locked?"

I glanced at the pile of clothes on the floor, peeked at myself in the mirror one more time, then marched over and yanked open the door. Mom stepped in, saying, "We're ready downstairs," before she paused to look up and see Cullen sitting on the bed and me in front of her, in my underwear.

"Cullen. Where did you come from?"

I planted my hands on my hips. Cullen wouldn't look at me.

"Front door this time, Mrs. O'Dell. I promise."

"Bri?"

Mom stared at me. I grinned like everything was perfectly normal.

"Yeah, Mom?"

"What are you . . . ?" She glanced at my bare legs and my

chest and then met my eyes. "I . . . I don't think it's a very good idea for you two to be in here with the door locked, do you?"

"Dad said it was okay."

Mom shook her head, confused. There was no telling what she was thinking—if she was thinking at all. She was dressed for church, but her face was pale. Her grimy, unwashed hair appeared more brown than red in the dark hallway. I knew she could be so beautiful and hated that she chose not to be.

"What are you two doing in here?" she said. "Where are your clothes, Brielle?"

"I was . . ." I laughed loudly—too loudly. Obnoxiously loudly. "Oh God, you thought we were . . . No! Mom! Come on. I was just getting dressed for church. I made Cullen look the other way."

She offered a look of disappointment, like it insulted her to know how little I thought of her ability to see through this most transparent, preposterous lie.

"I think you should get dressed right now."

"I know that, Mom," I shot back at her. "That's exactly what I was doing until you interrupted me."

"We're all ready downstairs," she said.

I nodded at her. She stared.

"Can you close the door?" I said. "So I can finish getting dressed?"

She was mad, the first time I'd seen her mad in I don't know how long. But she didn't do anything about it. She didn't even ask Cullen to leave. She stepped outside and, very carefully, very quietly, shut the door.

Later we sat five in a row in church—Mom, Dad, me, Cullen, Ray. The great hall of the chapel smelled of incense and pine, and the faithful huddled together throughout the business of the mass. Row after row of cardinal coats were thrown over pews. Impatient girls in black-and-white buckled shoes squatted at the feet of their fathers, while boys wriggled in their seats and fussed with their little ties. Mothers patted their nests of hair, and men with shaved faces, folded hands, and ashen suits nodded off under the weight of a desperate fatigue that was finally allowed to surface with the holiday break in the workweek. Ray sat at the end of the pew and didn't move throughout the mass. When the congregation stood, when they knelt, he didn't move. Hands resting on his thighs. Head bowed. Eyes blank.

A week earlier, Ray had shown up to the dinner table with a bloody, swollen eye and an awful bruise on his chin. Dad and I asked him one question after another, but all he did was eat and tell us that he was fine and to leave him alone. Mom ate her dinner, saying little. Thin and gray-faced, she wouldn't look at Ray. Could not be confronted with what she had been denying for a long time now—that something was wrong with her son.

Finally, when Ray rose and attempted to retreat to his room, Dad blocked his way.

"What happened to you?" Dad said.

Ray hung his head and said, "What do you think happened, Dad?"

"I have no idea, Ray. Tell me. Did you get in a fight?"

Ray laughed and wiped his nose. "Yeah," he said. "Yeah, that's it. I got in a fight."

He took a step back from Dad and unbuttoned his shirt. He hardly ever changed out of his school outfit anymore, like it didn't even occur to him to put on normal, comfortable clothes after school. Bruises were smeared all over his thin arms. He removed his undershirt to reveal more across his ribs and chest. A grotesque purple blooming of pain.

"A fucking fight, Dad," Ray said. "That's exactly what happened."

Mom put a trembling hand to her mouth and excused herself. Dad said, "Karen, please," but she waved him off and skittered past him. She walked so lightly we didn't even hear her going upstairs. You could see Dad wanting to chase her. Wanting to fix both his wife and his son at the same time, but only able to choose one. This time he stuck with Ray.

Ray held his arms across his torso. Dad turned back to him and looked pained—more frightened than concerned.

"Ray?" I said. "Who did it?"

Tears came out of Ray like a burst bubble, and he wiped his nose and choked it all in.

"I just want to go upstairs," he said. "Please."

"Okay, Ray." Again Dad reached out a hand, but again Ray flinched away. "Can you tell us who? And then you can go."

"Nick O'Dwyer. Okay?"

Dad nodded. "How about some ice?"

"You said if I told you."

Dad stared at Ray for a long time while Ray shrunk under his gaze. Finally Dad stepped aside, and Ray hurried past him. Dad picked up the phone and called the school. The office had cleared out for the day, but he left a stern, quiet message, insisting he be called back as soon as possible. Then he sat down across from me, picked up a fork, and stared at his pasta.

"Dad?" I said.

"Yes." He was stuck in that pose—fork poised, eyes unblinking, gaping at the plate of food.

"Can I go too?"

"You're not hungry?"

"Not really."

He put down the fork and exhaled. "Me neither."

There was nothing I could say to him that would change what we'd seen. It was all so sudden and terrible, but the truth is that as much as I was also concerned about Ray, I didn't want to be the one left behind with my father.

"So," I said. "Can I go?"

"Oh," he said. "That's fine."

Now, at mass, Dad snuck glances at Ray, rotating his head to Ray then back to the altar then back to Ray, hoping with each new glance to find some promising change but always finding the same glitch of his troubled son, like tonguing the tender roof of your mouth after a burn.

Father James recited a homily about joy. He noted the

crowds of celebratory families and called for us to fill the church with so much joy year-round, not only at Christmas and Easter. "Tonight and tomorrow morning," he told us, "we rejoice with joy. And not only because we're getting all those great presents." He paused to let the soft chuckles whisper through the cathedral. "We rejoice with joy because this is the day that Christ is born anew in our hearts. It is a day of hope for all the love that our lives can bring, here and ever after."

Ray's eyes were bloodshot and his cheeks hollow. He looked thinner than usual. When we all rose and snaked through the pews and down the center aisle to the altar to take communion and then shuffled back along the stained-glass sidelines of the chapel, Ray remained seated, lost in himself, a ghost. Mom put one hand on Ray's thigh, but he flinched at her touch, and she pulled the hand back. Ray moved to the very end of the pew, where no hand could reach him. The wound on his chin was scabbed and ugly.

Back at the house, Cullen stood tall and shook my father's hand. I stepped down the drive with him to his car. "Cullen," I said. "This thing tonight."

"Yeah."

"Please don't do it."

"You should talk to Ray about it," he said.

"He listens to you. Don't you think it's a dumb thing to do?"

"No," he said. "No, I think it'll be fun."

"But why?"

"You should talk to Ray about it. I'm not making him do anything he doesn't want to do."

"He won't listen to me!"

"He'll be okay. Trust me."

"The gun," I whispered.

"It's not loaded."

"You promise?"

He nodded. "I got it under control."

There was a pause during which neither of us said anything. Cullen gave me a quick kiss, and then I was watching him drive away.

The family dispersed for the night with little fanfare or discussion. Ray sat in the kitchen with a glass of water in front of him, and my father asked him if he was okay. Ray nodded, and Dad tilted his eyes up to the ceiling, lips colorless and pressed together.

"All right," Dad said. "Good night then."

At twelve thirty, the light in Mom and Dad's bedroom clicked off. I joined Ray in the kitchen, where he still hung a long gaze over the glass of water that had not been touched, and I informed him that I was coming with him.

Calmly, like he'd anticipated this very moment, he said, "I don't want to end up arguing and then Mom and Dad hear us, so fine, you can come, I don't care. But you have to wait in the car."

"Okay," I told him. "I'll wait in the car."

"And don't make me nervous. Don't worry so much."

"I'll just be there. That's all."

Ray pursed his lips and clenched his fists. I saw him leaving us—burrowing into some place within himself from which, I worried, we might never completely get him back.

"Why are you doing it?"

"I don't know," he said. "Why not?"

"A million reasons why not."

"Just feel like it, I guess."

"Are you mad?"

He looked at me as though this was the first time he'd thought to put the word to what he was feeling. "Yeah."

"Mad at what?"

"Just everything," he said. "Everyone."

At one thirty A.M., we walked out the front door without waking our parents. We hurried down our quiet street to the corner where Cullen waited for us. We passed houses whose holiday lights had been switched off for the night and whose children had long since fallen asleep, dreaming of Santa and all that the morning would bring. We passed the houses and felt the cold. I watched my brother rub his hands and I wished I had something to wish for other than that predictable hope of retreating home and crawling under the covers to encounter down there in the softness and whiteness of my childhood bed some familiar but long-lost dream.

At the corner we found Cullen's car idling and spitting white exhaust tinged cherry from the taillights. The driver's side window slid down to reveal not Cullen at all, but

Roman. We didn't move. A quiet hip-hop beat and a wall of warmth snuck out of the car. Roman clamped his hands between his thighs. "Well, get the fuck in. Freezing out here."

Cullen leaned over from the passenger seat and stuck his face up toward us. He blinked slowly when he saw me, not able to hide his surprise, then smiled and turned to Ray. "We need a driver, buddy. Roman's got this."

Ray hesitated. Stared at the ground, calculating.

"Hop in, guys," Cullen said. "It's cool."

"Ray?" I said.

Roman rubbed a hand across his jaw. "Nice neighborhood," he said, looking around. "Shit."

Finally Ray shook off his stupor and climbed into the backseat, and I followed. Roman talked the whole ride. "This is some shit," he kept saying. "This is sooome shit."

We drove into East Orange and cruised by a twenty-four-hour QuickChek that was lit up, radiant with fluorescent-tinted products.

"There she blows." Roman momentarily swerved the car across the double yellow line, then glided it back.

We pulled into an empty parking lot three blocks away and parked in the alley behind a mattress store. Roman killed the engine. We sat in silence. Cullen hadn't said a word to me during the ride, but I'd promised Ray that I wouldn't worry so much or make him nervous, so I kept quiet. The more he thought about my being there, the harder it would be for him to do the thing he had come to do. I understood that. And the truth was that I was as curious as the rest of them. A big part of me was just as electrified by the senseless act we were about to perform as the boys were.

Cullen handed the gun to Ray, who stared at it for a long moment and then fiddled with the handle.

"Careful," Cullen said.

"Safety's on, I'm fine."

"What are you doing?" Cullen asked.

"The clip," Ray said. "I want the clip."

"Why?"

"I want to check it."

"It's loaded," Cullen said.

"Here." Ray handed the gun up front to Cullen. "Show me."

"Ray, it's loaded. Just like we said."

"I believe you. Show me."

Cullen looked briefly at me and then at Ray. He sighed. "Look, Ray . . ."

"Where are the bullets? In the trunk?"

"There's no reason for it to be loaded!"

Ray stepped out of the car. "Are they still in the trunk? From the target-practice trip?"

Ray walked around to the back of the car. The rest of us sat in silence. I yelped when Ray pounded on the trunk.

"Open it!" he yelled.

Roman looked to Cullen, who nodded, and Roman reached down to pop the trunk.

"Cullen," I said.

"It's fine." He opened the door.

"Cullen, you promised."

"It's fine!" he said. "I promise. It's under control." He grabbed gloves and ski masks from the glove compartment and exited. I turned to see Ray, but the raised trunk blocked my view.

"This is some shit," Roman whispered.

The trunk slammed shut. Cullen and Ray, putting on gloves, hurried past the car, moved into the shadows of the alley, and then, turning the corner, disappeared.

Ray

Cullen and I hurried toward the store, and I wasn't thinking at all about God or Heaven or life before or after death, because none of that meant anything to me in that moment. What I felt, above all else, was emptiness. I trusted the emptiness. I had faith in the emptiness. *Bloodfire*, I thought. *Bloodfire. Bloodfire.*

"Get in and out," Cullen said. "No distractions. Got it?"

I nodded, even though I wasn't really listening to the words he was saying. They were just sounds, but I agreed with the general feeling coming from them.

"And do not shoot the gun. No matter what happens, for the love of God, Ray, do not shoot that fucking gun. You want him to think you'll shoot it, but you're not going to."

"Okay."

"You've shot it before. You know how to handle it. Show

him that. Show him this is your gun and you've used it a thousand times before and will not hesitate to use it on him."

"Okay."

"We get in and get out, and you don't shoot the fucking gun, and nobody gets hurt."

We stopped at a crosswalk and waited for the light to change, even though there were no cars. Behind us a slope of muddy grass covered with broken liquor bottles and losing lottery tickets rose to a small wooded area. The road to our left followed a line of green traffic lights into the depths of East Orange. In front of us, across the street, was the store.

Cullen nudged me with his elbow. "We're out there now, kid," he said. "You feel it?"

The whole thing took maybe three minutes, but it felt much longer. We paused at the curb to let the store's only customer amble into his minivan and pull out of the lot, then we put on our masks and marched inside. Without breaking stride, and without thinking about it, and with my head humming from a violent rush of blood, I sprinted up to the counter and held the gun at the guy and screamed at him just like Cullen had told me to do—just like we'd rehearsed in the garage of his grandmother's house.

"Show me your hands, hands up, show me your hands, motherfucker!"

The clerk was a dark-skinned, broad-chested guy who seemed somehow familiar. He looked about Cullen's age, considering that Cullen looked almost five years older than he really was. The idea was to submit him to my will. Tonight

I was going to puppet someone else the way so many had done to me. To flex and then watch someone cower.

The guy put his arms over his head and tried to duck away from the gun's aim. "Okay!" he said. "Okay, man, don't shoot."

"The register!" I said.

"Okay!" On the way to the register, he touched an alarm button under the counter.

"What are you doing?" I shouted. "What the hell was that?! You want to get shot over a few hundred fucking dollars?!"

"I'll get the money!"

"Get it now!"

I looked to Cullen to see about the alarm and what to do next, but Cullen just stood there staring at the clerk, not saying anything. The guy was taking such a long time getting all the cash out of the register, and I was terrified about that alarm, so I screamed—not even words, just a wild, maniacal noise from my throat—and I pointed the gun at a refrigerator full of beer and pulled the trigger.

The glass exploded. Beer poured out. It felt like some ancient door to the underworld had opened up inside me. I couldn't breathe, and I tried to stop my arm from shaking as I pointed the gun at the clerk, who had gone pale and appeared frozen in place.

"Open. The. Register," I said.

"Okay," he said. "Okay, Ray, just, Jesus . . . relax. I'm doing it."

The register slid open. The guy gathered the cash. Cullen

stared at him, but with a look that was somehow different from the one he'd been sporting just one minute ago. Because of the gunshot? Because he was scared? I looked from Cullen to the clerk and back to Cullen, trying to think. The guy pushed a pile of cash across the counter.

"Here," he said. "Go."

Cullen scooped up the cash and pulled my sleeve. "Come on."

"Wait," I said, turning to the clerk. "What did you say?"

Cullen grabbed my shoulder, pocketing the money. "The alarm! Let's go!"

My name. He had said my name. Hadn't he? I stared at him and instantly understood everything. I knew who this guy was and why he looked so familiar. How could I not have seen it right away? He was bigger, sure, wider in the shoulders, and older, but he had the same almond-shaped eyes and short, sloping nose. They could have been cousins. Or . . . brothers.

I smiled. "You think I'm stupid?"

"What? Ray, come on, there's no time."

"What'd you do? Deactivate the alarm?" I pointed with the gun to a security camera in the ceiling. "Turn those off too?"

"Just go," the clerk said. "Go!"

I tried to remember his name. Amir had told me about him. He went to Seton Hall. Worked part-time for their uncle. The name was in the blazer, I remembered. The hand-me-down that Amir wore.

"Malik," I said.

"Look, Ray . . ." Cullen started.

"How dumb do you think I am?"

"We need to leave right now!"

"What's the rush?" I said. "None of this is real anyway. We're not actually robbing a convenience store, are we?"

"No, but you did *actually* shoot up the beer case, genius."

I was so mad. Everything went hot and white, and there was a dizzy moment when I wasn't there. When I didn't exist. I heard the next explosion of the gun before I even felt the trigger give. The soda case. Boom. The milk case. Bang. I walked the aisles of the store, shooting as I went: blasting bags of chips, incinerating aspirin bottles. Cullen and Malik came after me. I shoved over one of the shelves. Candy bars and gum packs tumbled across the floor.

"Ray!" Cullen was shouting. "Calm the fuck down!"

"This is so stupid," I shouted back. "This isn't at all what I wanted. I wanted something real!"

I heard a door open in the back of the store. When I looked to see what it was, Cullen lunged at me, grabbing for the gun. He had my shirt with one hand and was grabbing for the gun with the other. I kept pulling away, but he wouldn't let go, and I couldn't see the clerk anymore, and someone was coming from the back of the store where that door had opened. Cullen and I tumbled to the floor of the snack aisle. He snatched the wrist of my gun hand, and I squirmed away from him. He scrambled across the floor at me like a spider, grabbing and crawling and screaming at me, and someone was coming from the back of the store.

He grabbed my arm and sunk his fingers into a bruise where Nick had hit me, and I shouted in pain and elbowed Cullen in the eye and bang! The gun fired into a shelf of groceries. Cullen rose and stumbled back, knocking into and tipping over the same shelf I had just shot. I heard Malik groan on the other side, pinned under the weight of the rack.

The fading echo of the gunshot rippled through me for a moment that seemed to last forever. I couldn't move. The world blurred. Malik was on the floor. I held on to a refrigerator door for balance. Cereal was spilled everywhere. Broken bottles. Glass. Malik moaned. His hand was on his stomach, and when he brought it away it was covered in blood. Blood on his hand. On his shirt. On the floor.

Something cracked open in my chest. I dropped the gun. And I ran.

It was only when I sprinted across the street and up the muddy slope into the trees, slipping in the mud, rising, slipping again, breathing like crazy and trying to stop the earth from spinning on me, that I dared to look back to see who had been coming out of that back room.

But of course I already knew. I crouched in the brush and looked at the store. There was Malik, Cullen, and this new third person. He was kneeling next to the injured clerk. I locked eyes with him. I knew I should run, but I couldn't look away.

He was right there. Holding his bleeding brother. Staring at me.

Cullen

DECEMBER 26 I was standing at a pay phone outside a deli in Jersey City. It was a little after dawn, and I looked down a street lined with row houses to the Hudson River. My cell battery was dead, and Amir wasn't answering his phone. It was six in the morning, but you'd think with all that was happening he'd be sleeping with the damn phone to his ear. My fingers felt like frozen glass. "Come on, man," I said, jumping in place. "Pick up the phone."

On Christmas night, Brielle, Ray, and I had holed up in what was once maybe a house or a hospital or a hotel but that was now an abandoned building that looked like a haunted castle. It was three stories tall and from each corner rose a redbrick tower with a pointed top. Stone steps, a big terrace, and double doors that I swear weighed a thousand pounds. It was at street level but hidden from view by a border of bushes, which were dead and brown but which you still couldn't see through. Once past this barrier, the place opened to a big lawn and beyond that a vacant lot filled with leftover construction machines and abandoned warehouses. Its windows boarded up, the house was splattered with graffiti. Horror movie–type stuff.

We camped on the third floor at the top of a spiral staircase where a heap of crumbled concrete gave us a little spot for a fire. Earlier that morning, I'd tiptoed down the stairs, careful not to send the whole thing crashing down and wake Bri and Ray. The building was filled with hostile signs of earlier visitors: broken bottles, glass pipes, graffiti symbols of anarchists, satanists, and gang members, with the satanists seeming to have outlasted the others in the turf war. At the top floor, where Ray and Brielle were still huddled against the wall, sleeping on each other's shoulders, someone had painted a red star around a black stallion's head and listed "The Eleven Satanic Rules of Earth" below it. It wasn't so bad in the light of day, but during the night, when we built the fire below where a hunk of ceiling had collapsed who knows how long ago, the flames had thrown a creepy-as-hell glow across the blood-colored scribblings.

Ray hadn't said much since we fled Rosewood the afternoon before. He stared at his feet a lot and kept shrugging his shoulders like he wanted them to swallow his head. I told him that I'd left the store just after he did—quick enough to get away but not quick enough to jump in the car with Bri and him. Ray was positive that the shot he delivered to Malik's gut had killed him, but he wasn't about to get anywhere near the place anytime soon to find out for sure. Of course I knew Amir's brother worked at the store. And I knew Amir would be there on Christmas Eve. After what happened with the stolen car, I wasn't about to let things go bad again. I was all for a good time, but I had no interest in letting Ray be questioned by the cops. It wasn't his fault that he wasn't the type of guy who could withstand interrogation. He just hadn't grown up lying to adults the way I had.

After I talked with Amir, I was going to buy some breakfast sausages from a nearby deli and cook them over the fire so we could all eat something hot. Then I'd sit back and wait for Amir to show up so we could get this done with and get back home before anyone got arrested or hurt or worse.

But Amir wasn't answering. I cursed myself for forgetting to charge my damn cell phone so I wouldn't have to keep hanging up before his voice mail answered in order to get my two quarters back.

I called Nana. She didn't answer either. She was usually up by four thirty A.M. but tended to drift off for nap number one as early as six, so I left a message with the usual report: food in the fridge, be back later, love you.

I dialed Amir one more time before deciding to try Roman.

Ro always answered his phone. Never thought twice about it. He usually fell asleep fully clothed, phone in his pocket, and he had no qualms about who was calling or what time it was or whatever. If it rang, he picked up. This morning, he had just woken, and his voice sounded like when you're lying on the beach and someone shuffles close by and you hear the sand below you move.

"Yo," he said. "Fuckers ditched me."

"I know," I said.

"Bitch just drove off without me."

"Listen, I need a favor."

I heard the flick of a lighter followed by Roman inhaling and then breathing out the phrase "No fucking way," before he fell into a brief coughing fit. "Look, I'm not messing with this shit anymore."

I stared down the block at the water that was so still it looked like black ice. "Listen," I said. "Everything's fine."

"Uh, no it ain't, bro. Your boy shot that dude."

"Ro. How long have you known me?"

"I don't . . . I mean . . . you want me to count?"

"No. I'm saying, you think I don't know what I'm doing?"

"Sure seemed like you didn't."

"I got this whole thing covered."

Again I heard the lighter and Roman pulling in a bunch of smoke. "I don't understand what you're telling me right now."

"Just get your ass out here. I need you to stop and pick somebody up. Can you do that?

"Who?"

"Amir Shadid."

"Who?"

"The brother of the guy from the store."

Roman coughed once and didn't say anything.

"Come on, man. We're having fun out here. Wouldn't be the same without you."

"You think I'm crazy?"

"What's wrong?" I asked him. "You afraid of a freshman who weighs all of ninety pounds?"

Again he was inhaling. And then coughing. And then he was silent. For a long time. It went on so long I thought maybe he'd fallen back to sleep.

"Don't know what the hell you're up to, man." He cleared his throat and sighed, insisting on being all over-the-top and dramatic about it. Finally he said, "Tell me what you want me to do."

Ray

I woke in my bed the morning after the robbery, trying to remember how I'd gotten there. I stared at the ceiling for a good while, rubbed my eyes, then moved to the edge of the mattress and rested my chin on the windowsill and thought about all the people out there in their houses. Christmas morning was sad and rainy. Even though it was daytime, some houses had their lights on because the sun wasn't coming out. I sat there and watched my neighborhood where nothing was happening and felt a feeling I couldn't explain. Like I was missing my home even though I was inside it, and missing my neighborhood even though I was looking right at it. There was a deep, whirring pain in the center of my head that made me dizzy.

I remembered being in Cullen's car with Bri. She'd been driving. And talking to me. When I thought about it now, I could almost re-create the sound of her voice but not any of the words she was saying. One time when I was little and we were at the beach, I had ducked my head under a wave and stayed underwater for as long as I could, and when I opened my eyes down there I looked up and saw the rushing foam above me, and all I thought about was how much more quietly the waves came in when you were underwater. That's what it felt like being in the car with Bri. Like I was under a wave—one of the really big ones—and couldn't hear anything, but also like I couldn't breathe and knew I'd have to come up for air before the next big one came rolling in.

I couldn't remember if we talked about where to go or whether or not to try to find Cullen. I couldn't remember coming home or walking upstairs and getting in bed. All I was thinking about at the time was Amir's brother. Malik. I'd killed him. I was sure of it.

When I finally left my bedroom window and went downstairs the next morning, I was so surprised to find Bri, Dad, and Mom sitting in the living room and all the presents waiting for us under the tree that I almost laughed. I don't know what I was expecting, but it wasn't that. *Maybe*, I thought, *everything is somehow okay. Maybe nobody will ever find out. Maybe last night never even happened.*

We sat and opened our presents, and for a while I thought it was nice, but very soon I started to understand that nobody was having fun. Dad was acting like we were all having the most wonderful time, which is maybe what tricked me, however briefly, into thinking that I was too. But if you listened closely enough and looked at his eyes when he handed the presents to me and Bri—some of them still signed "From Santa"—you could tell he was faking it. He so badly wanted us to be having a good time that he'd never admit to being less than happy himself.

Bri and Mom weren't faking it, though. They hardly said one word the whole time, and they both looked tired. Ever since I'd revealed the results of my latest beating from Nick, Mom had pretty much been a total wreck—she barely got out of bed and, except for last night at church, hadn't gotten dressed in days. I knew it was going to be bad when I ripped my shirt open like that. I told myself that Dad was asking for it and that I was doing it to shock him, but I knew I was doing it for Mom too. I saw her looking at me. I felt her sadness. And later I would feel bad about it, but in the moment, showing her the truth like that—forcing her to see the real me—and knowing what it would do to her filled me with a fierce, perverted kind of pleasure.

Bri was also quiet and moved slowly that morning, not looking at me even when I gave her a gift. I started to worry that maybe she'd end up like Mom someday and that I would be the one who had sent her down that path with what I'd done in the store. I wasn't exactly giving her a great present—it was a sweater Dad had bought at the mall that he let me put my name on. In all the excitement about the robbery, I never thought to buy anyone gifts. It occurred to me now that I hadn't thought at all about any of the days that would come after the robbery. I wouldn't have been surprised if, right after it happened, the world had stopped spinning and we all just disappeared.

It wasn't lost on me that today was supposed to be in celebration of the birth of Jesus. There was a little nativity scene set up on a table over by the Christmas tree. When we were younger, Bri and I used to fight over who got to put the little plastic baby Jesus in the manger on Christmas morning. I didn't know who put it there this year. Dad, probably. To me, Jesus was even more mysterious and confusing than God. I knew a lot of people found God through Jesus, and vice versa, but to me the two didn't have anything to do with one another. If I ever did find a way to believe in one, I was pretty sure that it would take me a whole other lifetime to believe in the other. In any case, none of that really mattered anymore. There was a part of me that still hoped God would, by some miracle, decide to reveal himself to me, but deep down I knew that after last night it wasn't going to happen. Why would He bother with someone like me?

But what first got me thinking about Jesus and how Bri and I used to fight over the nativity scene was that she got me a really nice present: Leo Tolstoy's *A Confession*.

"I don't know what type of confession they mean," she told me. "But I saw you reading the other one."

"St. Augustine," I said.

"Yeah," she said. "So I saw this and thought you might like it."

I did like it. Even before I opened it and read a single

word, I knew I liked it. And I wished I could have told Bri that, but something inside me kept me from doing so. Maybe it was what had happened the night before. Or maybe it was how badly I felt about the dumb sweater that she probably wouldn't even wear. Maybe it was Dad looking at the two of us with a sappy grin like he wanted us to hug or something. Most likely, though, even as awful as I felt about everything—most of all the shooting—it was simply that she was my sister, and I was her brother, and I couldn't remember how to get along with her like we'd done when we were little. Each day we seemed to wake up as two new people who had to introduce themselves to each other all over again.

"Cool," I said to her. "Thanks."

After breakfast, Mom had gone back to bed and Dad was at the sink washing dishes. I was sitting on the couch next to the tree in the living room. I hadn't eaten much at breakfast and now felt like I might pass out. I sat there feeling my heart beat like crazy, afraid that the underwater feeling was coming back and trying to make it stop. Bri walked by me on the way up to her room, motioning for me to follow.

"Why?" I said.

She glanced quickly at Dad, not wanting him to hear, and motioned again as she hurried away.

She closed the door to her room when I stepped inside. It smelled flowery and was really warm.

She paced the room. "We need to talk," she said.

I didn't say anything. Suddenly I felt nauseated. All the things I didn't want to think about came rushing in.

She tapped a nervous fingernail against her front teeth. "I don't know what to do."

My chest felt tight.

"Cullen?" she said. "Should we call Cullen?"

"Do you trust him?"

"Do you?"

We stared at one another, waiting for the other to answer. That's when the doorbell rang. As soon as I heard it, I was floored with the understanding of how badly I'd screwed everything up. Not only for myself, but for everyone. I couldn't keep Mom happy, and I couldn't keep Bri happy, and I'd just single-handedly ruined the life of my only friend in the world.

Bri was already in motion. She shoved open the window near her bed, letting in a burst of cold air, and moved to the door. "Stay here," she said. "If you hear the cops, go down the roof."

She was out the door before I could say anything, but if I had stopped her I would've explained that there was no point in sliding off the roof and escaping into the woods. I was fifteen years old and, I was certain, wanted for murder. All I owned was a twenty-dollar bill left over from the money I'd taken from Dad's closet. Where exactly did she expect me to go?

There was some talking downstairs that I couldn't make out. It sounded like a man at the door talking to Dad and Bri. I sat on the bed and tried to breathe. I don't know why, but I thought about how I hadn't showered yet, and I tried to straighten my hair quickly but then thought about how stupid that was and stopped doing it. I stood and paced the room. My heart beat. My stomach turned.

The door opened, and in walked Bri.

After her came Cullen.

Bri shut the door behind him. He smiled and winked at me. I was so mad at him that if my mom weren't sleeping in the next room, I would have tried to strangle him. But I was afraid of doing anything that might upset the balance of the day and somehow set off a chain reaction that led to my being found out. So I sat there and tried not to look at him.

For a long time nobody said anything. Cullen leaned against Bri's dresser, while Bri came and sat next to me on the bed.

"Anyway, I guess we should get going," he said.

"Going where?" Bri asked.

Cullen peered across the room, out the window. "I don't think it's a good idea to sit around here waiting, do you?"

"What the hell were you doing?" I said.

"When?"

"You tackled me. You . . ."

"I didn't *tackle* you."

"This is all your fault! You did this!"

"I didn't load the gun, Ray. I didn't pull the trigger."

My fists were shaking at my sides, and I told Cullen through clenched teeth—clenched so tight that it hurt when I finally relaxed my jaw moments later—"This is your fault."

He stood there in his cool leaning pose. I wasn't only

mad at him for what happened in the store. That was a big part of it, of course. But what enraged me even more was all the stuff in the days leading up to the robbery. How cool he always made himself seem. How strong. How brave. When the whole stupid thing was fake.

"I'm not going anywhere with you," I told him.

"Okay," he said. "Fine by me." He laughed a little. "I didn't shoot anybody, Ray."

This was exactly the type of thing Cullen would say, and he said it all calm and composed, which just made me angrier and angrier.

I felt hot and moved to the window.

"Maybe it's okay," Bri said. "Maybe he's not dead."

"He's dead," I said.

"But how do you know?"

"I just know!" I said.

"Well, you had the mask on, right? Maybe—"

"Amir knew," I said. "He knew everything."

"Okay, well, there has to be something we can do. Something . . ."

Bri trailed off, and it was just as well, because I'd suddenly stopped listening. Through the window I'd seen something move in the woods. Again I felt too hot, so I stuck my head out the window. It smelled like cold rain outside. A dark figure moved on the other side of our fence. It was a person, no doubt about it.

I heard Bri's and Cullen's voices but was no longer registering words. I was under the wave now. The figure moved closer to the fence and stepped into a gap in the bushes that separated our yard from the woods. My heart leaped when I saw his face. He was looking, one at a time, into each window of the house. And I shook with fear.

He found me in the corner window and smiled. An unhinged smile. The look of a person who had no fear. Who would do anything and go anywhere and take any risk or challenge posed to him. He pointed at me. *Why?* I thought. *Why is this happening?*

I wanted to duck away from the window, but something kept me standing there, staring at Amir like I was in a dream.

I heard Bri saying my name. "Ray," she was saying. "Ray, what are you thinking?"

Rain dripped from the trees, and Amir's damp hair looked like black paint smeared on top of his head. He reached into the pocket of his jacket and held something up between the bushes to show me—a gun. The same one I'd so stupidly dropped in the store.

"Ray," Bri said again. "What is it?" She stepped over to me and looked out the window to see what I'd seen. But when I turned back to where Amir had been, there was now only the woods, the trees gray and dreary but somehow innocent-looking in their bareness.

"What did you see?" Bri asked me.

I turned to Cullen. He gave me a look that seemed to say he already knew what I was going to say. Like he knew exactly what I'd seen.

"I know a place," he said. "Nobody will find us."

"And what then?"

"We lay low till we figure out our next steps."

I took a quick breath and nodded at him. He smiled a little, his eyes jumpy with excitement. This was exactly the type of stuff he got excited about. And it was, I remembered now, exactly the type of thing I had asked for.

"Ray," Bri said. "Can you talk to me? Are you sure about this?"

I looked out the window and didn't answer her. The screen door downstairs squeaked open. Dad's arm appeared briefly and out ran Lincoln, who sprinted to the spot where Amir had been, and you could see even from up here that Lincoln was trying to bark. But of course no sound came out. He rose with his two front legs against the fence, and he looked so sad, snapping his teeth, flinging his head all over, warning everyone about invisible demons, wishing, just this once, that someone could hear him.

Brielle

THE MINUTES I HAD SPENT in the car with Roman during the robbery had been awful. He'd pulled a thin bottle of vodka from the pocket of his cargo pants. He wouldn't stop gulping down liquor, pulling at his pants, and talking—constantly talking and wiping a spittle of saliva that fizzed at the corner of his mouth.

"I like blondes," he told me.

"Okay."

"I don't even like brunettes."

Anxiety over Ray in the store with that loaded gun welled in me almost to the point of exploding, and if I could have pushed a button and made Roman disappear from the world forever, I would have done it.

"Cullen can keep you," he kept saying, his words sloppy, while he held a chapped hand to the side of his head as though trying to keep his skull from tipping off his neck. At one point he tumbled out of the car and stepped into the neighboring alley, polishing off the vodka and tossing the bottle against the side of a dumpster, where it shattered in one high, clean note. Beside the dumpster, Roman unzipped and relieved himself.

One benefit of our visit to the Pine Barrens was that I could recognize a gunshot, though I would have recognized this one anyway. It was just one of those unmistakable things. Roman didn't even flinch at the sound of it. He kept drunkenly at his business without looking up, so I climbed into the driver's seat, hit the gas, and left him there.

And that was how I found myself staring into the store, looking for my brother, and meeting, so oddly, the eyes of Amir. The resonance of the shot still dying in my ears, I saw a masked Ray scrambling down from a muddy slope to the sidewalk, leaping into the passenger seat, slamming the door, and screaming at me, "Go!" Cullen stepped into the door frame of the store. In the rearview mirror, twenty yards away, Roman lurched down the road, pointing at the car.

"Go!" Ray shouted.

Once again, I hit the gas. The tires squealed and whined, and the car fishtailed briefly before I righted it.

I drove without purpose or direction until Ray breathed, "There," pointing to a sign for the Turnpike. I don't know why he pointed there, and I don't know why I obeyed him. We had no destination in mind. We were just getting away. Once we passed through the toll, Ray mumbled something about pulling over that I was sure I'd misheard, until he hunched over like he'd been kicked in the stomach and said again, louder this time, "Pull over," which finally I did. Ray rolled out of the car and into the halo of a pale orange streetlight, where he doubled over and vomited.

When he was back in the car, as we approached a sign for the George Washington Bridge, I asked him what had happened.

"I shot him."

"But what happened?"

"I shot the guy. I don't know. I shot him."

"Where should we go?"

He tightened his jaw, said nothing.

I gazed north up the Hudson and felt sick. The river disappeared into the black horizon, which was dotted with spots of light where people were living lives that were not mine. Ray breathed shortly and wiped a palm across his eyes. I exited just before the bridge. Again I asked Ray where to go. He was looking at his hands, lost, not hearing me.

So I took us home. I didn't know if it was the right move, but I couldn't think of anywhere else to go. For all its faults, home was where things were safe. Where we could think. And plan. And wait for Cullen.

Less than twenty-four hours later, on Christmas Day, we ran away from home. Cullen drove us across the Pulaski Skyway at dusk. The structure's tangle of steel flitted past, and beyond that was a drab industrial landscape. To the east, a low fog blurred New York into a figment of sickly pale colors. Cars whipped by on the left. The lanes were too narrow and the edge of the bridge too close. I had the car's heat blasting on my face because Ray was intent on keeping his head propped next to his opened window in the backseat, his eyes, I could tell from the passenger side mirror, watering against the nasty whip of cold. The wind echoed through the car, and behind it thumped the rhythmic roll of tires over bridge joints.

We crossed into Jersey City. Cullen explained that he'd come here once for a thing with Roman and had taken note of a perfect hiding spot, in the event he ever needed it. I was certain "a thing with Roman" meant drugs. With Roman it was always drugs—buying them, selling them, taking them.

By the time we parked across the street from the abandoned house where we were to spend the night, the day had grown dark. Just four thirty, but already night. We stood on the sidewalk and eyed the massive building rising above a border of long-dead, overgrown shrubbery. Ray was so pale and looked like he might vomit again. The place reminded me of the front building of a run-down insane asylum in our neighboring town that everyone always claimed was haunted. When Cullen directed us through the bordering thickets and then proposed investigating the house, Ray finally burst into tears.

Cullen and I were silent. My eyes drifted again toward the

dilapidated house. A demented, demonic star was painted across the front door, visible in the glow of nearby street-lights. Shutters hung at twisted angles. Weeds and roots pushed up through the concrete steps, slowly ripping them apart. Ray cried silently. I put a hand to his shoulder, but I don't think he felt it.

Cullen was eyeing the house too, but in a different way than Ray and I were. He was calculating, not worrying.

"I don't want to go in there," I told him.

Cullen reached into his pocket and produced a wallet. He flipped through a thin stack of bills. "Okay," he said. "How about we get some food? Something hot to drink. And then come back."

I moved to speak, but Cullen cut in: "We could sleep in the car, but I honestly think we'll be better off in there. Police will bother a bunch of kids in a car, but nobody's been inside this place in a long time. If we're freaked out, so is everyone else. We'll be safe in there. I'm telling you."

I glanced at his stack of bills again. "What about a hotel?"

"We need this money to eat. It's not much."

I knew Cullen had more money than that. Why hadn't he brought more with him?

We walked maybe a mile through Jersey City, out of this run-down, seemingly abandoned part of the city to where the place started to come to life—brownstones, parked cars, the glow of corner markets—and slipped into a mostly empty diner on a quiet street. A Christmas tree, doused in blue-silver tinsel, stood beside the counter, which was strung with primary-colored bulbs. Some old version of "Frosty the Snowman" crackled through unseen speakers.

Against our protests, Cullen ordered food for all of us, insisting that we'd find an appetite once it arrived. This proved true for me. I chewed down a plate of eggs, bacon, and toast, and as the warm food settled in me, I realized how light I'd felt throughout the whole day—as though gravity might betray me and let me float away like in a recurring dream I had where, in a panic, I would grasp at the brittle ends of tree branches before drifting up into the suffocating atmosphere. But the food weighed me down now, and I felt centered for a moment. Ray was supporting his head with his palm, staring off to a place I would never see, his heaping plate of food untouched.

By the time we'd trekked back to the castle, we were exhausted enough to be brave about entering. All three of us yanked and pried away a rotting plank of wood that had been nailed over the front door. Cullen and Ray shouldered open the door itself, pushing a blockage of concrete and lumber out of the way. We paused in the great hall of the building, waiting for our eyes to adjust to the dark.

We followed Cullen up a decaying staircase. On the second floor, Ray stopped and stared into an adjacent room. Moonlight spotlighted the far wall of the room, where the carcass of a cat had been nailed, legs splayed like a star. Ruddy handprints and spots of mold dotted the wall around the cat. In the morning we would see that the prints had been made with blood, dried now and faded. We would also see the roiling nest of maggots in the cat's innards on the floor. I took Ray by the arm and led him away. He kept his eyes fixed on the pinned carcass and tripped along behind me.

The next day I woke at dawn, cramped close to Ray around the remains of a small fire. Cullen had worried about the smoke escaping through the hole in the roof, but we couldn't light a fire in an enclosed room, and it was too cold to go without one. Cullen was gone now, though. It was only Ray and me.

I squirmed out of our sleep pile, leaving Ray to stir briefly and then curl back up on the floor. I stepped out into a crisp and pale day-after-Christmas morning, watching Cullen climb through the bushes and pull specks of leaves from his hair as he walked toward me.

"I need to call home," I announced to him.

We walked two blocks to a pay phone, and I took a quick breath as I slotted in two quarters and dialed, steeling myself against whatever lingering softness squirmed deep down inside me.

Dad picked up on the first ring and said, "Hello," in a quiet voice. No doubt he was lying in bed, Mom asleep next to him.

"Dad, it's me."

"Brielle?"

"Ray and I are okay. I wanted you to know."

Any story I told him would have to involve being

somewhere with one of my friends—people he could call, lies he could check up on. And I didn't have any friends I could trust to back me up.

"What do you mean?" he said. "Tell me—"

"We're okay, but we can't come home. I'm so sorry. We're okay. I love you."

I hung up so he didn't hear the rupture of tears that followed. It felt like a cheap seam had split apart on my face, and I cried and cried, wondering how I would ever repair the gash. I walked, wiping my nose, heaving dry, hollow breaths, reining the world back in through the hot blur. Cullen paced two or three steps behind me, which was exactly where I wanted him for the moment. Finally I stopped at a street corner one block from the water, realizing I didn't know where I was going or how to get back to Ray.

"What's the plan, Cullen?"

"It's okay." His hand was on my hip. "Amir's coming."

"Amir? Why?"

"We'll talk to him about what happened, and everything will be fine. I promise."

"What about his brother?"

"He's not dead."

"What? How do you know?"

"I know. Trust me. We're in the clear. Everything is one hundred percent totally fine."

"Oh God. We need to tell Ray!"

"We will," he said. "We will. Let him rest for now. He needs it."

I knew enough by this point that a promise from Cullen didn't mean what he wanted it to mean, but, at the same time, it was hard not to believe him when he knew what you really wanted. And what I wanted was for everything to be okay. He kept promising me that it would be. Malik was alive. I so wanted to believe that. It was only a matter of time now, I thought, before this somehow worked itself out and we could go home.

The morning was warming up, so I shed my heavy coat and soaked up the precious bit of sun fighting through the gray. We toed a narrow wall along the water's edge, walking south toward the castle, the water slurping against the narrow, rocky beach. Normally I'd have cherished the sight of the Statue of Liberty glowing out there, a speck of beauty in an otherwise drab, wintry landscape, but today I didn't feel like looking at it.

We moved through a construction site toward a redbrick warehouse. A rusty backhoe sat in a ditch of weeds. A finished condominium tower stood at the far end of the lot, with an unfinished one right next to it. It was impossible to tell which parts of this place would come alive again after the holidays and which parts were dead for good. The door to the warehouse was chained and locked—a slipshod job that reminded me of the chains they put on the front doors of our school after hours.

Cullen yanked on the doors to no effect except to startle a group of winter sparrows nesting in the eaves three stories overhead. I watched the birds boomerang an arch across the low-slung sky and then flit back into their hooded nests. Cullen tromped through the debris and pried a concrete slab out of its hold in the dirt. The building's windows were paneled with what looked like wrought iron but must have been something much weaker because when Cullen wound up and heaved his concrete block at the glass, the crashing blow left a gap where both the obliterated glass and its paneling had just been.

"Want to try?" Cullen glowed with a sense of destructive wonder. He bent to hoist up another giant rock and then shuffled it over to me.

"Bend your knees," he said.

I did, and he shifted it into my hands.

"Got it?"

"Yeah."

But I didn't have it and almost shattered my toes by dropping it before Cullen stepped back in and secured the other side of the block. My back ached, and my fingers threatened to gave way.

"We'll do it together," he said. "On three."

"I can't hold it!"

"Three!"

We swung the slab back once and then tossed it through the window, blowing open a fresh gap in the pane. The sound of the punctured glass and the rock hitting the floor— one initial crack and then a rolling pitter-patter—struck my nerves with a sparkling switch. I told Cullen to find me one I could throw myself.

We heaved one block after another into the window that rose twice as tall as us and stretched just as wide. We worked at it with such fervor that our faces blushed. We mocked the winter cold with sweat on our foreheads. We cried out against the world with every toss, and the cracking glass echoed our anger back to us. We screamed out demented versions of "Jingle Bells" and "O Holy Night" while we flung rusted lengths of pipe and discarded wrenches at the window, working until only a stubborn few shards and wiry splinters of paneling clung to the corners. When we finally stepped through the breach and into the warehouse, we navigated clumsily over the piles of rock and concrete we had created.

The floor of the gutted interior was checkered with blocks of light from glass ceiling panels. Piping webbed the upper reaches in what was once some mad map of water and electricity. Cullen held his leather jacket in one arm. He snuck his other arm around my waist and fit his hand in the back pocket of my jeans. The place smelled like metal and mold.

"What do you think they did in here?" I asked him.

"I don't know. Built things. Shipped things. Received things."

We stopped walking. He leveraged my waist around to face him, and we kissed. We were still warm from our rock tossing, but I felt the cold tip of his nose against my cheek.

Cullen laid his jacket down on a square of sunlight, spreading it out in what was, under the circumstances, a welcoming patch of protected ground. He took my coat from me and laid it out on top of his. Then he unbuttoned his flannel shirt, slipped it off, and laid it smoothly over the coats. I stretched my sweatshirt over my head, then a gray tank top, and added them to the pile. He flipped off a stained white undershirt, and we both shimmied out of our jeans with a few nervous chuckles. The cottony pile grew at our feet.

He moved against me, one hand tracing over the surface of my bra and the other scratching the skin of my back. I tugged his boxers down and touched and then squeezed him there. He led me down onto the pile of clothes, lips touching lips, neck, breasts, navel, thighs.

I tried to focus on Cullen—the sensation of him, the reality of his being here with me, doing this thing. I wanted to look into his eyes, smell him, synch my breathing up with his, feel his weight on top of me and the weight of the world underneath me. I wanted to get closer to him than I'd ever been to anyone else ever before. But it was too difficult, the moment too momentous. All I could think was: *This is sex. Screwing. Humping. Fucking.* What was I supposed to do? What was I supposed to feel?

The simplest thing changed all that. His hand—a tender hand, and gentle—cupped at my neck, thumb near my ear, fingers tickling at my hairline. Something about that hand there brought me out of myself and nearer to him. His eyes met mine.

"You okay?" he asked.

"Yes," I breathed.

He exhaled and put his face close to mine, the warm skin of his cheek settling against my shoulder.

When it was over, the cold bit at us while he breathed naked atop me, our clothes newly spoiled. We dressed awkwardly. Cullen made a joke. We wandered our way outside and back to the house through the outer stretches of Jersey City. He held my hand—a gesture that grounded me, a defender against my own invading armies of doubt. I couldn't help but wonder how many girls he'd done this with and for how many it had been their first time. Had he learned to hold their hand through some early missteps? Or had he just known all along?

"What time is it?" he asked.

I showed him my watch: eleven A.M.

He nodded and looked off. Calculating. Planning.

I felt lonely and hugged his arm. The oily smell of his leather jacket was almost overwhelming. I'd never been to Europe or any place like that, but being at the waterfront at dawn felt a lot like what it must feel like to walk the streets of Rome or Athens, only instead of walking through the history of civilization with millions of other tourists, we had it all to ourselves. The ruins and the ghosts and the silence. Far off, all alone in the middle of an empty field, there was an enormous clock with COLGATE written under it. There was an inescapable feeling that shades of life watched us from behind these empty warehouses, abandoned project buildings, closed storefronts—a lost society of men and women pausing from their toil to eye us, thinking, *There goes that future we're building in here* . . . and I couldn't help but wonder what they thought about that.

The place was so quiet, we heard Ray's running footsteps before we saw him turn the corner. When he did appear, his face projected a look I'd never seen before, on him or anyone else, and yet I could identify it immediately: It was the look of a boy who was running, literally, for his life.

Ray

I DIDN'T PLAN ON RUNNING when whoever was going to come for me—the cops, Amir, or anyone else—finally came. I wanted to let whatever was going to happen to me happen, so during that night in the castle I sat awake a lot, shivering badly and hoping the end would come already. I didn't want to fight, and I didn't want to run. I didn't want to live anymore, and so I hoped the one who came would be Amir and that he'd end it for me himself—much cleaner than some dumb ordeal with cops and lawyers and judges and parents. Amir was capable of it, wasn't he? Maybe he'd show up in the night, sneak through the house real quiet, and strangle me or cut my throat or bash my head in. That would be fine, I thought. Because if God was an illusion, then so was Heaven. And when I died, I'd be nothing. And if you were nothing before, and you'd be nothing after, then the part in the middle was just a fantasy—a long, pointless car ride between two places that don't exist.

While Bri and Cullen were gone that morning in Jersey City, I grabbed a piece of broken glass from a heap of debris in a second-floor room. I stared at its pointed edge for what felt like hours. Sometimes I'd set the sharp edge against my gut, clench my teeth, and close my eyes, but I couldn't put even the slightest bit of pressure on the glass. One time I acted the whole thing out. I held the glass out in front of me and pretended to jab myself in the throat, falling back from the imaginary stabbing, trying to hold together my torn-apart neck, coughing up blood, moaning and crying and stumbling around the room like some Bugs Bunny death scene, tripping on piles of wood and broken pieces of roof, until I landed on my butt in the corner and died, my feet stuck out in front of me and my arms hanging at my sides. The whole thing made me feel better in a funny way. At least for a little while. Then I remembered that part from *The Catcher in the Rye* when he pretends to be shot in the stomach and stumbles around his room, and I felt like an idiot. I couldn't even come up with my own weird way of doing things.

Eventually the reality that I was afraid of doing it wrong— that I'd have to live without a voice box or something horrifying like that—set in and made me feel doubly bad about all the things I wanted to do but couldn't.

I dropped the glass at my feet and went on with my waiting. I spent most of the morning pacing the floors, flipping through Tolstoy's *Confession*, which I'd been carrying around in my back pocket since Christmas morning, and ducking into rooms where everything reminded me of death. I eyed the dead cat nailed to the wall in one room, studied the satanic verses scribbled above our makeshift fireplace, imaging all the maniacs who'd been in this awful place before us and all the awful acts they'd performed.

I read the "Eleven Satanic Rules of Earth" written in red across the wall of the house. Some of them were pretty straight, even moral. *#9: Do not harm little children. #10: Do not kill nonhumans unless you are attacked for your food.* This one made me think about the cat and how nobody could follow their own rules, not even satanists. *#7: Acknowledge the power of magic if you have employed it successfully to obtain your desires. If you deny the power of magic after having called upon it with success, you will lose all you have obtained.* I thought about satanists in the same way I thought about Christians—did they really believe? Could they? Was there really any difference between worshipping the devil or God? Could you worship anything and let that count as faith? The sun? The stars? A car? A gun? Yourself?

Tolstoy said, "Where there is life, there is faith."

He said, "Without faith it is impossible to live."

He said, "Faith is a knowledge of the meaning of life, the consequence of which is that man does not kill himself, but lives."

Well, I must have had some faith of some sort, even if I couldn't put words to it, because I hadn't been able to use that glass on myself, and when it came time to run, I ran.

I was standing next to the little fire pit at the top of the stairs when a fluttering caught my eye and I looked up to see snow sifting through the hole in the roof. It came from an invisible sky—low and gray and smothering. I moved to a room at the front of the house. The windows were boarded up, but there was one missing slot in the center frame, and I peeked through the gap to see the snow. You could spot Roman at a hundred yards—he was all elbows and knees and a giant head and nose, making his way across the street toward the house.

I didn't think much of it at first. It made sense that Cullen would call Roman. He was already very much a part of this. But then, from the passenger side of Roman's old pickup, I saw Amir looking up at the house. He looked right at the window, and for a moment I was sure that he saw me but I just as quickly thought that it was impossible. I was too far away, and only my eyes and nose were showing through the narrow slot. At first, he didn't move or blink or do anything at all—just stared at the top story of the house, where my eyes were exposed. Then he stepped out of the car, holding in plain sight that same gun he'd had yesterday.

I thought maybe I was making this happen. Like Amir kept showing up because I was invoking him out of my dreams in some confused, hallucinogenic fever. Giving birth to him in a series of manic fits. If I could just get a grip on my thoughts, I might make him disappear as quickly as he'd arrived.

I raced through the hall to the stairs, grabbing at the wooden knob of the post at the stairs' edge as I ran, hoping to wheel myself around on its pivot, but the rotted wood gave way. I crashed down the staircase in a painful tumble, until I managed to throw out a leg as a kickstand that popped right through a soft spot in the wood. The wood clamped against my shin like a bear trap.

The front door moaned open, followed by the sounds of Amir and Roman hurrying across the sawdust of the house's bottom floor. I kicked at the step with my free leg, splintering and cracking through the stair to free my foot, screaming, "Fuck, come on!" and then, when I was free, I hurried to the back of the house, where there was a big floor-to-ceiling window with many missing slats of lumber.

I slipped through some loose pieces of wood and out into the crazy winter storm. I ducked through a bunch of leafless bushes and onto the sidewalk. The whipping snow hurt my cheeks.

I needed to find Cullen.

Cullen

THE THING YOU HAVE TO UNDERSTAND about Amir is that he knew Ray better than any of us. Sometimes two people can meet and instantly understand all the most important truths about each other without ever talking about them. It probably doesn't happen often. But it happens. I thought that's what happened with Brielle and me, but who knows, maybe I was wrong.

After Ray had fled the convenience store that night, Amir looked up from his brother, who was squirming out from under a rack of groceries, and said to me, "Told you."

"Yeah, yeah," I said.

"I *told* you he'd see through it. He's smarter than you think."

Malik stood, and I noticed his hand—a deep gash across the palm. He wiped blood onto his shirt—a white shirt, already covered in blood across his stomach.

"You okay?" I said.

He nodded. "Glass cut me pretty good."

Amir handed a fistful of napkins to his brother, who sponged at the blood. I looked at Malik's shirt, then outside to where my car had just been before Brielle peeled off with Ray, then back to Malik, then back to the door, then back to Malik. The red mess of his shirt.

I laughed when I figured it out.

"What?" Amir said.

"Ray's smart," I said. "But not that smart."

I was content to walk right over to the O'Dells' that night and break the news to Ray. Maybe I would've had a little fun with him, let him have one or two good freak-out moments before I told him that he had not, in fact, shot Malik, let alone killed him. But I wasn't imagining anything like what Amir came up with later that night.

Malik called the cops and reported a robbery. We had to empty the register of a few handfuls of cash, which I felt bad about, but Malik said he'd figure out a way to get it back to his uncle, the store's owner. The cops showed up and took witness statements. I hung out in the back alley until they were gone. No need to have my name on the report, even as a witness. Malik and Amir told the cops he was a big guy—maybe six foot three, 250 pounds—dressed in a New York Jets sweat suit, and driving a blue minivan. He crazy, they said. On drugs probably. Came in shouting, tossing over shelves, and shooting at stuff while he demanded the cash. Amir told me the cops were pissed about the security camera malfunctioning, but they seemed to buy the story. Why wouldn't they? Amir and Malik's uncle showed up to assess the damage and, yes, go a little nuts over the security camera thing, but not to the extent that he wasn't, most of all, relieved to find his nephews mostly unharmed. Finally, Amir and Malik's parents appeared and took Malik to the ER for stitches. Amir and I stayed behind to help his uncle clean up the store.

All of this took forever. By the time we were ready to leave, it was almost five in the morning, but Amir and I were still wired from the wildness of the night, so we stopped at a diner on the way home.

"He wants something better than what we gave him," Amir said. "So let's give it to him."

"It's pretty fucked up," I said. "Letting him think he shot someone."

"But that's exactly what he wants—something fucked up! He wants to go through this, like, totally insane experience, right? And you tried to give it to him, but you played it too safe."

"Oh yeah?"

"Yeah," he said. "Admit it. You did. We have to go deeper. Ray needs it. He deserves it."

I won't lie; the gun stuff freaked me out. Things could have turned out a lot worse than they did in that store. But what freaked me out even more was that Amir, rather than showing any signs of being spooked like I was, seemed energized by it all.

"He said he wanted a vision." One of his legs bobbed frantically, shaking the table. His fingers tapped on his water glass. "This is exactly the type of thing that can help him see whatever he wants to see. I think . . . oh man. I just think we can really do something that's just totally insane and awesome. You know? I mean . . . imagine the look on his face when he sees Malik!"

"Malik? You're gonna keep him involved?"

"Well, yeah. It won't work without the big reveal."

I took a bite of my breakfast sandwich, thinking.

"What is it?" Amir said.

"I don't know. He's your brother. I don't even really know the guy. But you really think he'll go along with that? After tonight?"

"I'll talk to him."

"Just like that?"

"How do you think I convinced him to do this tonight?"

"Beats me."

"He used to beat me up all the time when we were little. Wanted to look cool in front of his friends. Now that he's grown up he feels bad about it."

He was talking fast, forking eggs into his mouth, chewing on toast, gulping juice. He wasn't looking at me—his manic eyes darted all over the place.

"See this?" He pointed to a scar that sliced diagonally across his eyebrow.

"Yeah."

"He pushed me off a skateboard when I was twelve,

and I gashed my head on the curb. Got eighteen stitches. So, yeah, whatever. You know what? I won't even tell him the whole plan. I'll just ask him to stand in some place at a certain time and wait for Ray. He'll be cool with it. Trust me."

He ate. The leg bobbed, table shook. I realized I was suddenly no longer in control of this enterprise. That Amir would probably go through with whatever plan he was cooking up whether or not I decided to participate. And that maybe he and Ray needed me there to keep it from going too far.

"Well," I said. "What exactly do you have in mind?"

He held a fork full of scrambled eggs in front of his mouth, thinking. Outside the window to our right, a New Jersey Transit train sped by, on its way to the city. Amir watched it go. His eyes narrowed. He nodded slowly.

And he smiled.

"Cops and robbers," he said. "The ultimate chase."

So . . . Jersey City. Day after Christmas. Ray ran toward Brielle and me. We couldn't see yet what he was running from, but obviously I already knew. I led the three of us away from the street, back to the huge abandoned lot at the waterfront. Brielle ran slowly. From somewhere not too far away, I heard sirens. Amir appeared, coming at us from the castle, a small, blurry figure leaning into the snowy wind.

Ray's mouth hung open in perfect goddamn holy terror. From the direction of the warehouse that Brielle and I had shared earlier that day, I spotted two blue-jacketed officers sprinting across the empty property.

"Oh shit," I said. "Look."

Amir must have seen them too because he immediately pulled back. I took us south along the water, hooked across a concrete lot filled with huge piles of stones, then vaulted the outfield fence of a rundown baseball field. I had to boost Brielle over the fence, and Ray eased her down on the other side. By the time we reached the infield, the officers had hurdled the fence with ease and were closing in on us at a steady, uncaring pace.

This is bad, I thought.

This is bad, this is bad, this is bad.

I took Bri's hand and pulled her onward. When we stepped off the field and onto a small deserted street, a kid in a hoodie sprinted out of a nearby patch of trees toward us. I heard him breathing and knew it was Roman. He shouted, "Wait up, yo!"

"Get out of here," Ray told him.

"I'm here to help," he breathed.

Bri eyed Roman, trying to make some signal of disgust push through all that exhaustion on her face.

We kept running. Four of us now. The place was all vacant space. Nowhere to ditch the cops. We moved across yet another parking lot, this one with enormous red, blue, and orange cargo containers scattered all over it. The police were close enough to shout at us and threaten to shoot, but so far no shots had been fired. When they caught us, I didn't think they'd be gentle.

"Watch this," Roman said.

Roman unzipped his pants as he ran and pulled out his dick—a hilariously massive thing. He turned, keeping pace with us as he stumbled backward, and waved it at the police, shouting, "You want some of this, you pig fuckers, you gotta catch me first!"

He hooked east across the parking lot, peeling away from us, his dick still bouncing wildly from his fly. One of the officers broke away to chase him. Roman crawled up the ladder of one of the cargo cans like some sort of demented orangutan, with the cop going after him.

The other cop still came at us. There was nothing to do but run. Abandon the plan. Find a hole to hide in, regroup, and take it from there. I was thinking about how to explain everything to Ray, fearing that if he got caught he might confess to an imaginary murder, and, actually, I was looking forward to revealing the truth. We'd taken this as far as it could go. I no longer thought the way that Amir wanted it to end was smart or useful or necessary, and I was eager to ditch these cops and get home.

A gunshot popped and echoed somewhere nearby. Our pursuing officer eased up, listening. Then another shot, from the direction of the castle. The cop glanced back once more in our direction, then peeled off down a side street toward the blast.

Amir's shot diverted the cop away from us, and in another few moments, by some miracle of his wit, he found us again. We were catching our breath on some random street corner, wiping melted snow from our chins, and I said, "Ray, listen . . ." when Amir appeared, moving methodically toward us down the slippery sidewalk, a mischievous flash in his eye.

And in that one quick moment, I shoved away my hesitation for good. *Okay*, I thought. *Whatever. Forget it. This is fun. Everything's fine. We're just having fun.*

I snatched the O'Dell siblings by their arms and led them toward the PATH station, just like Amir and I had planned.

Ray

THERE WAS ONE DAY when Amir and I went for a run after school. No cops and robbers—just a warm-up jog we sometimes took with Cullen, but this day it was only the two of us: up South Mountain Avenue and then into the reservation toward Hemlock Falls. The falls were mostly frozen and brown, the rock covered with tons of graffiti. We moved across a big, flat stone to the top of the falls, where a little stream worked through the middle of the frozen river. It'd been a full month since I'd started training with Cullen, and I felt strong—actually refreshed after the run rather than totally destroyed.

"Do you have a girlfriend or anything?" Amir asked me.

"No," I told him. "I barely even know any girls."

"Me neither."

"There was this one girl, at my old school. Cheryl Kennedy. I was totally in love with her."

"And what happened?"

"Nothing."

"Nothing?"

"I don't know," I said. "There was a party once. The only reason I was invited was because it was next door to my house, and the kid—Tim Mason—and I were friends when we were little. It was his birthday party, and I'm positive his parents made him invite me. But anyway, later in the night we were in his backyard playing truth or dare, and someone dared Cheryl to take me to the woods and make out with me."

"Sweet."

"Yeah," I said. "I thought so too. So I went out there. She smiled at me or whatever and said she'd be right there."

I stopped telling the story and watched the gray sky.

"What happened?"

"Like I said . . . nothing. She never came. I stood out there for a long-ass time before I realized. The worst part was I tried to listen to everyone laughing or joking about having tricked me, you know? But it didn't sound like that at all. They just went on with their party. Like they forgot I'd ever been there in the first place."

"Assholes."

"Yeah."

"People are fucking assholes, man. I don't know why they have to be like that."

"You know the weird thing about Cheryl Kennedy? I was totally in love with her. I swear. Like I was *positive* she was put on this earth just for me. And it took me so long to realize that everyone else was in love with her too. It's funny how that works. It's like the good-looking people get together with the good-looking people. But if you're ugly, it's not like you're attracted to other ugly people, right? So what about the rest of us?"

Amir nodded. He lay back on the rock and sighed before he said, "Sometimes I'm pretty sure I don't even like girls." He closed his eyes, like he couldn't stand to see what might happen to the world after saying something like this out loud.

I scratched at a patch of moss in a crack at my feet and let enough time pass so that the next thing I said could be a totally new topic. Of course I had the same doubts as Amir, or at least similar ones, if not exactly the same. I had all sorts of strange feelings about all sorts of people that I couldn't seem to control, no matter how much I tried. I remembered reading a book about puberty in seventh grade and getting hard when reading the part where a bunch of guys talked about how much they jerked off as teenagers and how it was totally normal. I remembered the hard-on I got the first time I shaved the darkening hair above my lip. A boner from shaving. It was funny, when you thought about it. Then there were all those times when some thickheaded bully would call me gay or a homo, and I'd shrug it off in the moment but then later have to figure out if maybe those kids knew something about me that I didn't. And if so, what then? And where did that leave my urgings for someone like Cheryl Kennedy? I knew the way I felt about Amir wasn't the same way I felt about someone like her, but I couldn't help but think that he felt differently than I did. That he maybe liked me in some other way. Or maybe not. I never got to find out. Either way, it didn't bother me. What did I care? I'd never known anyone like him. He changed me. Even more than Cullen did, he woke me up.

When I looked over at him, he was still lying on his back with his eyes closed. "What's the worst thing you ever thought?" he asked.

I laughed in a strange way—feeling weird about being asked such a straightforward, out-of-the-blue question—but was actually glad I did, because Amir's face went from being serious to kind of smiling out of the corner of his mouth.

"What do you mean?"

"I mean, do you ever have thoughts that, after you have them, you're like, holy shit, where did *that* come from?"

"Sure."

"So . . . what's the worst one you ever had?"

"You go first."

"No way, I asked the question."

I took a breath and held it in, watching a woman walk her tiny, yapping dog along the edge of the water below us. "Sometimes I think it would be easier if I were dead instead of alive."

Amir nodded. The woman pulled her dog back from the ice, and they walked the path into the woods. "Me too," he said.

"You think that too?"

"For sure. Things would definitely be easier if you were dead."

He laughed and tossed a small rock into the stream.

"I think about that all the time," he said.

I shoved him, laughing, "Fuck you."

"You've been holding me back, man."

"Right."

We rose and moved across the rock toward the trail. I brushed off the cold, wet gravel stamped to my sweats.

"So that's it?" I said. "I pour my heart out, and you're not going to answer the question?"

We walked for a while and didn't talk. We jogged across South Orange Avenue, back toward school and the late bus. While we were waiting for a traffic light, three blocks from school, he told me.

"That time I ran across 280," he said, looking at the ground.

"Yeah?"

"It wasn't like I wanted to get hit or anything. But when I got to the median, right before I started up again, I had this image of a car hitting me and it causing a massive, like *all-time* massive, pileup of cars."

He stared off. The light had changed, but we didn't walk. I jumped in place a little to keep warm.

"And I thought . . . that would be so. Fucking. Awesome. You know?"

"Yeah."

"Which is so crazy," he said. He wiped his nose, which was red and chapped from the cold. "It's so fucking crazy! I don't know those people. They don't deserve that. Why would I think something like that?"

"It's okay," I said.

"It's not okay."

"I get it, though. That's all I mean. I get that feeling."

"It's not like I wanted the people in those cars to get hurt. When I imagined it, they weren't even really there. It was only the cars themselves, just . . . smashing together. The fucking noise of it all. And right there in the middle of it . . . was me."

He sniffled and wiped his nose again, and I wanted to reach out and hug him or put an arm on his shoulder or . . . something. Of course I knew what he meant. That's the whole reason we were here. But before I could muster the courage to reach out for him, he stepped into the street, and so I followed him, saying nothing.

Standing now in Jersey City with my hands on my knees, breathing hard, three blocks down the street from the castle, which was just as marked up with graffiti as Hemlock Falls and whose towers you could see poking through a line of leafless trees, I watched Amir come at me, and I took a breath, and I said out loud, "Amir, please just let me go," before finally standing upright and following Cullen.

We ran for what felt like hours with Amir a steady two blocks behind us. Ran in the snow and cold and across intersections, which became busier and busier as we moved into the heart of the city. There was a passage from St. Augustine that I'd read and reread until I'd memorized it: "If I did anything against my will, it seemed to me to be something which happened to me rather than something which I did, and I looked upon it not as a fault, but as a punishment."

I knew that I played some mysterious role in the unfolding of my own fate. Otherwise why would I exist as a conscious being at all? But still it felt more like this was happening *to* me rather than because of me.

Cullen led us down the steps of the PATH station. At the bottom of the stairs stood two enormous men in camouflage, each with an epically fierce machine gun slung over their shoulder. Cullen pulled out a MetroCard, swiped it, and motioned me through the turnstile. He did the same for himself and Bri. I was dumb. So clueless. Why would he have a MetroCard? It didn't seem strange until long after the fact. But there were all sorts of things about Cullen I didn't know, so I let it happen.

We hurried onto the train. Navigated from one car to the next, slipping between holiday travelers, opening and closing the heavy doors between cars, all the way to the front of the train. I peeked out the windows and did not see Amir. The doors closed with three warning beeps and a hush.

The train lurched forward, and soon we were rocketing under the Hudson toward New York. I watched the door at the end of the car. If Amir was on the train, I wasn't sure if he could move between cars while in the tunnel. Maybe the doors automatically locked or something. I wasn't about to walk over there and check.

"Tell him," Bri said, hitting Cullen on the knee.

"What?"

"Tell him what you told me."

"About what?"

"Malik!" Bri said. "He's not dead!" She nudged my arm. "Ray? You hear me?"

"Yeah," I said.

"He's alive. Right, Cullen?"

Random colored lights flitted past the window—green, red, blue. Cullen stared at me and didn't say anything.

"Tell him! Tell him now!"

My ears popped as we came out of the tunnel.

Bri punched Cullen on the shoulder. "What is the matter with you?" She punched him again and again. Across the aisle, a family with two little kids watched us. I looked at our reflections in the black window and tried to see ourselves as they saw us: dirty, wild, unsupervised. Delinquents.

The train stopped at Christopher Street, and Cullen shook his head no at me. I understood. Amir would expect us to get off here. We stayed put until Ninth Street, then exited. As soon as you were in the city, everything was faster. People swarmed on the platform when we stepped off the train, tossing bags over their shoulders, shoving strollers through the ruckus. The three of us huddled in a corner. I was too afraid to move, hoping that if Amir had been on the train and by some horrible stroke of luck exited at this station, he'd be swept along in the flow of traffic and end up looking for us at street level.

Bri was agitated. "Ray, listen to me. He told me. Cullen *told* me that Malik is alive. It's okay. Okay? Can you listen to me, please?"

Yes. Okay. I was listening now. I understood. Not everything—not yet. But enough.

At the far end of the platform, through the crowd, I saw him. His eyes. His hand in a jacket pocket. He moved against the momentum of the crowd, pushing upstream toward us. He was my friend. He'd brought me here.

Cullen looked down the black tunnel. "We gotta go."

"Go where?" Bri's hands were shaking. She was trying not to cry.

"We'll pop out at the next station."

"Are you crazy?"

"It's our only chance!"

"No! No, no, no!"

Amir came toward me, stalking through the crowd. I understood what he wanted me to do. I knew how to win the game.

"I'll go."

"Ray, no . . ." Bri tried to grab my coat, but I pulled away and looked down the tunnel to make sure no trains were approaching.

"I need to do this!" I said to her. "You stay!"

Bri was crying for real now. "You don't have to! Cullen, please, tell him he doesn't have to!"

Cullen stood with his arms crossed over his chest—maybe he was grinning a little.

"Stop it!" Bri shouted so it echoed throughout the tunnel. "Cullen, why are you letting this happen? Please! Stop it!"

Bri again tried to grab my coat to keep me from going, and as I turned to pry her hands off me I saw Amir shove his way between two people, gun in his pocket, eyes wild. This was it. My turn had come.

I pushed my sister away, leaped onto the tracks, stumbled once, rose, and sprinted into the darkness. I turned back just long enough to see Amir taking the leap, chasing after me. The single track opened up to a cavernous maze of tracks. I hurdled the third rail and landed on the middle path, where the express trains come screaming through.

I ran. A cold wind came through the tunnel. It was so loud that I worried I might not hear an oncoming train, but then almost immediately the ground shook with a roar and a spotlight came out of the black. I tripped across to the neighboring tracks—there were maybe six of them in all—but wherever I went, the light seemed to come right at me. It grew and grew, and the whole world shook, and I looked back, expecting to find Amir but instead seeing another train, just as bright, just as loud, screaming at me from the other direction. The air exploded when the two trains crossed paths with me standing upright in the space between them, clutching a steel beam. The sensation was like if you were falling through the sky and got caught in a storm cloud full of lightning.

The trains passed. The place went black again. Footsteps came at me. I didn't move. Again the ground shook, and here came the shriek of another train. The light made Amir into a shadow. He ran at me, leaping over tracks.

Like the last two, this train came in quickly. Too quickly. At first it was a distant light—just the idea of a thing, not even the thing itself—and then it was real and deadly and right on top of us. Amir looked up from running with a face that I thought was a smile, like he had something funny he'd been waiting to tell me for a long time. Like he still wasn't afraid. Like he was having a great time playing this game where no one could ever get hurt, not even when you crashed a car into the woods at seventy miles per hour. Not even when you played with a loaded gun. Not even underground, in a subway tunnel. And I smiled back at him. Because I already knew what he wanted to tell me.

He had the gun in one hand, and he came at me so fast. Out of control. His shoulder was lowered, and his arms were held out like he wanted to tackle me. Or hug me. He tripped. Lost his balance. Arms flailing, he almost recovered, but then didn't. He tumbled across one track, and his momentum took him all the way into the next one.

When the train hit him, it didn't make any sound at all.

PART TWO

Brielle

AMIR'S MEMORIAL SERVICE was held on a clear, sunny January day. Ray did not attend, nor did Cullen. I pleaded with Ray, but he was resolute about staying home. The service itself was devastating, and I did not stay very long. There were tears and screams and total emotional breakdowns everywhere you looked. Nobody bothered to be polite. There was not much in the way of composure or self-possessed, quiet suffering like you might have found at an O'Dell memorial service—like I remember at my grandfather's funeral. I thought about going to talk to Amir's brother, but couldn't bring myself to do it. Malik looked so angry at the world, and at himself, that I feared how he'd react to someone else who was a part of the ridiculous plan that got his brother killed. I understood then why Cullen didn't go, and I understood too that, no matter how much any of us may have wanted to, we would never be able to make this right for Malik or any other member of Amir's family.

I knew Amir primarily through watching Ray interact with him, but I really liked him. I knew what he meant to Ray. And it wasn't only because I knew he'd regret it someday that I urged Ray to attend the service, but also because I was afraid of leaving him alone. I knew what he was capable of. He proved that to me with the subway tunnel stunt, yes, but even more so right afterward.

When Amir jumped onto the track after Ray, Cullen and I raced aboveground to the next station. By the time we arrived, a team of EMTs, firemen, and police were already hurrying down the steps, closing off the entrance. Of course a stunt like this, I thought, in a city under twenty-four-hour surveillance, wouldn't last more than ten seconds without a swift and brutal response from the authorities. I was waiting for Ray to be led out of the subway in cuffs, already planning his defense for the events of Christmas Eve, working out a way to scapegoat Cullen for the whole thing, when a handsome, quiet-eyed young guy came walking down the sidewalk, shielding his face from the snow, and nodded a greeting at Cullen.

"This is Brielle," Cullen said.

The guy lifted his face briefly to greet me, and I knew instantly who he was.

"Brielle, this is Malik," Cullen confirmed.

Malik had a small bandage wrapped around his hand

but other than that did not appear to be injured at all—no signs of a gunshot recovery.

"I got out of there," he said, nodding to the subway stairs. "Before the cops came."

"I'm sure everything's fine," Cullen said.

I shook with a wet shiver and moved under the too-short awning of a Duane Reade. Except for a few hurried travelers pausing briefly at the yellow tape strung across the station stairs, nobody noticed or gave more than a cursory thought to the firemen standing guard beside their truck while some mysterious tragedy played out underground. This relentless movement of the city made me sick. The three of us stood in a row with pocketed hands and waterlogged feet.

I still didn't know what the whole scheme had been, and I didn't have a full sense of Cullen's role in it, but I knew enough to understand it was a dumb idea that had been taken too far. I also knew I was just as complicit in its conclusion as everyone else.

Even pressed against the glass as we were, people brushed against us as they marched into the pressing storm. The city resisted our stillness. Bullied our waiting. The storm briefly died down, and the wind let up. Oversized flakes sunk down so slowly it seemed like they would keep falling and falling and never touch down. I closed my eyes and inexplicably saw summer. A sort of childhood I'd never really had, with lakes and docks and bare feet. I pictured that image of Mom and me at the beach. Snowflakes touched down on my cheeks and eyelids, and I let the summer daydream dissolve to feel the quick touches of cold and then the melt slipping down my chin. It would be nice, I thought, to come apart like a cloud. To watch as a thousand million specks of Brielle drifted away to some other place. It would be just the right amount of hurt: a scattershot of quick, burning pinpricks, minuscule flecks of skin, muscle, tissue, and bone, each one a unique marvel of biological intricacy, plucked by gravity from the whole and snared by the wind.

I looked to see if Cullen was watching me, but he was not. Despite it all, and against all good reason, I wanted him close to me. To touch him and smell him. I wanted to reach out and take his hand in mine, but the space between us felt impossibly far.

Two police climbed out of the station, untacked the yellow tape, and stood somberly at the steps. It was another two minutes—agonizing minutes during which I imagined all sorts of calamity and terror—before a team of EMTs appeared, carrying a gurney on which was strapped a faceless bundle of person. Instinctively, ready to shatter with mourning, I stepped toward them, but Cullen caught my arm. I looked where he looked—across the street, catty-corner to us. Even with the snow and the crowd, which was gathering now around the ambulance where the body was being deposited, I could make out Ray's figure—thin and slouched with a windblown flop of hair.

Malik saw him too. And Cullen saw Malik seeing him. Cullen pushed me away from the scene. Malik let out a harsh, piercing cry—like a small boy who's broken his wrist badly—and scrambled to the ambulance, shoving people out of his way, pedestrian and police officer alike. I looked again for Ray, but he was gone, and Cullen was pulling me in the opposite direction. I fought against him, but he tugged me harshly, and I went with him because I didn't know any better, because I was in a total, mindless panic, and because I didn't want to listen to that noise coming from Malik anymore.

Our best bet was that Ray would retreat to the castle. When we'd first arrived in Jersey City, Cullen made both Ray and me swear that if we ever got split up, for whatever reason, until further notice we were to meet at the castle. Ray didn't have a MetroCard, and I was pretty sure he didn't have any cash or even the wherewithal to jump a turnstile, but it was our only hope. As soon as you lost someone in a city like this, they were gone. There was no sense in wandering the streets looking for them.

Once we stepped off the PATH back in New Jersey, Cullen pulled me by the arm the whole way to the castle. If he hadn't, I might have collapsed in the nearest snowdrift and curled up to let the storm bury me. On the steps of the house, I suddenly found my strength and erupted at Cullen, who couldn't meet my gaze as I screamed at him.

"You did this!" I told him. "You! You! You!"

I was just getting warmed up, but at that very instant Ray appeared through the bushes—he must have ridden on the same train as us. He moved past us and into the house, ignoring our questions about what had happened and was that really Amir on the gurney and had anyone followed him here. We chased him inside, where he plodded up the stairs, head drooped, on a mission. I tried to position myself in front of him, but he only squirmed away and moved into a bedroom on the second story, where he picked a piece of broken glass off the floor. He went right for it like he knew it was it there.

At the sight of the glass, Cullen and I paused at the threshold. I saw in Ray's eyes what he meant to do with it, and I guess Cullen did too.

Cullen held a hand out to Ray. "Ray," he said. "Listen to me."

Ray smiled at Cullen in the most awful way. His head was tilted down like his neck was broken—the head of a discarded puppet—and he gazed at Cullen through possessed eyes. He raised the glass. Cullen shouted. I took two desperate steps toward Ray. Ray went to jam the glass into his throat, but Cullen dove at him, tackling him, sending the glass piece across the floor. Ray fought against Cullen, the two of them kicking and squirming on the ground. I grabbed the glass and tossed it into the hallway.

"Stop," Cullen shouted. "Stop!"

Ray kicked and slapped at Cullen, trying to bite his shoulder as they wrestled.

"Ray, stop! Stop it!"

Cullen fought his way on top of Ray, pinning his arms to the ground. He screamed so loudly it made me dizzy. "RAY! CALM THE FUCK DOWN! RIGHT NOW!"

The world tilted. My lungs tensed. Ray seethed under

Cullen's grip—a trapped beast. Cullen held him until Ray stopped fighting. It took a long time. Ray screamed and kicked and spat and thumped his head against the floor, until finally he just lay there breathing heavily.

"Let me go," he mumbled.

"You gonna do anything stupid?"

"Just let me go." He said it so sadly that Cullen released his grip on Ray's wrists and moved off him. Ray didn't move. He just laid there, his arms outspread on the floor.

Cullen explained it all. He told us about Christmas Eve. Explained that Ray's sprint through the subway was meant to serve as a rite of passage and that Ray was supposed to find Malik—a living, breathing second chance—waiting on the platform on the other side, and be forever redeemed. He made sure to emphasize that this last part—the tunnel run—was Amir's idea. Amir wanted to be there with Ray when he made it through.

"Ray," I said. "Are you okay?" It was such an obvious, pointless question, but it was all I could think of to say.

He watched the ceiling. Did not move. Didn't even blink.

"What about Amir?" Cullen said.

Ray said just one word, but we knew what it meant. He barely parted his lips to let it come through.

"Crushed," he said.

God, did we know what it meant. And for as much as Ray had to be blaming himself, and even though I knew Amir at least well enough to believe that the tunnel run was in fact his idea, I knew the real culprit. I knew the identity of this immeasurable hurt inside my brother and me. The only thing we were guilty of was not calling it by its proper name before it had metastasized. *Cullen Hickson.* That cancer.

He offered to drive us home. I didn't respond.

"Take the car then," he insisted. "I'll take the PATH to Hoboken and get on a train."

Again, I didn't say anything. What I wanted most of all was to leave him alone at the castle to soak in its viciousness. I wanted to walk away from him for good. But it all seemed too much. And I don't just mean the actual process of figuring out how to get home—navigating to the PATH and then finding the right train in Hoboken. Those things were intimidating, sure, but even more so I was paralyzed by a fear of detaching from Cullen. Because if I walked away, I was on my own. And on my own, I'd be adrift. Unmoored. But if I stuck with Cullen—if we climbed into that Buick again and let him steer us home—I could continue to glide along in this same manner. To define myself by way of this boy. To keep the blame for what had happened, and would happen yet, aimed squarely at him.

Ray

FATHER JOE WANTED ME TO TALK. It was a freezing January day outside, and his office was too cold—he didn't control the thermostat, he explained, and there was no way to make any more heat come from the radiator behind his desk. Music played from the stereo on his bookshelf. Something '90s and grungy. Pearl Jam maybe? I didn't know, and plus the volume was so low I could hardly hear it. Maybe Father Joe didn't even like the music. Maybe that's why the volume was so low. He put it on, I thought, so kids would come in and sit on his couch—kids like Nick O'Dwyer—and hear the music and think, *Wow, a priest who listens to music! What a cool guy!* For the first time, I thought I could see through Father Joe. I was starting to see through everyone lately. Everything everyone did was meant to make you believe they were someone they weren't. All for the sake of vanity.

And that's why I hadn't said a word to anybody in five days. Father Joe insisted on calling it my "vow of silence," but it wasn't a vow. I wasn't about to make a promise to him or God or anyone else. I just didn't feel like talking.

I kept a piece of paper in the inside pocket of my school blazer, crinkled and torn now from too much folding and unfolding. Father Joe was telling me about the memorial assembly coming up for Amir. On Friday the whole school would gather in the auditorium for a mass in Amir's memory. He wanted some of Amir's friends to come up during the time normally reserved for the homily and "say a few words" about him. Would I do that, Father Joe wanted to know. If not for him, and if not for myself, then at least for Amir?

My hand went for the note in my pocket, and Father Joe was rolling his eyes and shaking his head before I even pulled it out. He knew what was coming. I unfolded the note, flattened it out on his desk, and pointed to the word scribbled across the paper: *vanity*.

"Honoring your friend's memory is not vanity, Ray."

I pointed to the paper.

Father Joe looked past me and didn't say anything. He looked sad. Like he felt sorry for me, but not for the reason you might think. Not because my friend had died. For some other reason that I couldn't understand.

I retrieved my paper, folded it, and secured it inside my blazer. I liked having it there in the pocket next to my heart. Sometimes walking the halls or sitting in class or riding the bus home from school, I'd tap my hand against the outside of the blazer, right over the St. John of the Cross crest, and feel the note press against my chest, listening to its soft crinkle. It reminded me of why Amir had died. That even if it had been his idea to chase me through the subway tunnel, and even if Cullen had led me to the platform and pointed the way, the only reason we were down there was for my own vanity. Because I thought I was worthy of something more than what I'd been given.

I hadn't stopped talking right away. In fact, at first, I did a lot of talking. Two days after the funeral, I went to the Rosewood cops and told them that I'd been in the subway tunnel with Amir when he died and that I'd pushed him in front of the train. There were two reasons I did this: One was for Amir, and the other was for me. I did it for Amir because there were so many questions about why he'd been in the subway tunnel and why he'd been carrying a gun, which, by the way, was not loaded. The newspaper articles suggested that he jumped in front of the train on purpose and that he maybe even had bigger plans for being down there. They never stated this exactly, of course. But the writers always made a point to mention that his parents were Saudi Arabian and, of course, Muslim. And they always referenced how smart Amir was, as if that were a bad thing. Like maybe he was *too* smart. And of course he was quiet. Always some dumb quote from a guy at school or a neighbor or a soccer coach from five years ago who pointed out that Amir was a quiet kid. That he kept to himself. Which wasn't true at all. They only thought he was quiet because they never bothered to listen. By the time you finished reading about the accident you were supposed to put the newspaper down and think, *Well, gee, what* was *that smart, quiet Muslim kid doing in a New York City subway tunnel?* And then you were supposed to start thinking, *Who else might be down there? And what are they planning?*

So I hiked to the police station and demanded to speak to a detective, and after waiting for two hours I was escorted to a dreary, fluorescent-lit office toward the back of the building. I planned to leave out Bri, Cullen, and Malik. I didn't want them to get punished for any of this—not even Cullen. I made my own choices. I understood that now. So the second reason I was there: myself. I had come to receive whatever penance I deserved. Because just like those readers, I had been afraid of Amir too. And I should have known better.

So I told this guy—Detective Clift—that I'd been in the tunnel with Amir Shadid on December 26, that Amir wasn't doing anything wrong, that he was only in there because of me, and that I'd pushed him into that F train.

And what he said was "You too?"

I blinked at him.

He tossed a pen across the desk and then a pad of lined yellow paper. "Write it out," he sighed. "I'll add it to the others."

"What do you mean?" I said again. "What others?"

He wheeled around in his chair and grabbed a folder stuffed with pieces of that same lined yellow paper.

He plopped the folder on the desk. I stared at it, not understanding.

"Look," he said.

Inside were dozens of confessions to the murder of Amir Shadid. All hand-written. All signed by kids I knew or had at least heard of: David Garfield. Alice Cochran. Jennifer Chang. Tim Mason. And there were faxed pages signed by kids from St. John's. Cesar Navarro. Michael Russo. Troy Jardin.

"Other precincts started sending them in to us. They couldn't be bothered anymore. They figure since Rosewood is where it started, this shit is my problem."

"It started . . . ?" I began, but then stopped, digging to the bottom of the pile.

"I don't understand this generation," Detective Clift said. "This is your idea of fun or what? What happened to stick-ball and shit?"

At the bottom of the stack of papers, I found it: the first confession. Meticulously hand-written in perfect cursive. Handwriting I knew well. And the signature at the bottom: *Brielle O'Dell*.

"Girl came in here couple days ago, says she was in the subway tunnel with the kid who got hit by the train. I say, 'Okay, tell me about it.' She knows what he was wearing. Knows what the gun looked like. Identified a couple stand-ing on the platform who saw two kids jump onto the tracks. Couple reported they witnessed two *males*, but I figure, what the hell, maybe they weren't looking that closely, right? Neither one of them could offer a reliable description of the other kid who jumped anyway. You should see the sketch—looks like it could be any kid in America—which, as you can see before you, turns out it is *every* kid in America."

"But it's me," I told him. "I was there! I pushed him!"

"Write it down. I won't stop you. But if you think I'm running this over to NYPD again, you're crazy. I called in that first one—the girl. Expected them to whip on over here and pin a fucking medal on me. You know the rest."

"But I don't! I have no idea . . ."

"Well, whatever. Next day, three more confessions come in. Day after that, four more. So on and so forth. Every single one of 'em knows all the right details. They recite it like a prayer. What the Shadid kid was wearing, what the gun looked like, what the couple on the platform looked like. So you know what I gotta do?"

I shifted uncomfortably in the plastic chair.

"I gotta call these high-and-mighty Manhattan jerkoffs and tell 'em about all these bogus confessions. Tell 'em I'm the asshole getting fucked with by a buncha dipshit kids. You all picked a helluva time to be messing with NYPD, I'll give you that. They got real police work to do over there these days, you know."

"And what about you?"

"Me?"

"Yeah, what kind of work do you have to do?"

He sucked something through his teeth and didn't say anything.

"Look," I told him. "My name is Ray O'Dell, and Amir

Shadid was my friend. He was my best fucking friend, okay? And I killed him. I didn't mean to, but I did. And you can't just . . ." I choked a little, because I was crying now. Because the whole thing was coming apart right in front of me. "You can't just do that! You can't just take this away from me!"

The detective seemed to understand me this time, or at least sympathize. His eyes went soft, and he said, "Look, man. You ask me, he comes out okay in this. It was an accident. That's the official call as of this morning. Accident. Not a suicide." ˙

"Suicide?"

"Yeah."

"Why would it be a suicide?"

"You kidding? A kid don't go running around a subway tunnel unless he's got a death wish. So, like I said, you ask me, he comes out okay in the end."

I was about to respond, but just then the door behind me cracked open and a woman poked her head in.

"Got another one, Pete. Want to double 'em up?"

She opened the door wider to reveal the person standing behind her.

Cullen threw a crooked smile in my direction. "I'd like to confess to the murder of Amir Shadid."

I turned back to Detective Clift. He shrugged and raised his eyebrows at me like *What can I tell you?*

I was so mad, and there were so many things I wanted to say. To Cullen, and to the detective, and to Bri, and to all the kids Cullen had duped into being a part of his most recent, infuriating scheme. But I didn't say anything—not in that moment or for five days afterward. I swallowed it all— the hate and disappointment and every other boiling-hot feeling erupting inside me. Choked them down like cough medicine. Cullen and Bri thought they were saving me when in fact they were doing no such thing. They were saving themselves. Scrubbing clean their own consciences. And I wasn't about to give in to that same kind of vanity. That smug self-satisfaction.

The whole of humanity by this point was disgusting to me. The planet a filthy nest of insignificant life. It was funny, really, when you thought about it in a big-picture sort of way. We were just these grubby little creatures who imagined ourselves blessed. *I am large*, Walt Whitman said. *I contain multitudes*. Which was such a load of bullshit. Everything we did—Amir and me included—was based on the irrational idea that we were special. That our own individual lives—no matter how short or painful or pathetic or whatever—that each one actually *meant* something. And of all the terrible things we did in the name of vanity—fought, stole, cheated, murdered, raped, whatever—the search for God was by far the worst. Because at least that other stuff was honest about its own vileness. The search for God was an illogical, child- ish way to make ourselves feel better. To turn away from the hurt and the gloom and the astounding meaningless- ness of our own actions in order to warm ourselves in the make-believe glow of some imaginary creator's loving gaze. To convince yourself there was a God was to deny the cold facts of being human, which had nothing to do with immortality or salvation or purity, and had everything to do, I was finally understanding, with death and cruelty and pain and an unending series of one devastating disaster after another.

And no, Amir didn't have a death wish. I knew exactly why he led me into that tunnel, and it didn't have anything to do with suicide. He was giving me exactly what I wanted, because he knew that I wasn't going to get that close to the edge on my own. He had brought me as close as you could come to finding the truth—to seeing through to the other side. To really, truly living. But it didn't work. Because there *was* no other side. And now Amir was gone. And what a stupid waste of time it all was.

So that was the moment—in that cramped detective's office—that I stopped talking. Because talking was exactly what everyone expected me to do. The detective was waiting for more pleading, and Cullen was waiting for some manic outburst, and Bri was, no question about it, at home waiting for me to storm into her room and demand something as trite and clichéd as her minding her own business.

But I wasn't going to do any of that.

I was finally ready to take control.

The mass for Amir, like all masses, was long and boring. We were supposed to be thinking about Amir the whole time, but it was impossible to keep something like that at the front of your mind every single second, even for me, one of the only people in the crowd who actually knew him. The seats of the old auditorium were cramped and hard, and guys squirmed and creaked in their chairs, unable to get comfortable for more than three seconds at a time. Some guys slept. Some guys whispered inaudible jokes to each other, chuckling too loudly. An altar dominated the stage; four priests sat in a line to the left of it. Usually Monsignor Murphy, our school head-master, would say a mass like this, but today Father Joe did it. During the homily, Father Joe tried to sell us on the idea that loss and pain were side effects of love and awe, and that experiencing love and awe, loss and pain, was really a way of coming to know Christ, and that even though it may seem like Amir had been taken from us, what really happened was that God had welcomed Amir back into His heart. He then asked for volunteers to "say a few words" about our classmate.

There was a horrible silence that went on forever. Nobody moved. Nobody laughed or cracked a joke about it. You could feel the whole room tighten up with a hot, heavy feeling. It wasn't fear, exactly, but something like that. A feel-ing of wanting, above all else, for the moment to pass. For the pressure to be relieved.

From the back of the auditorium came the squeaking of a chair. We all turned to see a row of students stand in order to let someone by. Of course it was Cullen. He'd taken off his blazer at some point during the mass and, realizing that he'd left it at his seat as he stepped into the aisle, motioned for it to be passed down the row. He walked down the aisle, slip-ping into the blazer, flipping down the collar, straightening his tie, pushing strands of hair out of his eyes.

His speech was short. People barely had time to react to it. He said, "Amir was my boy. He was smarter and cooler and better than all the rest of you. I wish he was still here. It sucks that he's gone." Then he took two steps away from the podium, but at the last moment he leaned back to the microphone and blurted out, "Ray O'Dell was Amir's friend too. Maybe he has something to say."

He marched up the aisle toward the back of the room. He didn't look at me, probably didn't even know where I was sitting. Nobody else looked at me either. Hardly anybody knew who Ray O'Dell was, so nobody knew where to look. Except Father Joe. He saw me.

My stomach flipped over itself. Father Joe stepped to the microphone. "Ray," he said. "Would you like to speak?"

I shifted in my seat, which squeaked loudly. The whole room was quiet now and watching me. Hundreds of boys. Nobody was asleep anymore. Nobody shifting in the creaky seats. Nobody bored.

Okay, I thought. *Fine. Fine! If they want me to talk, then that's exactly what I'll do.*

Once I was at the microphone, I said, "This isn't a funeral. They already had the funeral. I didn't go, but this isn't one. This is . . ."

I paused, reaching into the shelf within the podium and grabbing what I knew would be there. I flipped through the book until I found the passage I wanted—the one that had first given me the idea for the note in my pocket—and read: "Ecclesiastes 1:14. 'I have seen all the works that are done under the sun; and behold, all is vanity and a striving after wind.'"

I looked up from the book and scanned the enormous room. "That's all this is. Vanity. A striving after wind. Amir's not even here, so how could it be for him? How can this be an 'honoring of his memory,' like some people want it to be? It's just us trying to make ourselves feel better. Which is so dumb, isn't it? I mean, it's so dumb!"

I said this last part like I was pleading with someone who I assumed would agree with me. I expected to see heads nodding, guys who also felt like me—but didn't have the courage to say anything—agreeing enthusiastically. But nobody was nodding. Mostly everyone stared. Not shocked or surprised, necessarily. Not even amused. They just looked at me blankly.

"There's no sense in being here—like, on earth, I mean—if being here only means pain. Between pain and nothing, wouldn't you choose nothing? Especially if the pain . . . I mean, it would be one thing if the pain *meant* something, wouldn't it? If there was some *point* to it and all. But if it's just this randomness, if it's just pain all the way around, well, then . . ." And here I glanced at Father Joe, who was sitting next to Monsignor Murphy, who was motioning for him, it seemed, to come up to the podium and stop my speech. But Father Joe wasn't getting up. He was looking past me with that same sad face he had shown me in his office.

"Well, then Amir was one of the lucky ones. Because he got out. And you know what? I'm going with him. It doesn't make sense to stay. Why would I not kill myself? Why wouldn't any of us?"

And now I felt a hand on my elbow and another on my shoulder, tugging me from the podium, gently at first, but then more forcefully as I fought against it. I grabbed the microphone as they yanked me away. "Give me one good reason!" I shouted. It was Monsignor Murphy, I realized now, and another priest—not Father Joe—who escorted me from the podium.

"Okay now," the one priest was saying. "Okay, son."

"Give me one good reason!"

I flung my arm away violently and charged up to the microphone. "One reason we shouldn't all kill ourselves right now! I dare you!"

There were a lot of arms around me now. I was being lifted into the air and hauled away. I heard the auditorium erupt in applause and laughter. I stopped struggling and let it happen. My whole body relaxed. I felt my breathing ease up, and—very slowly—I felt a sense of absolute happiness wash over me. It was a feeling of surrender. Of calm. Of total, utter clarity. There *was* no good reason. That was the big secret. And knowing this made everything clear. It was so simple, in the end, that as I was carried over the shoulder of a priest through the curtains of the stage and into the dark wings of the auditorium—carried aloft to the roaring applause of the student body, like I was an all-time great football hero being treated to one final, rousing send-off—it was so simple that I had to smile.

Cullen

IN THE DAYS AFTER AMIR'S DEATH—before Ray went to the cops about it, and before the moment when he totally lost it in front of the entire school—I converted the basement into my new bedroom. I needed to occupy my mind with something, I suppose. *Converted*, though, is probably overstating it. Mostly it was the same basement that had been there before Dad died and Nana moved in to take care of me: some adult male's half-assed version of a hangout spot with an oak bar across one wall, mirrors and tin signs and snuffed-out neon writing all celebrating cheap American ale, wood paneling, a thin green carpet thrown over the concrete floor, an old television set, and a dank, cobwebbed stairway in the corner leading to the hatch of twin cellar doors. The major additions were a waterbed I'd bought at a garage sale for $200—situated against the wall opposite the bar, under

Dad's black-light Led Zeppelin poster—and a PlayStation 2 hooked up to the TV.

It was pouring outside the day Brielle came over. The rain drummed against the doors of the cellar hatch. The doorbell rang three times, and Nana called down for me to come do something about it, before I paused my game of *NBA 2K* and climbed the stairs. By the time I got there, Nana was sleeping in her La-Z-Boy. The bell must have woken her, and, after calling for me, she had slipped right back into sleep. I spied through the living room curtains to see a frigid, soaked Brielle standing at the front door.

I had, prior to this appearance on my porch, resigned myself to never seeing Brielle O'Dell again. Which doesn't mean that the resignation didn't hurt. It did. Because I liked Brielle. A lot. And I anticipated a blowback to the initial subway-chase plan, of course. But convincing her brother that he'd killed someone when in fact he hadn't was something I could work around. I didn't have a blueprint for doing so, exactly. I just figured that eventually, someday, somehow, she'd forgive me for the Ray-killed-Malik stuff—not only for the plan itself but for not trusting her enough to let her in on it from the start—and we would go back to falling in love and living in a state of complete, uncompromising astonishment.

The thing with Amir, though. Pretty sure there was no coming back from that.

And yet . . . here she was.

Thank God she was dripping wet when I let her in,

because it gave us an immediate, awkwardness-squashing task on which to collaborate. I grabbed a towel for her, and she bent over and went to work drying her hair. Coming back upright, rope of damp hair smacking her back, wiping raindrops from her hairline, she was stunning. She was paler than usual and shivering and wearing no makeup, but she was Brielle O'Dell, and she was in my living room, and I could hardly stand it.

"You want to take your jacket off?" I whispered. "I have like a button-down or something you could wear if your shirt—"

"I'm fine," she said. "I can't stay long. I need a favor."

"Okay."

"It's a big one."

"Okay."

Nana shifted her in her chair, murmuring. She could sleep through any noise coming from a television—laugh tracks, gunfire, explosions, sirens, someone winning the jackpot on *Wheel of Fortune*—but the tiniest noise from an actual living human tended to shake her alert.

I put up a finger to Brielle, asking her to hold on. I tiptoed over to Nana, slung the oxygen mask over her face, and turned the knob on the tank. I grabbed her plate of half-eaten apples and crackers, dumped them in the kitchen sink, and then motioned for Brielle to follow me downstairs.

She joined me on the basement couch—me at one armrest and she at the other, a full square of cushion between us. We sat like that and kept quiet for a long time, Brielle watching me.

"So," I said. "A favor?"

"Is she okay?" she asked.

"Who?"

"Your grandmother?"

"Oh. Yeah. Why?"

She fiddled with the frayed edges of the couch fabric. "You take care of her?"

"Sure," I said. "When she needs it."

Of my many long-running lies, the idea that Nana took care of me instead of the other way around was maybe the biggest. Something I kept from everyone. When Nana's health and mind started to slip, she'd covered up her inadequacies with a snarkiness that she brought to every public appearance. She'd shout to customer service at the market about the state of the produce, attend city council meetings as the only voice speaking up against new traffic lights and crosswalks and any other safety measures proposed for the town that she thought were a waste of her tax dollars when people should be capable of avoiding goddamn calamitous bullshit on their own. For a long time, even as she started to need me more and more at home, she was loud and present around town, so nobody bothered to question her ability to raise me adequately. Even when she finally stopped showing her face in public, stopped leaving the house altogether, nobody really thought to check in.

Which was fine by me. And, as far as I could tell, fine by
Nana too. I even thought that maybe she'd acted that way in
public because she knew what was coming and knew that
the two of us would be fine on our own.

I didn't think about this while Brielle stood in my living
room, though. All I could think was that she was here and I
wanted to be with her. Couldn't wait to get downstairs with
her, even if all she wanted was a favor. *Yes*, I thought at the
time. *A favor. Of course. Anything you want, whatever it is,
I will do it.*

And helping Nana with the mask was a simple enough,
routine action. One day I went with her to the doctor, who
told us that people her age with lung issues—lifetime smok-
ers, especially—might suffer sleep apnea to the point where
they stop breathing and their bodies don't start up again in
time. Of course I wasn't home every time Nana fell asleep,
but for the times I was, I slipped the mask on her to be safe.
I'd done it so many times now it was like a reflex.

And Brielle saw it.

"It's not a big deal," I said, and my breath tripped when
I said it.

Little by little, for reasons I couldn't explain, everything
in me was suddenly going soft. All the walls were coming down. I tried my best to hide it, but Brielle must have
noticed it. She scooched across the couch and leaned her
head on my shoulder.

"I didn't mean for it to be like this," I told her.

"Seems like you two are doing okay."

But I wasn't thinking about Nana anymore. It wasn't until Brielle said what she said that I was forced to identify the source of the feeling. The thing I'd been ignoring all week.

"With Amir, I mean."

"Oh."

"So stupid," I said. "So, so stupid."

We listened to the rain. At some point I sighed, and she tilted her head to kiss my neck. Her hair was wet on my shoulder. I noticed her shirt and pants were still soaked through, and I told her so, and right away she stood and shimmied out of them. I put my head against the cushion and closed my eyes to her unbuckling my belt. She jimmied my legs out of the jeans, and then she was bare-bottomed and on top of me, adjusting me into her, wincing at first, then sighing. It never occurred to us that I still wore my shirt or that she still wore her raincoat.

She shifted rhythmically in my lap, and the weirdest thing happened. Something I didn't think could happen to me in a thousand years. I'd had sex all of eleven times in my life, with two different girls, including Brielle. The other one was this girl Carmen who I dated for a little junior year, and every time we did it—every single damn time—it lasted maybe ten seconds. *Maybe.* And the first time with Brielle, same thing. But now, in this moment with Brielle, it seemed like it might go on forever. I could hardly even feel it.

The problem was that I started thinking. Partly about Nana. And about Amir, and Ray. But also about her. What was in her head right now? Why, after all I'd done, was she on top of me like this? Was she enjoying it? And what was her exit plan? I wasn't wearing a condom. Was she even thinking about that? Did she really like me? And if so, for Christ's sake, *why*? Wasn't Brielle O'Dell—the girl I'd been obsessed with all those months leading up to the moment I leaped in front of her car—wasn't she smarter than this? Wouldn't she be better off without me?

She leaned over and breathed into my neck. I stared at the paused video game on the television, then closed my eyes and tried to get back into it, but it wasn't going to happen.

She put two hands on my shoulders and looked at me.

"What's wrong?"

"This is not . . . okay," I said.

"What do you mean?"

"This isn't . . ." I couldn't explain whatever realization I'd just had. At least not to her. Not yet.

"Am I . . . does it feel good?" she said.

"It's not that."

"Well, then what?"

"I don't know, Brielle. It just doesn't feel right."

She shoved off me. Stood and pulled her pants up.

I did the same.

"Whatever." She pushed wet hair from her face. "I felt *bad* for you, Cullen. It's not like I'm . . ."

She waved away the rest of the thought. The part she'd said stung, though. Never imagined myself the beneficiary of a pity-fuck. Still, I wasn't sure I entirely believed her.

There was something else simmering beneath her desire to have sex with me in that moment. Something bad inside her. Something I wanted her to see for herself. But how to show it to her?

A wind gust sent rain against the tiny ground-level window near the basement ceiling. "Listen," I started, but she cut me off.

"Is that a waterbed?"

"Yeah."

"Oh my God."

As in *Oh my God, how pathetic you think that's cool.* As in *Oh my God, I can't believe I fell for the shtick of a boy who thinks a waterbed is cool.* She laughed, rolling her eyes. She was doing her best impression of those girls she used to worship so much, and I couldn't stand it.

I glared at her. There was a long, uncertain pause before she continued.

"Look, I just need a favor," she said. "And then I'll go."

"What is it?"

"For Ray. I think he's going to turn himself in. For Amir."

"I don't think he'd do something like that. He didn't do anything wrong."

"He will," she explained. "I know he will. I said *I think*, but I meant *I know*."

"How?"

"I just know."

She was shivering again, and her hands were jittery.

"Okay," I told her.

"Okay, what?"

"Okay, I'll think of something."

"He can't turn himself in. You can't let him do that."

"I know."

"You owe him that, at least."

"I know," I said. "I'll help him. I promise."

She nodded and did the quick breathing-in thing again. Like someone had pushed a fistful of air down her throat when she least suspected it.

"You can go out the hatch, if you want." I unlocked and tossed open the cellar doors. Freezing rain slammed into the room.

At the top of the stairs, standing outside in that same frigid pose as she had on the front stoop, she said, "Your front yard is still a mess."

"I know."

"You should fix it."

"Yeah."

She gazed up into the rain, blinking against it. She looked at me again for an extra moment, and then she threw her hood on and splashed away.

I stood there with the door open, staring at the space where she had just been, letting the rain dump on me.

Brielle

IT WAS EASY TO KNOW that Ray was going to seek out some form of official, irreversible punishment for the subway accident. There weren't any sleuthed-out clues. No diary entries or thread of Internet searches. No overheard phone calls. You only had to know Ray.

I was grounded when I went to see Cullen about it, and so I had to sneak out. Again.

I splashed through the woods in an old pair of Mom's galoshes, my determination to be angry and unyielding only growing stronger when I saw on the lawn the muddy, tire-dug trenches that had delivered me into Cullen's life, and the stoop that was still cracked and crumbling where Meghan's car had smashed into it. And, of course, next to the stoop, standing there in her little shell overseeing the wreckage, the Blessed Mother Virgin Mary.

Later, though, when Cullen was sitting on the couch in his basement-turned-bedroom, all alone with his grief, so handsome and so sad, I didn't care what else had happened. I wanted to be with him. Needed to be.

Even after I left—after the sex went all wrong, and after we tried to make each other feel worse than the other one felt about it—I still wanted to be with him. Could not stop thinking about him. It was the opposite of how people sometimes say, "I'm in love with the *idea* of him." I hated the idea of Cullen Hickson. I hated what he'd done to Ray and Amir and how he'd no doubt thought he was doing the right thing all along. But I was irreconcilably enraptured with Cullen Hickson the tangible piece of matter. With his scent and his sound and his shoulders and his filthy, unwashed clothes and how his eyes got quiet and sad when he didn't think you were looking at him. These real-life pieces of him made me believe he was the only thing that could keep me from floating away.

And I was so pissed at myself for believing that.

Dad was waiting for me when I returned. I emerged from the woods and climbed over the fence to find him at the back door, looking out at the yard. Lincoln did circles on the welcome mat outside, stopping intermittently to scratch at the door. But Dad didn't open it. He waited for me to slog across the swampy grass.

Apparently, we were overdue for a talk. He allowed me a brief interlude to dry off and change clothes—five minutes that I stretched into thirty, during which I brushed the memory of Cullen's breath from my mouth, showered, shaved my legs, dried myself off, retreated to my room, and lay naked on my bed. While I lay there, not wanting to move at all, let alone move downstairs where Dad waited, I heard him step into his and Mom's bedroom next to mine. A familiar scene played out. I couldn't hear many of Dad's words, but I could hear well enough to sense the tone in his voice— earnestness, pleading, desperation. I wanted to be on Dad's side—wanted to root for him—but somehow I couldn't do it. It made me so mad listening to him beg like that.

A few months ago, around when school started, I found a newspaper clipping on the dining room table, which, due to its prolonged lack of use, had long ago been unofficially converted into Dad's desk. The clipping was from September, when everyone was talking about the one-year anniversary of the attacks. The headline was something like "Never Forget? Some Wish They Could." It told the story of people suffering from the trauma of having survived or been first responders during the attacks, and there were a number of quotes from Dad, whom the writer called "a New Jersey–based psychiatrist who has been commuting to Manhattan once a week for the last year to volunteer his time to first responders."

I admit that at the time I was proud to see him mentioned like this, but since then I couldn't stop wondering why, even after cutting out the article and saving it for himself, he'd never shown it to the rest of us.

"Karen, please!" came the shouting from the room next door. "We *need* you."

And I thought now maybe this is why he never showed us. Because he can help all these total strangers, but he can't even get his own wife to have a cup of coffee with her daughter. It was pathetic, really, when you thought about it.

When I heard Dad walk, defeated, back downstairs, I rose from the bed. I dressed in black jeans and an old, too-small, faded purple hoodie, pulled my hair back as tightly as I could possibly pull it, gathering it in a wet bun, stared at myself in the mirror for what felt like forever, tried to stop being angry, tried to decide if I was pretty, or if I even wanted to be pretty, cried, tried to stop crying, wiped my tears, rubbed my swollen eyes, applied the darkest shade of lipstick I owned so that my mouth looked like a plum-colored bruise, and then finally trekked downstairs, where Dad was waiting for me at the kitchen table with two cups of coffee.

Dad didn't know we'd been with Amir when he died. A week earlier, about our Christmas Day disappearance, I'd claimed that Ray and I had been invited to Katie's ski lodge in the Poconos. I explained that Katie's parents had flown to the Caribbean for the weekend but that Katie had to stay home for track practice—the field hockey season having ended weeks ago. She was throwing a secret bash up at the lodge, I told him. And I knew he wouldn't have let us go. So we had to sneak out.

It seemed like a decently believable tale, filled with enough random details and supported by a rebellious back-drop that made it seem more like a confession than an excuse. But it didn't matter whether Dad believed it or not. All that mattered, from his perspective, was that we had left. And all that mattered now was that I was grounded and that, again, I had left.

He pushed a cup of coffee across the table to me. I stared at it a moment. For all my recent ventures into the forbidden fruits of adulthood, I'd never had a proper cup of coffee. Dad nodded at me, acknowledging it was permitted. A gesture of respect, I thought. *We're both adults here*, this offering of a hot beverage seemed to communicate.

"It *was* hot," Dad said, nodding at my mug.

I sipped. "Tastes fine."

It didn't taste fine—too cold and too bitter—but the caffeine would maybe help me stay alert during the upcoming lecture, so I gulped it down while Dad spoke.

He talked about responsibility. About accountability. Trust. Love. He tried to remain calm at first, but soon his composure cracked and broke away. We'd pushed him to his limit—that much was obvious. He moved between flinging his arms around and shouting up at the ceiling at some points and, at other points, leaning over and earnestly searching my eyes for any measure of enlightenment, so desperate to have me see things the way he saw them.

The words made sense, though the whole time I was

thinking only about what I'd just heard upstairs. I hardly looked at him and remained silent, waiting for the lecture to conclude, drinking the terrible coffee.

At some point Dad said, "Mom and I are very worried about you."

"Oh yeah?" I said. "Where is Mom?"

He tilted his head and glanced once at his coffee and then back at me, running a finger over his eyebrow—a nervous gesture I was dismayed to know Ray had inherited.

"She's . . ." The finger rubbed and rubbed at the eyebrow. He couldn't say.

"What's wrong with her?" I said.

"What do you mean?"

"I mean what's *wrong* with her, Dad?"

"Bri . . ."

"She's depressed?"

He gave me that earnest look again, like he wanted to reach a hand out to me but couldn't, for whatever reason, do it. He took a deep breath, seeming to steel himself against the turmoil triggered by saying this one word: "Yes," he said.

"Why haven't we talked about it?" I said. "Isn't talking about stuff like this, like, your whole thing?"

He sighed. I drank my gross coffee. His eyes darted back and forth, like he was wrestling with what to say and what not to say.

"I'm sixteen, Dad," I said.

"I know."

"Was she ever happy?" I asked.

"Yes," he said. "Yes, of course."

"Before me and Ray?"

"Yes, then. But also with you guys."

He looked at the window, and to my surprise, he smiled briefly. Just the slightest bit. I'm not even sure if he knew it happened. Only a flash, though—gone as quickly and mysteriously as it had come—and then he turned somber again.

"She was happy," he said. "You know how people say to kids, *If you keep making that face, it'll stay that way?*"

I nodded.

"When a person has a depressive episode—that's what it's called, like those months after she lost the baby, you remember that, I'm sure . . ."

I nodded again, remembering the dismal days I had spent so much energy trying not to remember.

"After one, they're twice as likely to have another one. And after the second one, even more likely. The more you have, the more they come."

"So every time she goes into one . . ."

"Yes."

"It's a downward spiral like that? Forever?"

"No. You can't think that way."

"Well, then can't you fix her? It's your job!"

"We've tried, we . . ." he said, then paused, resetting and finally—if only for a moment—letting go of his insistence that everything was going to be okay. "It sounds strange, but with things like this, I think sometimes the more you care about someone . . . the harder it is to help them."

Now it was my turn to stare out the window, trying to put all this together.

"But you're right," he said. "It can feel like a downward spiral. And it's worth saying . . . this is something, I'm sure you've noticed, I've had a hard time admitting to myself, even. But you're old enough now . . . I mean, you've been old enough for quite some time, and I regret not doing this sooner . . ."

He went silent. Outside, the wind bent the trees in the woods.

"What?" I said.

Dad shook his head, hesitating, stalling. Because if he said it out loud, to me, that would mean he too would have to accept it as truth.

"Dad, what?"

"It's not like she's going to wake up a different person one day, Beaker. There'll be good days. I do believe that. But . . . Mom's sick. In one way or another she always will be."

I stood and stared into the far corner of the room. My chest went tight. I could feel him watching me. I wanted so badly to stop myself from crying, but I couldn't do it. I felt childish. The tears came. Dad rose and stepped forward, but I moved away from him, shaking my head, begging him, *please, don't touch me, not right now, just leave me alone.* I searched for the worst thing I could possibly say to him, and I found it.

"Just because you're terrible at your job doesn't mean Mom can't get better. And what about Ray? Is he a lost cause too?"

He stepped back and looked like he felt sorry for me. "That's not fair," he said. "Look, we'll talk tonight. How's that? All four of us."

I shrugged and rolled my eyes. Because that was always the plan, wasn't it? Forcing Mom to talk about things she didn't want to talk about, as if that would make any difference at all except to make her pull even further away.

"Fair?" he said.

"Fine," I said.

He sat back down and worked the finger over his eyebrow like he meant to erase it. He told me I could go. Reminded me I was still grounded until further notice, but we'd talk more tonight. All of us.

I retreated upstairs to lie down, but with the caffeine buzzing in me I couldn't sleep. I wanted to put music on, but I didn't know what to play. All of the music I owned had been purchased because someone else—someone I thought was cool, or popular, or pretty—liked it: Shakira, Britney Spears, John Mayer, Phish. I didn't even know what kind of music I liked. It might seem like a simple enough thought, but in that moment the realization was terrifying to me. I could make fun of Scarlett for singing along to NSYNC all I wanted, but at least she knew herself well enough to enjoy something on her own terms.

My backpack lay on the floor next to my desk. I had a test

in French the next day and another in chemistry the day after that, neither of which had I even begun to study for. I had history homework. I was supposed to read five chapters of *The Red Badge of Courage* for English, but I hadn't even read the five previous chapters that were due the week before. I felt hot. I grabbed the backpack, tore at the zipper, emptied its contents onto the desk, then shoved everything—books, notebooks, pens, pencils, a calculator, a stapler, a lamp, et cetera—off the desk and onto the floor. I shouted, "Fuck you," at my backpack before flinging it across the room. I thought, *Fuck Amherst, and fuck Dartmouth, and fuck the whole stupid thing*. I almost cried again but decided that twice in one day was enough, so I held back the tears and just lay in bed staring at the ceiling in silence.

Hours passed. The day grew late. I cleaned up the books and everything else I had knocked off the desk. The room became darker and darker until finally it was night and I could hardly see beyond my own hands.

I went downstairs. The kitchen was empty and dark. I poked around the house—Dad in the dining room, bent over bills, loose sheets of paper fanning out around his laptop like colorless flower petals. Somewhere in there was his cherished newspaper article. Ray's door was shut. Mom's room was dark but for the arrhythmic blinking of a television light.

I stepped back into my room, turned on the light, locked the door, put the Shakira CD on repeat, slipped into a ratty pair of Chuck Taylors, stepped out the window, and scooted carefully down the slick roof.

Across the yard.

Over the fence.

Through the woods.

Into the darkness . . .

Cullen

AFTER BRIELLE LEFT ME ALONE in the basement, I spent much of the night going through closets while Nana slept upstairs. My initial plan was to go on a trash binge. It was just like my move to the basement—my head was crowded, and I needed a distraction.

But when I started examining all the trinkets, bric-a-brac, empty picture frames, chipped and cracked Hummel statuettes . . . I couldn't bring myself to get rid of any of it. I emptied the living room closet, inspecting moth-eaten blankets, throw rugs, faded, tattered tapestries, and then, when I was done, instead of chucking everything into the enormous garbage bag I had prepared for the mass disposal, I put it all back exactly as I had found it. In a shoe box under the coffee table, I found a picture of Nana with my dad when he was a little boy. Nana sat in a folding chair by an aboveground pool wearing a big, beautiful pair of sunglasses, and Dad stood beside her in the grass, sporting tri-colored bathing trunks. His hair was wet, and his teeth were stained red from an ice pop melting in his hand. He was little-kid skinny— you could count every rib.

I sat on the floor with my back against the couch and tried not to think about all the people who were gone. I hated my father when he died. He was supposed to take care of me, and he didn't. In time that feeling had grown duller, but it never went away. He wasn't a bad guy before the accident. He drank a lot of beer, but so did Mom. There were always parties in the backyard on summer weekends, and at night when I went to bed and the adults were still partying, sometimes it was hard to differentiate between the shouts of joy and shouts of anger. But we had fun. I remember one Fourth of July when Dad and Cousin Sal came back from New York with a garbage bag filled with firecrackers and Dad and I spent the whole afternoon blowing holes in the lawn with M-80s while everyone else was busy talking and barbecuing on the deck.

I felt thoroughly fucking exhausted thinking about all this, mostly because I couldn't shake the feeling that the unspoken agreement I'd made with Ray and Amir was that I was supposed to take care of them. And just like Dad, I'd failed.

The house was so quiet. I was about to turn on the television just to hear the sounds of one of Nana's shows when the doorbell rang again. Brielle had come back—this second appearance of the day just as miraculous and welcome as the first one.

She and I sat on the couch. I still held the picture of Dad in my hand, and when she took it from me, her eyes went soft for a moment, but then she steeled herself in preparation for the following line of questioning:

"I need to know something."

"Okay."

"I need to know what's real for you."

"What do you mean?"

She placed the picture on the coffee table. "You know what I mean. Most people steal a car because they actually *need* a car."

"I guess."

"Most people have a girlfriend because they actually like that person."

"I do like you. I . . . love you."

"But how do I know? How am I supposed to know that, Cullen? You live on this, like, plane where nothing is real. It's like your life is a movie. You're writing it, and directing it, and watching it, but you're not actually living it."

"It's all real. Isn't it? I love you, Brielle."

She put her chin in her hand and sighed.

"I mean, how does anyone know?" I said. "You just have to decide. One way or another you have to decide if you trust me."

"Yeah." She said it softly, almost a whisper—not exactly a resounding signal of faith.

And then, in the next moment, I had a sudden, God-awful realization. The mention of the stolen car sparked something horrifying in my memory. Just like that. Boom. It hit me.

Gripped with a sudden, insane panic, my face all at once flooded with a terrible heat, I hurried to the front door and opened it to feel the cold air.

"What is it?" Brielle said.

"Jesus Christ."

"Cullen, what?"

"What's the date?"

"The date? I don't know. The tenth?"

"Oh fuck. Oh Jesus Christ."

She was standing now, moving over to me.

"Cullen, what is it?

"My court date."

"Oh my God. You missed it?"

For weeks I'd ignored the doom. Before Christmas break the disciplinary board at St. John's had met with me to discuss the grand theft auto charges and the possibility of the school doling out their own punishment in addition to whatever criminal mess was around the corner. At the time, I was just happy to get out of that room and away from those nasty-eyed teachers, which is what they never realize with kids like me. The threats don't matter until they become real. Moment to moment, we think only about wriggling out of any particular situation. I'd gotten phone messages from a public defender who assured me he'd have no trouble getting the charge reduced to joyriding, but I'd ignored them all. I could say that I didn't care, but that's not totally true. I was, in truth, so terrified of what would happen that I couldn't face it. Like not going to the doctor when you know it's something bad.

"What are you going to do?"

I shook my head. I couldn't even think about it. Brielle was back. She'd offered up a chance for me to save Ray from himself—something I hadn't done for Amir. So what my missed court date really meant was that in order to have any chance at rescuing the O'Dells from their burning building, I would have to haul ass.

Ray

After my outburst at Amir's mass, I met with Dad, Monsignor Murphy, and the dean of men. Time off from school was discussed, but it was decided I'd be better off in class. Getting back to work, moving on from the grief, all that stuff. As the meeting progressed, and more potential penalties were proposed and dispensed with, it became clear they weren't going to dole out any official discipline at all. I was *bereaved*. I was *troubled*. I was a young man in need of *help*, not a scolding. They insisted that I meet with a guidance counselor once a week; I negotiated my way into a meeting with Father Joe, who wasn't a counselor but who, we all agreed, could provide equally useful services.

So on Monday I was back at school like everything was normal. But it wasn't normal. Because I wasn't a real person anymore. I was temporary—counting down the days until I would, once and for all, disappear completely.

I opened my locker that morning to find St. Peter gone, replaced by a black-and-white picture of a dead woman lying on top of a dented car. It was weirdly similar to the Caravaggio: The woman's head was at the bottom of the image, her bare feet elevated and perfectly crossed, like they'd been nailed in place. Her face was perfect—still and clean and white even while everything else around her had been destroyed. She'd jumped from some great height onto the car—that much was clear. The hardest part of the photo to look at was her hands. She wore white gloves, and one hand was still wrapped around her necklace.

A caption at the bottom: "The Most Beautiful Suicide: The body of twenty-three-year-old Evelyn McHale rests atop a crumpled limousine minutes after she jumped to her death from the Empire State Building, May 1, 1947. *TIME* magazine."

I searched the hall for Cullen. Obviously this was his work, and obviously he'd be lurking around some corner, secretly trying to catch my reaction. But it was two minutes before class started; the place was jammed with kids.

I stared at the picture again. That hand on the necklace. Her grip on it, even in death, was tense—one look at the knuckles and you could transform the whole peaceful pose into an image of the fall: her face twisted, warped, and screaming like crazy; her legs flailing, kicking at air like they thought it was water and they could swim her back to the top.

Nick arrived at his locker next to mine. He was all business, digging out books like he didn't even see me. My locker door was half-open, so I could frame him and the Most Beautiful Suicide in the same view.

All last week, in the halls and in the locker room, Nick had ignored me. He felt bad for me, I guess. Or maybe he just didn't care about me anymore. Maybe he had other things to worry about. I wanted to ask him about that day in Father Joe's office. *What are you afraid of, Nick O'Dwyer? What makes you cry? What makes you so angry? What makes you, deep down in a place you would never want to admit exists, just like me?* I asked Father Joe about it one day, but all he'd said was "You never know what people have going on at home." Which was true enough, but it didn't exactly tell me why a guy as tough and mean and strong as Nick O'Dwyer would be reduced to tears. In the end, Nick was the bully, and I was the bullied. I'd never know more about him than he knew about me.

I decided in that moment that I missed the old Nick. That I didn't like him ignoring me. And if I was serious about killing myself—and I was—I needed him to continue contributing to the pathetic catastrophe that was my stupid life.

I removed the Most Beautiful Suicide from my locker door.

"Hey." I crumpled the paper and tossed it at the side of Nick's head. "Hey, shithead."

He slammed his locker shut and glared at me.

I grinned. "Want to smack me in the nuts today?"

"What?"

"You haven't done it in a while. I thought maybe you'd want to get a hand in there. They're available, if you do."

"The hell's your deal, man? It's like you *want* to get your ass kicked."

"Would it matter?" I asked him. "If I did?"

"You're a cancer, O'Dell. You know that? World just turns to shit everywhere you go."

This was more like it.

"Maybe I'll grab your balls." I reached for his crotch as he tried to remove himself from what, from his perspective, must have been a pretty unwelcome twist in our relationship. "Is that what you've been waiting for all this time?"

"The fuck, man?" He slapped my hands away, and when I reached again he snatched my wrist and pinched the bones together. Instant, blinding pain.

"There's my boy!"

Nick and I turned to see Roman dancing like some prehistoric, flightless bird through the mass of students, a full head taller than everyone else. Arms flailing, he skipped into the space between Nick and me, breaking the grip on my wrist, bouncing Nick away from the lockers.

"Better watch your ass!" Roman's voice carried all the way down the hallway. "My boy O'Dell is one bad-ass dude!"

He acted like he didn't even know Nick was there. Maybe he didn't. But his arrival, a tornado of limbs and bony angles, had removed Nick from the scene. Made him an inconsequential bystander to Roman's antics. Nick moved on to class without another glance my way.

I had algebra in the opposite direction, and Roman bounced along with me as I went. "That was some hilarious shit the other day."

"What?"

"At mass!" He flung open the door to the stairwell so it slammed with such force against the wall I thought the glass pane would shatter. He wore his collar popped and shirt untucked—small acts of rebellion at St. John's that exasperated the faculty, who were always having to remind him, *Thank you, Mr. Calvecchio, the dress code applies to you too.* Underclassmen cleared out of his way as we walked downstairs.

"No joke," he was telling me. "That was hands down the best shit I *ever* saw in that auditorium."

What could I say? That it wasn't meant to be funny? That I really was going to kill myself? That, even if he didn't know it, he was laughing *at* me, not with me?

With another violent tossing of the door we exited the stairwell and emerged into the first-floor hallway. "I got German with Nazi Gerber. Where you headed?"

"Uh . . ." I pointed to the right. "Algebra II."

"As a freshman?"

"Yeah."

"Shit, man! You ain't just crazy, you're crazy smart too. You got Joyner?"

"Yeah."

"Hate that fucker. Thinks he's the shit."

I tried to laugh agreeably—I struggled with algebra, but Mr. Joyner was all right.

"I fingered his daughter one time, though."

I stammered out some combination of half words that didn't make any sense, with a lot of *umm*s and *oh*s thrown in.

"She's on the soccer team at Franklin Academy? Defense?" He laughed his stoner laugh—high and nasally—and then said quietly, like he was in confession, "Fucking bomb-ass thunder thighs, dude." His eyes went big, and he made a "shh" motion. And then, loudly again, "I know you know what I'm talking about! Anyway, I'll catch up to you later. We'll hang with Cullen or something."

He moved down the hallway, bouncy and jostling, announcing his presence to all he passed, leaving me too stunned to nod or say goodbye or offer a wave, unable as I was to shake off one lingering, perplexing, yet strangely invigorating thought:

Roman Calvecchio wanted to hang out with me?

The one big mistake I made during this time, in terms of avoiding major obstacles to ending my own life, was asking to meet with Father Joe instead of the guidance counselor. The counselor was some guy I'd met once during the first week of school. He hardly knew me at all, and I thought at the time that if I were sentenced to meeting someone once a week, I might as well see a familiar face. But pretty soon I saw that meeting with the counselor would have been much easier. He no doubt would have worked through a check-list of generic questions, and I could have recited generic answers, and he would have dispelled generic advice. Boring, sure, but pretty much painless.

Father Joe knew me too well. He insisted on pushing and prodding and poking. Trying to get to the root of my behavior. He asked about Amir. He asked about God. He asked about Nick O'Dwyer—a situation he knew about because Dad had reported it to the school, at which point I went back on my word to Dad and denied the whole thing, and when they asked, *Well, then how did you get the bruises?* I just told them, *I forget,* and none of the adults involved were exactly thrilled about this stance, but there was nothing they could do about it.

He talked about infinity.

"Give me an example," Father Joe said, "of infinity."

I didn't know where this was going. I didn't care. I was wasting the minutes. Counting down until the end of every-thing. "I don't know," I said. "Space?"

"Space. What space?"

"Like, outer space?"

"Okay, good. So, in outer space, the universe extends to infinity. Is that right?"

"I don't know. Is it?"

"There are different theories," he admitted. "But that's a decent guess, don't you think?"

I shrugged.

"Stand up."

I moved slowly, begrudgingly.

"Come on, up, up, up."

He shoved the coffee table away from the front of the couch. We stood five feet apart.

"I saw this in a movie once," he said. "I won't make you do it, because I had a cheesesteak with onions for lunch and my breath is poisonous, but imagine you and I each take a step to halve the distance between us. Okay?"

I nodded.

"And then imagine we halve the distance between that new distance. And halve that one. And so on. Moving in ever smaller, infinitesimal distances. What would happen eventually?"

"We'd bump into each other."

"In reality. But *theoretically*, imagine we can move in those infinitesimal distances. What would happen?"

I was dreaming about those generic counselor questions.

"I don't know," I said. "What would happen?"

"Theoretically, we could just keep halving the distance between us, right? Forever?"

"Sure."

"So right now, in this room, between you and me, there is an infinite amount of space. You and I are literally separated by infinity."

He was so excited about it. He really wanted me to get it.

"So it's a metaphor," I said.

He laughed. "Sure. A metaphor. For what?"

I shrugged. "Beats me, it's your metaphor."

He caught me glancing at the clock. Three minutes to four. Time to catch the late bus.

"Go," he said. "But think about it, Ray. Okay? Will you think about it?"

The next day during theology, I was paged to the headmaster's office by a man's muffled voice over the PA system. For a moment I didn't move, thinking maybe I'd imagined it. But soon the desks creaked as everyone turned to see me, and at the front of the class Father Joe motioned silently at me, like *That's your cue, Ray.* So I grabbed my things and hurried toward the door while a series of amused mumblings moved through the room and Father Joe continued with his lesson, working up to some breakthrough about the meaning of John, chapter 20—the part where Thomas sticks his hand into the gash in Jesus's side.

There was a small room outside Monsignor Murphy's office where his secretary, Mrs. Carlyle, sat. Her door was always open, and behind her, Monsignor Murphy's door was always closed. Only now she wasn't there. And Monsignor Murphy's door was cracked open. I sat in one of the waiting chairs by the door but soon rose, daring to approach the monsignor's door and knock.

"Come in, Raymond."

It was a weird, murmuring voice. Not the headmaster's voice, yet somehow familiar. The same voice from the PA announcement.

At the far end of the room, across a plush, velvet carpet, and on the other side of a coffee-colored desk the size of a small house, in the monsignor's big leather rotating chair, sat Cullen.

I hadn't seen him since that day in the detective's office. Now he had a hand cupped over his mouth and spoke in that muffled voice. "Close the door, son."

I whispered furiously, "What are you doing?"

He grinned and motioned for me to step all the way in the room. "Shut the door before someone sees you."

I did so and stood with my back against the door. "Are you crazy?"

"Did you get my gift?"

"What? In my locker?"

"What do you think?"

"Where's my Caravaggio?"

"I got it. Don't worry. What did you think about the idea?"

"What idea?"

"Empire State Building!"

I felt light-headed. I reached for the door handle—just for balance, not to make a run for it. Cullen leaped out of the big chair.

"We can do it!" he said. "I've been looking into it. It's not easy, obviously. But it's not impossible."

"How did you even get in here? Where's Mrs. Carlyle?"

"I'm still the same guy, Ray. I can get us in and out of anywhere."

I shut my eyes and tried to stop hearing him. It was happening all over again. Cullen the Unmoved Mover.

"No," I said.

"Just think about it—"

"No!" I shouted, and then went back to a whisper. "I won't think about it. I don't have to think about it. Jumping off the Empire fucking State Building isn't at all what I'm interested in. That's not . . . something like that just misses the point completely."

"What is the point then? Tell me."

"It's none of your business."

"Okay."

"This is *my* thing."

"Okay. You're right. I'm sorry. But look, Ray, can I ask you one question? And then I'll let you go and never bother you again?"

I shook my head no and closed my eyes to what was about to happen, because I knew he was going to ask anyway. And I knew he wasn't serious about never bothering me again. That was the whole problem. As long as you were alive, somebody would always be bothering you about something.

"If you're so sure you can handle this," he said. "If you know exactly what you want and how you want to do it . . . I have to ask . . . why haven't you done it yet?"

Cullen

I WAS PICTURING 'roided-up SWAT-team guys rappelling like human spiders down the sides of Nana's house, bursting through windows, smashing through drywall to catch me as I fled down the driveway, pinning my neck to the asphalt with their M-16s . . . all for missing my court date.

I put into motion a plan to abandon the house. Packed up the Buick with some nonperishables from the kitchen and a pile of blankets and sleeping bags for freezing winter nights spent huddled in the car, which I planned to stash in some abandoned parking lot somewhere over on Route 10. I was going to call Cousin Sal to tell him that someone needed to come take care of Nana because I was just a kid, after all. Right before I did this, though, I called Roman. Just to talk to someone. Workshop the plan. Ro laughed and told me that his cousin once missed a court date for dealing and went through the same panic until his lawyer told him he had thirty days to surrender. I looked it up online to confirm: He was right. Thirty days. But in the meantime, I had to be invisible. I stayed away from school. I wasn't sure if the dean of men could somehow force me to turn myself in, or actually do the turning in himself, but I'd been on the guy's radar for the past three and a half years, so I wasn't about to take any chances.

There was only one good scare during this time. One night, around ten P.M., I spied a car parked across the street with a man planted in the driver's seat. I watched the guy sit there for a good thirty minutes before he finally stepped out, and I saw it was Officer Esposito.

Come on, man, I thought. *Give me a break, would you?*

He ambled across the street in his slow-as-hell cop walk, and just as he was looking over the ruined yard, I bolted through the house and out the back door, toward Brielle's.

It was a Monday night. I did the porch climb again, hearing the dog scratching at the living room's sliding door, thanking God for those cut vocal cords, not wanting to deal with more admonishing from Brielle's dad. It was real cold, and the roof was icy. I tapped on Brielle's window. Waited. Tapped again. So cold.

She came to the window, squinting, and when I saw her I thought, *I love you. I love you, and I'm sorry for everything, and I'm going to fix it, I swear.*

She let me in. She wore flannel pants and a T-shirt, hair in a ponytail. While she shut the window I explained why I'd come.

"I can't go back home."

"Okay . . . ?"

I glanced at her bed.

"What? You mean, stay here? No!"

"Just for a few hours," I said.

"Cullen! No!"

"I don't snore. Nobody will ever know."

She rubbed a finger into one of her eyes. "Not a good idea."

"I'll go back out the window before anyone wakes up. They'll never hear me."

She sighed and looked at the clock.

"Well, look," she said. "We're not going to . . . do anything."

"No," I said. "That's fine. It's not about that."

"Oh God. Take your shoes off."

I kicked them off, and Bri climbed into bed and stared at me while I stood there, stuck in place.

"What?" she said.

"You're going to bed now?"

"So?"

"It's ten thirty," I said, laughing.

"I'm tired. And unlike you, I have school tomorrow."

I smiled and shook my head at her.

"Just get in, will you?"

She shifted to make room for me. I climbed under the blankets with all my clothes on. Me on my back. Her head near my shoulder. Crisp sheets. Her toothpaste breath.

"Cullen," she whispered.

"Yeah?"

"Ray tried to turn himself in, didn't he?"

"Oh," I said. "Yeah."

"And it worked? Your plan?"

"Yeah. Seems like it."

Her hand on my stomach, under my shirt, not moving, not exploring, just resting there. A sleepy sigh.

"Thank you."

The room so warm. Schoolbooks piled on the desk.

"You're welcome."

But there's more, I thought. *There's still more to come.*

Glow-in-the-dark star stickers on the ceiling. Her bed as soft as a dream. Just before dropping into sleep, I thought: *You'll be okay here, Brielle. When this is over. Without me.*

I managed to slip onto school grounds one day to find Ray. Later that afternoon, he and I rode to the Livingston Mall, found an unoccupied computer in the back corner of an Internet café by the food court, and scoured the web for some all-time brilliant suicide ideas.

I showed him the research I'd done on the big leap off the observation deck at the Empire State Building, not because I thought he'd go for it—I'd miscalculated in thinking that would be Ray's kind of thing—but because I still had some work to do to convince him I was the man for this job. We also scrolled through images of a monk who lit himself on fire in Saigon in 1963. Dude sat there peaceful and cross-legged in the middle of the road while a colossal flame ate him alive. We read about a news journalist who said, on air, "In keeping with Channel 40's policy of bringing you the latest in blood and guts, and in living color, you are going to see another first: attempted suicide," and then pulled out a pistol and blasted her skull wide open. A janitor in a Singapore zoo jumped into the tiger cage. A prisoner in a Florida prison choked himself with toilet paper. This guy Cato in ancient Rome knew that Caesar was going to kill him so he stabbed himself before Caesar could get the chance. And then, when he saw a doctor rushing over to save him, Cato reached into the hole in his stomach, grabbed his own bowels, and ripped them out.

I had set all this up beforehand—the links scribbled on a torn piece of notebook paper in my pocket. When I'd shown Ray everything, he shook his head, staring off. The corner of the store was poorly lit, and the light of the screen shone on his face. Two seats away from us, a group of middle school boys huddled together, pointing at the screen, giggling.

"Obviously we're not going to reenact any of these outright," I assured Ray. "This is purely for inspiration."

He stood, stretched, and yawned. Like he was bored, and it was my fault.

"Thanks anyway," he said.

"Ray, wait—"

He moved to stand, but I snatched his wrist and pulled him back into the seat. The store clerk—a college-aged girl with bored eyes, walked over toward the kids on our left, who were cackling even more loudly at whatever porn sites they were no doubt surveying. I closed our own browser window and logged out. Ray tried to stand again, and again I grabbed for him, but this time he twisted out of my grip.

"Ray, listen . . ."

He spun around to face me. "Have you ever wanted to kill yourself?" He said it loudly. The clerk paused her uninterested march toward the horny adolescents. The kids stopped laughing and looked at us. Ray registered them gaping at him.

"Sorry," he said. "Sorry. Whatever. I'm leaving."

I chased him out of the store. "Ray."

"I mean, have you ever even thought about it?" he said, pacing through the mall. "Like, not seriously, but just a moment maybe. A fantasy."

"Sure," I told him. "Who hasn't?"

"And what do you think about?"

"What do you mean?"

"I mean, in that little moment when you're thinking about killing yourself, what do you picture?"

"I picture . . . I don't know. I guess I picture my funeral."

"And all the people there."

"Yeah."

"Who are they?"

"The people?"

"Yeah. Who's there? Am I there? Bri?"

"No."

"So who?"

"I guess it's . . . guys from school," I said.

"The whole school."

"Yeah."

"And what are they doing?"

"Uh, they're sad, I guess. They're really sad."

"Yeah," he said, reaching for the door. "Exactly."

"So I get it! I understand what you're going through!"

He wheeled around again, shouting at me. "You know what I picture when I think about it?"

"What?"

"Nothing. Absolutely nothing. Just . . . total, empty, quiet blackness. So, no, you don't get it. I don't care about the funeral. I don't care who will be there or how sad they'll be. I'm not doing this for anyone else. I don't want to send a message. I only want to disappear. Completely. Forever."

Ray

I SAW THE KEY the night I took the money from Dad's closet. It hung from a nail in the wall just inside the door. Dad— ever the pragmatist—had labeled it: *Hill spare*. *Hill* as in Hill Avenue, the street of Dad's office.

It was a small building, one of those offices that used to be a house, or at least looked like a house. Dad split the space with a dentist. Every Tuesday, Dad commuted to New York for his volunteer work, and one Tuesday after school I walked from the bus stop to his office. The secretary from the dentist's office saw me through the blinds of their office. I offered a friendly wave, and she waved back. *Perfectly normal*, I thought. Nothing weird about a son using a key to enter his father's office.

I was there to find out about dying. Who had seen it? Who was haunted by it? What did they say about it? Had one of his patients ever killed him- or herself? If so, how had they done it? I was conflicted because, on the one hand, I knew that if I was serious about my war on vanity, I would just choose an ordinary suicide like anyone else. Taking a bunch of pills or jumping off a bridge would fit just fine with my thinking that I wasn't special and didn't deserve anything other than a normal, forgettable-enough death. But at the same time I couldn't shake the idea that how I chose to kill myself was my last chance to get something right. I wanted a method that would *mean* something—not to anyone else who would be left behind, but to myself. I had no idea what that meaning would be, but I knew I'd recognize it when I saw it. Maybe there was a clue somewhere in Dad's records.

I sat at his desk in an enormous, swiveling leather chair. I tried to imagine him sitting here, listening to his clients, nodding his head. "Yes, yes. I understand completely. Tell me more. Here, have a tissue." Or maybe it was nothing like that. All I knew about therapists, I realized, came from TV and movies.

I started up the computer and guessed four or five login passwords—names, birthdays, anniversaries—before giving up and digging through Dad's drawers. Taped into the back of a datebook from 1999 was a torn piece of yellow paper with maybe ten passwords listed on it. The first one did the trick. I poked around the computer files until I found a bunch of folders, each titled "Progress Notes," with different codes attached to them. I tried to open "Progress Notes_ FGH_99," but these were also protected by a password, so I went back to the list until I found the right one. I clicked on a document: "TinReach." I scrolled through it, reading quickly, catching key words and phrases: "Tina Reacher," "Compulsive," "Body image," "Purging."

What I needed, I realized, were the guys who were there that day. The policemen. The firefighters. The random do-gooders. The ones who'd seen people go the same way I'd seen Amir go.

I searched for an hour, plugging in passwords, clicking through one document after another, glimpsing the secret worlds that all these random people had revealed to my father. At one point I thought, *If God has any interest in saving me, now would be a pretty good time to chime in.*

I found what I needed within the folder "Progress Notes_ ABC_02" in the document "JosBenit."

Here is what I learned: Jose Benitez was an NYFD dispatcher. He was answering phones that morning. At eight forty-seven—he remembered the time exactly—he got a call informing him a plane had crashed into the World Trade Center. He sent every fireman he could—every company available—to the towers. "Pretty much all those guys I sent in there are dead now," he told my dad.

He got calls all morning from people trapped in the buildings.

He told my dad, "This one guy just kept shouting at me:

'I'm trapped! I'm trapped!' And I told him help was on the way. I thought it was. I really, really thought it was."

He told my dad: "I would have rather been there myself than in that stupid office on the phone."

He told my dad: "I'd rather be dead than have to live with hearing their voices."

Jose Benitez had PTSD. He had anger-management issues. He had insomnia. He was experiencing what my dad called "hypervigilance." He was addicted to painkillers, which he took for sleep. He had nightmares.

My chest went tight while I read. I thought about Amir. *I'm so sorry*, I thought. *I'm so sorry I let you do all that stupid stuff with me. For thinking there was Something Else out there. And for letting you believe you could help me find it.*

"I'm so fucking sorry," I said out loud.

Jose Benitez told my dad: "I'm in there with them. The rubble crashes down on me. My mouth fills with dirt. I'm choking. Choking. Choking. I'm trapped. I can't move my legs, my arms, even a finger. I can't open my eyes. I want to explode my body just so I don't have to die under all that heavy shit."

I wiped away tears. I tried to keep more from coming, but they wouldn't stop.

I closed my eyes, slowed my breathing, and brought back that old image of the lake: *Bloodfire. Bloodfire.*

Calmer now, focused, pushing away the sadness and finding something else—something much worse—I read Jose Benitez's dream again:

"My mouth fills with dirt."

Yes, I thought.

"I'm choking. Choking. Choking."

This is the way.

"I'm trapped."

This is exactly the way I need to do it.

Brielle

I HAD A NIGHTMARE during this time where I was playing bas-
ketball in gym class. Play had been suspended amid a lot
of confused chaos. Blood was all over the floor and had
been smeared on some of the girls, including me. It was
sticky in my hair and trickling down my neck. We were
looking for the source, until gradually, horribly, it became
clear the blood came from the sides of my head—I'd cut my
ears off that morning in the shower, my dream-self remembered, and had tried to cover up the wounds with two tragically inadequate Band-Aids. There was laughter. Someone
whipped the ball in my face. Katie and Scarlett—whom I
hadn't spoken to in real life since the incident with Cullen
in the lunchroom—appeared as two floating, disembodied
faces, cackling like banshees.

It was infuriating that I still couldn't leave them behind

like I wanted to. I tried not to think about them all day. I told myself I was fine eating lunch all alone in the freezing cold on the back steps of school while trying to complete some last-minute chemistry homework, not brave enough to face the lunchroom, let alone find a spot to sit or try to converse with some new group of potential friends. But it didn't work. Katie and Scarlett still haunted me. The memory of our lost friendship waged a constant war in my psyche, fighting for space, reminding me what life had been like then and that I was kidding myself now in thinking being with Cullen was enough.

I started sneaking out of my room at night, slipping through the woods with a flashlight, and arriving at the cellar door of Cullen's house. The sex was fun. Freeing. Each time a little less awkward than the last. Sometimes we'd start like two little kids, playing, giggling, naked under the covers, lurching on his ridiculous waterbed, experimenting with new ways to make skin touch skin—hand on neck, knee between thighs, fingertips on back, chest against chest. At some point, inevitably, mysteriously, it would turn serious, and we'd engage each other solemnly, in slow motion, almost like we were praying.

But always afterward came these inexplicable waves of shame. And why? What were these post-sex demons that came for me? Where did they come from? Was it because of Amir? Didn't we deserve to be going on with our lives? Exploring new ground? Finding new pleasures? Or maybe it had nothing to do with that. Did Cullen feel the same? Did everyone? Is this just what sex was like? Maybe after being as close as you could possibly be to someone—physically speaking, anyway—the adjustment back to being alone in your own body was always an unsteady one.

I had no answers. It only felt like all the things I'd been doing lately were things a normal girl—a good girl—should not be doing. Which left me wanting to do those very things over and over. It left me wanting to make a clear break away from the field hockey girls once and for all. To do whatever I needed to do to erase them from my dreams.

"I need your help," Cullen told me one night, post-sex.

He explained that he had one final, guaranteed-to-succeed plan for Ray—how to save my brother from himself once and for all.

"Look."

The basement was connected to a crawl space, and from that space, Cullen, wearing only his boxers, dragged into the room a poorly constructed homemade casket: Ray's casket.

"We've been building this. Together."

Cullen detailed the plan. The idea was to bring Ray to the very brink, even to let him jump, so to speak, and then to watch him pull himself back over the edge. I tugged a sheet up to my shoulders and stared at twin tubes of fluorescent lighting on the ceiling. Even as I continued to sneak out and undress with this boy and do things with him I'd never done before, I was still stuck with the same old question I hadn't yet found an answer to: *Do I trust him?*

"So," Cullen said.

"Hold on."

"Okay, but—"

"Hold on! Please. You just showed me a freaking coffin in which you plan to bury my brother, so please don't talk for one minute."

I was angry. Partly I was angry at Ray. I'd forgiven him the awful moment in the castle with the piece of glass—chalked it up to a desperate notion on a horrifying day. And I knew Ray had gotten into trouble at school, even knew what he'd said at Amir's mass. But there was a part of me that didn't want to believe he was still serious about this. I was hoping Cullen's scheme to disrupt his confession had allowed Ray to get it out of his system without any permanent harm. Now Cullen was telling me that Ray was, in fact, very sincerely committed to disappearing and leaving me here, alone, with Dad—and with Mom, and I couldn't even in my wildest dreams imagine what she would do or what kind of total wreck she'd turn into if Ray killed himself. That was a kind of shock from which someone like her would never return. And I'd have a hard time forgiving Ray for doing that to her, and to me.

Also, though, I was mad at Cullen—bitter that he knew this about my brother before I did and had, in typical Cullen fashion, stoked the fire rather than making any reasonable attempt to snuff it out.

He handed me a glossy suicide-prevention pamphlet.

"Pick your favorites," he said.

"Huh?" Still naked, suddenly so cold, I reached over to retrieve my underwear and a sweatshirt from the floor.

Cullen opened the pamphlet for me. Inside were ten warning signs of suicide. "From the list. Pick one or two."

"For what?"

"We're not gonna plant Ray out there and just hope he comes back on his own. I will not let this one go wrong. We're going to give him a damn good reason to save himself and never think about suicide ever again. So, Brielle O'Dell, you may not know it yet, but you are in the business of offing yourself. What are your warning signs?"

I glanced at the pamphlet, not committing yet, not even fully understanding the idea.

1. Talking about wanting to kill oneself
2. Increased use of drugs or alcohol
3. Loss of interest in things one cares about
4. Sudden, jarring changes to appearance
5. Saying goodbye, settling affairs, or giving away possessions

I shook my head as I read.

"Just hear me out," Cullen said. "Can you do that? For Ray?"

I fiddled with the pamphlet. Ran a finger across the eyes of the sad-looking woman on the cover being comforted by a man who was presumably her husband.

"First of all," Cullen said, "Ray wants to kill himself. I'm sorry to be blunt, but that's what he said. And he means it. See for yourself. Talk to him. I promise he means it. So he needs help. And we're the ones who have to help him because, you know, who the hell else? So that's my plan. To save Ray. And if you don't want to be a part of it, I totally get it. That's cool. I don't blame you after . . . well . . . Anyway, it's your choice. But the thing about Ray is . . . he's crazy about you. Maybe you don't see it—probably he doesn't even know it. He takes it for granted that you'll be there. Because you're *always* there for him, Brielle. You're the only one. And if we can shock him into action by making him think that maybe you *won't* be there, if we can make him believe that *you* need *him* to save you . . ."

"I do need him."

"I know."

"Not to save me, but . . ."

"Say no more. I get it. So, look. This is the best way I can think of to show him what his life means. Why it matters. If you're not into it, I'll find another way. But I promise you that plan B, whatever it ends up being, will not be nearly as effective."

It was a good argument. Cullen had been crafting his case for days, maybe weeks. And he made all the right appeals except one—a quiet murmur trembling deep within me, just like the one I'd felt before I decided to go along on Christmas Eve. I wasn't even aware of it enough to recognize it or put words to it. But I felt it nonetheless. It came in ecstatic waves full of possibility and menace. The feeling told me: *You're doing this for Ray, but also for yourself. Because, whether you're willing to admit it or not . . . you like it. You need it.*

I couldn't help but wonder, even though he hadn't said as much, if maybe Cullen knew that about me too.

"I want complete access," I said.

"To what?"

"Your plan. No tricks. Nothing like the after-Christmas stuff."

"Done."

"No lies. Not to me."

"I promise," he said.

"Fine." I pointed to the pamphlet. "This one."

Cullen sat at the edge of the bed. The liquid rolled beneath us. He leaned over to see where I'd pointed and read it out loud: "Sudden, jarring changes to appearance."

Two nights later, after bombing my French and chemistry tests because I'd spent all my time thinking about how, exactly, I should go about suddenly and jarringly changing my appearance, I was back at Cullen's with rubbing alcohol, a needle, and an eyebrow stud.

I sat in a folding chair in the middle of the room. Cullen sat on my lap, facing me, pulling over the bedside table, on which lay all the essential items. He rubbed an alcohol-soaked cotton ball first over my eyebrow and then over the needle. Then he touched the ice cube to my brow. He held it there until it was so cold I told him to pull it away. He pinched the skin of my eyebrow and tugged it away from my face, holding the needle in the other hand.

"Okay?" he said.

"Okay."

"Sure?"

"Yeah."

"You're gonna look so badass."

I offered a frightful laugh, trying not to move my face too much.

"Okay," he said.

"Okay."

He inhaled, exhaled, and then plunged the needle through. I felt the pressure of the needle and afterward a dull burning, and that was about it. It hardly hurt at all. Cullen dabbed a tissue at the blood, reached for the brow stud—a thin rod with a red ball at each end—and secured it into place. He tapped the tissue against the piercing, and it came back with more spots of blood.

"Done," he said. "Take a look."

I rose to look at myself in the mirror. The numbness went away, and the pain crept in. I dared a finger to the two red beads above my eye. Tilted my head to see myself from different angles. *Is this me?* I thought. *Are we real? Am I here?*

"What do you think?" he asked.

"You say first."

"Fucking beautiful," he said.

"Yeah?"

He nodded, eyes shining suggestively beneath his brow. "You mean it?"

He nodded again, slowly.

I took a step toward him. I felt like I'd jumped from some great height and was falling and falling and didn't want to ever stop falling.

"I want to dye my hair too," I said.

The doorbell rang. We stared at each other. It was twelve thirty A.M. The bell rang again.

"Who is that?" I smeared blood off my eyebrow, rubbing it onto my jeans. The bell rang again and again and again. Cullen didn't move. *Please*, I thought. *Tell me you know who that is. Tell me this is a scheme. Something you have planned down to the last detail. To the very second. Something that will work out in the end.*

Silence. No more ringing. We exhaled. Entertained the fantasy that it was over, that maybe we'd imagined it. Cullen handed me a tissue. I patted my eyebrow. And then a knocking. The kitchen door, upstairs.

"Shit," Cullen said. "Shit, shit, shit."

"Would they come for you now? In the middle of the night?"

"I don't know."

A furious knocking boomed out on the basement hatch. My breath left me. Cullen raced to the doors—they weren't locked—but in the next moment the steel doors creaked open, clanging against the backyard patio.

I watched, of all people, my father march into the room.

I held a trembling hand to my eye as he inspected every element before him: Cullen, daughter, folding chair, needle in Cullen's hand, bloody tissues on the floor, a freaking casket against the far wall. His eyes came back to his daughter. Her face. Her eyebrow. Her blood.

"What is happening in here?"

Cullen said nothing. He shrank into the corner. He knew, I could tell, there was no use in explaining.

Dad came closer, inspecting my face. His eyes went soft. His shoulders drooped. "Beaker," he said. "My God, what are you doing?"

"I'm fine."

He put a hand out to touch the piercing. "Beaker . . ."

"Please!" I said. "Dad. *Stop* calling me that."

He pulled the hand back and looked like he might cry, but I didn't feel bad about what I'd said. *We know things you don't, Dad*, I thought. *This isn't even real. We have the situation totally under control.*

Cold came in through the opened hatch. I shivered. Dad's gaze landed on the casket again. I thought for sure he'd ask about it, but he quickly turned back to me and said, "Let's go."

"Where?"

"*Where?* Home, Brielle. We're going home."

I scoffed, like that was the most preposterous next step he could have proposed. He reached for my arm, but I pulled away.

"You're gonna drag me out of here? Is that your plan?"

"If I have to."

"I'm fine."

"We're going home now."

"I. Am. *Fine!*"

"You are not fine! Nothing about this is fine! You obviously need help!"

"Oh, okay." I said. "Thanks, Dad. Who's gonna help me? *You?*"

"What does that mean?"

"Forget it."

"I've been here, Brielle. I'm trying. You have to meet me halfway."

"Oh God, Dad. You're so far off. Can't you see that? You're not even fucking *close* to halfway right now."

"Look at yourself! It's the middle of the night. You weren't in your room. How do you think that makes me feel? And so I . . . I have to go looking for my daughter? And I find you here? With him?" He turned to Cullen. "Is there even an adult here? Where's your grandmother?"

"It has nothing to do with him."

"Everything! It has everything to do with him. This is not—"

"Mr. O'Dell," Cullen said.

"Don't interrupt me."

"Okay, but listen—"

"You . . . you of all people . . . do not dare interrupt me right now."

Cullen nodded. He went silent. We were all silent.

Dad was seething. He breathed hard, wiped a hand across his face, and looked at me in a way he had never looked at me before. "You," he said, "are a child. Do you understand? You are . . ."

He slowed himself down and gazed at the ceiling, exhaling mightily. Then he looked at both of us in an earnest, desperate manner, as though this were the most essential piece of information he would ever deliver to us.

"You are *children*," he said.

A muffled thump sounded from upstairs. I hardly noticed it, thinking, more subconsciously than not, that it was just one of those noises an old house makes. Dad didn't react either. But Cullen, I saw after a moment, had gone rigid. He looked at the staircase, put a finger up to my dad—as in *Sorry, just one second*—and then raced up the steps.

Dad turned to me, confused. I went after Cullen.

At the top of the stairs, I heard Cullen saying, "Okay, okay, okay," in a quiet, panicky voice.

I hurried into the living room, where Cullen kneeled over his grandmother, who was on the bottom step of the stairs, collapsed against the wall.

"Oh God."

"She's okay," Cullen said. He was lifting her off the ground.

"Cullen, don't move her! If she fell—"

"She's fine," he said. "She just got dizzy and sat down a little quickly."

I turned to find Dad right behind me, moving toward

Cullen. He took one of Nana's arms, and he and Cullen eased her down on the La-Z-Boy.

"What are you doing out of bed?" Cullen asked.

Nana coughed. "Asshole," she said, sucking for breath.

Cullen smiled. "Huh?"

"Ass . . . hole," she said again, coughing more. "At the . . . door." She jabbed her index finger like a person pushing a doorbell over and over again. Cullen grabbed a plastic mask from the coffee table drawer and hooked it up to the tube running from the oxygen tank.

Dad cleared his throat. "The doorbell," he admitted. "That would be me."

Cullen slipped the mask over her face. "There you go," he said. "Get some air."

I watched Dad as his eyes swept across the room—the old, torn couch, the dusty La-Z-Boy, the oxygen tank, the mold on the ceiling, Cullen holding his grandmother's hand, Nana breathing, coughing wetly, her eyes awake but mostly lost, focused on nothing. The look Dad gave me was a question—even without words I knew what he was thinking. And I nodded: *This is what it's like*.

Cullen

AFTER SCHOOL, for three weeks, Roman, Ray, and I locked ourselves in my basement bedroom for two and a half hours to
construct the coffin. We taped black garbage bags over the
tiny rectangular windows near the room's ceiling. We didn't
tell Ro the plan. He never asked. After what happened to
Amir, he didn't want to know, and he didn't want to be there
when whatever we were planning went down. But he liked
hanging out, so he lifted some tools from his dad's garage
workshop and sat in the corner of the basement, alternat-
ing between watching us and playing video games. He was
surprised as hell, of course, when he found out the thing
we were building was a casket, but even then he didn't ask
questions or demand to know what the plan was. He only
shook his head and laughed, grabbing the controller and

unpausing his game, saying, "You two are some crazy, crazy dudes."

We made three caskets, in the end. The first one started badly, but I kept thinking we could salvage it right up until we carved out a lid and tried to fix it on the base and the result was like something made by two blind preschoolers with hooves for hands—unmet edges, gobs of wood glue everywhere, bent nails poking through. And the second one began just as pathetically. The only improvement this time was that we knew to scrap it rather than push on.

We were standing one day in the middle of all this old woodworking machinery that for the life of us we could not figure out how to operate with, like, even the most microscopic level of effectiveness. We were drenched with sweat, and sawdust was pasted to our arms, necks, and foreheads. By that point, I was ready to quit the whole damn thing.

"Fuck it," I said. "New plan."

"No way," Ray said. "It feels like we're on a treadmill, but we're not. We're moving forward. We're getting better."

I motioned to the misshapen monstrosity on the floor that was meant to be a rectangular box.

"We're getting there!" he said.

"What makes you so sure?"

"I don't know, but—"

"We're oh for two."

"Yeah."

"With not one shred of evidence that would lead us to believe we're figuring this thing out."

"Yeah."

"So? I'll ask again. What makes you so sure?"

"I don't know," he said again. But then he stared off to the corner of the room, gathering his thoughts. "It's like when you have a shitty day but you're sure that tomorrow will be better. You know? Nothing *makes* you sure about something like that. You just are or you aren't."

"Sorry. When have you *ever* thought tomorrow will be better?"

I said it lightly. An innocent joke at his expense. But in an instant, he turned dark and angry.

"Before I met you," he said.

The work, much like our training leading up to the robbery, tended to free Ray from himself. And that freedom, over and over again, would take us pretty close, even in these astoundingly sad circumstances, to sharing a decently enjoyable moment. But as soon as Ray realized I'd caught him being a real person for half a second, he'd cower back into his own shadow and disappear, like he had to remind himself he wasn't supposed to be happy.

The next casket was better. Not perfect, but better. We'd be able to nail it shut, at least. It'd sustain the pressure of a few feet of dirt without collapsing. Against his assurances that he wouldn't need it, I went ahead with constructing a bailout mechanism. We drilled a hole near where Ray's head would be and jammed a length of PVC piping into it. Then we dropped a string through the pipe, glued a rubber washer to the aboveground end, threaded the string through the washer, and tied the string to a bell. So whenever Ray was ready to admit to himself that he didn't want to be buried alive—which I was sure he'd do after pondering a few gently dropped but all-important pieces of information from myself at his supposed gravesite—all he had to do was pull the string and I'd deliver him back to the whole freaking rest of his life.

On a Sunday, in the early afternoon, Ray and I loaded up Roman's pickup truck with the following: the empty, homemade, slightly off-kilter coffin, the last-minute-change-of-tune-get-me-outta-here apparatus, two pickaxes, two shovels, one hammer, eight bundles of firewood, one stack of kindling, four bags of charcoal, one can of lighter fluid, one pair of jumper cables, six gallons of gasoline, four flashlights, two work lights with clamps, one generator, two gallons of water, one cooler with ice, six sodas, four turkey sandwiches, three bags of beef jerky, and one box of Oreo cookies.

Ray was quiet on the drive. Classic rock played on the radio: Billy Joel, Springsteen, Zeppelin. The Parkway was wide-open; we cruised south. Exits for shore towns clicked by: Belmar, Point Pleasant, Toms River, Manahawkin. The gear, hidden beneath a canvas top, rattled in the truck bed. At one point, Ray reached down for the suicide-prevention pamphlet I'd planted near his feet. He read, unfolding it and, I hoped, looking carefully through those warning signs.

We followed the same route into the Pine Barrens that we used for our target-practice excursion, with only a few wrong turns within the maze of pitted, sandy roads. When we arrived at the clearing by the pond—only half-frozen now, thanks to a week of warm late-winter days—we unloaded the truck and sparked two fires with the kindling we'd gathered at home. As the fires grew, we built them toward each other so they connected in the middle. We spread charcoal around the edges, allowing the heat to spread across the frigid ground.

There was a lot of waiting for the flames to catch and spread. We drank the sodas and ate the sandwiches and cookies. We didn't say anything beyond what was necessary—which for the time being consisted of guessing when and where to place logs most strategically so the ground would be sufficiently softened by the heat.

We shoveled one corner of the fire toward the center and then took pickaxes to the dirt. It broke up easily; the fire had done the trick. But as we dug, the ground became hard and frozen again, so we scooped some burning coals into the ditch and started with the pickaxes on another corner.

In three hours we had the hole dug and were dead tired.

"How about dinner?" I said.

Ray agreed. We retreated to the truck's cabin, where we each scarfed a second sandwich, gulped down a soda, and immediately fell asleep. I woke with a shiver to find the cabin light on and Ray awake, silent, head in a book.

I started the car with painfully cold fingers, sticking my hands down my pants while waiting for the heat to kick in. It was night now. Fully dark. Damn cold.

"How long you been up?" I asked.

"Not long."

"Didn't feel like waking me?"

"Figured you needed the rest. Your job's not done."

The pants weren't working, so I blew warm breath into my hands and then put on my gloves. I yawned and rubbed my face. "Man," I said quietly, as though to myself. "Hope the next one's easier."

I ran a hand through my hair and stretched my shoulders back.

"Huh?" Ray said.

"What?"

"What next one?"

"Next one?"

"You said something about the next one being easier."

"Oh yeah. I just meant . . . you know. The next stunt or whatever. You ready?"

He didn't say anything.

"Ray?"

"Yeah."

"You ready?"

"Just a minute."

I nodded. He read his book.

Put it together, I thought. *Your sister, Ray. Your sister. Your sister.*

He seemed somehow unlike the Ray I knew, but I couldn't tell if this was a good sign or not. He was quiet like always, but his usual everything-sucks-and-most-of-all-I-suck silence had morphed into this stoic kind of . . . *confidence.* Like he didn't give a shit anymore what anyone thought of him. And this had me thinking, on the one hand, that maybe he'd hardened himself against a choice as dumb and pathetic as suicide, but on the other hand that maybe it was easy to be stoic—or cool, or arrogant, or whatever this was—when you had nothing left to lose. Not even your own life.

"What're you reading?" I asked.

He showed me the beat-up cover: *The Confessions of St. Augustine.*

"Good?"

He flipped back a few pages and, finding what he was looking for, read: "Behold with what companions I walked the streets of Babylon, and wallowed in the mire thereof, as if in a bed of spices and precious ointments. And that I might cleave the faster to its very centre, the invisible enemy trod me down, and seduced me, for that I was easy to be seduced."

The car hummed, and the heat whistled. The New Ray held his stare on me—a hard stare.

"All right," he said. "Let's go."

Ray

CULLEN HAD HOOKED UP yellow work lights to a generator, which buzzed and growled near the truck, and then he hung the lights from some trees. The casket—my casket—was in the ground, waiting for me. I wasn't afraid, exactly. But something wasn't right.

"Change your mind?" Cullen asked.

I squinted into the lights. It felt like we were two highway workers adding a carpool lane in the middle of the night. "Do we really need all this?"

"I thought . . . you know, to see."

"What's there to see?"

He motioned to the casket, out of which rose a long, white pipe with my safety bell attached to the top.

"What if you're trying to ring the bell but it malfunctions or something? Maybe I'll see the string moving."

"I'm not going to pull the string."

"You say that now."

"Can we turn the lights off?"

"Hey," he said. "It's your funeral." He walked to the truck, shovel in hand, leaping over the mound of dirt we'd removed from what was now my grave, and flicked a switch on the generator. All at once the world went quiet and dark.

"Okay?" Cullen called over.

"Better."

I climbed into the casket and was lying with my arms across my chest by the time he returned. I didn't want him to mistake my complaints about the lights as hesitation. I'd tried to remain quiet and businesslike all day, hoping to avoid what I believed was the inevitable moment when he would, I was positive, lay the "you have so much to live for" speech on me.

Cullen stood above me. Way above him trees swayed, black against the hazy, grayish night sky. It definitely wasn't an ordinary Sunday night, but I got an ordinary-Sunday-night kind of feeling anyway, looking at the winter trees and thinking about how dark and sad Sunday nights are. Sunday's always the day when you wonder how you'll ever make it through the rest of them.

"That's it?" Cullen said. "No fanfare?"

"I've been ready for a long time now."

He disappeared from view, then returned carrying the lid and a hammer.

"What about you?" I asked. "Not gonna talk me out of it?"

"You think I did all this work for my health? When some-one asks me to help them kill themselves, I take that shit seriously."

This comment—like the one he'd dropped about "the next one" being easier—caught my attention, but not enough for me to do anything about it. They were two puzzle pieces that didn't yet form a coherent image. So, for the time being, I let them go.

"Last words?" he asked.

I shook my head. No more words. The fewer words, the more he'd take me seriously. The more he'd be left with only his own thoughts about what was actually, truly, no-bullshit happening right now.

I watched the safety string dangle briefly beside my head as the lid came down, and then it, along with everything else, disappeared in the darkness.

The hammering was more efficient and less excruciat-ing than I thought it would be. Three strikes per nail, four at the most. And then the dirt—early trickles followed by a tsunami. Then the claustrophobia. The sides of the coffin seemed to shrink, pinning my legs together and squeezing me at the elbows. The wood creaked and, a few terrify-ing times, cracked as the mounds of dirt piled on. Probably there was still plenty of air in the box, but I felt my lungs go tight and my heart speed up. *How long?* I thought. *Oh God. How long can I last?*

A blackness beyond black. Beyond dark. Like the

blackness had invaded my body and turned me inside out so that I became the blackness itself.

I tried to meditate. I'd been trying all day but failing. On the car ride south, for example, I'd closed my eyes and focused on my breathing, trying to think about nothing. But I couldn't do it anymore. Amir was always in there, and I couldn't remember how I used to let unwanted thoughts pass by before they did their damage. There was suddenly no more blood and fire to call up. When Amir floated by, he always stayed for a long time.

I pushed those same thoughts away now, and Bri came flooding in, and then a sudden realization about Cullen's puzzle pieces.

Earlier that week, Bri had knocked on my bedroom door after dinner. My room was a mess because of a weird thing that had happened the previous night. At three in the morning, I'd woken up in a panic and ripped a bunch of pages out of my books—the Gospel according to Thomas, Kant, St. Augustine, Aquinas, the Bible, the Tolstoy book. I went through the texts, overheated and sweating, tearing pages out, ripping them into pieces, and spreading the pieces across the floor. Then I got dressed for school—khakis, undershirt, button-down. I even wrapped a tie around my neck, though I didn't manage to fix it under my collar nor tie it. It was like sleepwalking, except I was more conscious than not. In the morning, I had woken with the fabric of the tie scratching my throat, looked over the floor of shredded pages, and remembered the whole thing.

Bri had knocked again, saying, "Ray? I know you're in there."

I sat at the desk and didn't say anything.

She opened the door. "Can I come in?"

"Oh . . ." I looked over my shoulder to see her poking her head in. Her hair was purple. She'd dyed it two days earlier. "Sure," I said. "I guess."

She tiptoed between the pages to the bed and gave me a look like I was crazy. "What are you doing in here?"

I told her about the previous night.

"You were sleepwalking?"

"Sort of, but I remember doing it. I don't remember what the reason was, though. I woke up all panicked and knew I had to get dressed and rip all these pages to shreds. And then I went back to sleep in my clothes."

She laughed. "That's pretty weird."

We were silent for a while. I tried not to stare at her eyebrow—the swollen, slightly bruised one with the two red beads peeking out. The one that dared you not to look at it. The one that, when combined with her hair, made you want to ask why she would do something like that to herself.

"Anyway," she said. "Oh hey, you know how to do Lincoln's food, right?"

"What do you mean?"

"You do one scoop of the dry food from the big tin and then spoon a can of the wet stuff on top of it."

"Okay . . . ?"

"He needs it every day after school."

"Why are you telling me this?"

She shrugged. "Just in case you're around and I'm not."

I nodded, still not understanding.

"After school, I mean. In case you're around after school and I'm not. Can you do that? Lincoln can't wait until Dad gets home from work. And God knows Mom can't be bothered."

"Okay," I said. "Sure."

"Okay!" she said. "That was all!" She smiled big—too big—and hopped off the bed with a peppy sort of flair.

She motioned to a poster on the wall as she went. "What is that, anyway?"

It was a haunted-looking painting showing a hilly landscape and medieval city backed by a stormy sky. "El Greco," I told her. "We learned about it in Spanish. It's where John of the Cross was taken when he was arrested."

"St. John like your school?"

"Yeah," I said. "They tortured him there."

"Huh." She studied the painting for another moment. "The cans are in the garage, by the way."

"Okay."

"Cans of food, I mean. For Lincoln."

"Yeah. I got it."

"Great. So long, little brother."

And it was only now, lying under the dirt, trembling with the horror of being trapped in this much-too-small box, that it all made sense. The pamphlet in Cullen's car. The top ten warning signs:

4. Sudden, jarring changes to appearance
5. Saying goodbye, settling affairs, or giving away possessions
6. Suddenly happier; unusually or unnaturally perky

I focused on my heart, trying to slow it down. Honed in on my muscles—arms, legs, stomach, face—trying to completely relax them. So that was Cullen's big plan. That once I put the pieces together about Bri supposedly wanting to kill herself, I would pull the string and race off to save her.

But here was the funny part: This time, I had a plan too. This time, I was one step ahead of Cullen.

Two days before I climbed into the casket, I decided I didn't want to die. That line of thinking started, oddly enough, with my first deciding that I *did* want to kill myself. My life as a ghost unstuck me from the day-to-day world that once seemed so unbearable. I wasn't afraid anymore. I wasn't so guilty. I was free to open my eyes, and what I saw when I did . . . well, I had to admit it wasn't all that bad. I joked around with Roman. I learned how to use a buzz saw and a hammer. I laughed. I sweated. I even started doing my homework after school instead of poring over those religious books that only made things worse. Moment to moment, I was becoming a real person again. I've never called a suicide hotline or anything like that, but I swear if I could talk to the people who run those things I would tell them that the best thing you can tell someone who's thinking about

maybe possibly offing themselves at some point in the unde-
cided, distant future is this: Pick a date. Mark it on the cal-
endar and exist as a ghost until that date. You will come to
believe things you never thought possible.

All this work was almost undone one day when I saw
Amir's brother. I was walking from school to the market on
the corner for an after-school snack, and I saw Malik pull
up to a traffic light. On his way to work, probably. It was an
uneventful enough moment. We stared at each other. Said
nothing. The light changed. He drove off. But then, in the
next instant, the full extent of Amir's death hit me again. And
all my guilt came rushing back.

So on Friday afternoon—two days before Cullen and
I made the drive south—I met Father Joe during my free
period, the last period of the day, and interrogated him
about the Infinite Space.

"Are you saying that's God or something?" I asked him.

"What's God? The infinite space?"

"Yeah."

"How so?"

I knew he would turn the line of questioning back on
me, yet I couldn't help but pursue it. Before I drove south
with Cullen, I needed to know.

"Well," I said. "I've been thinking that, like, even though
there's this infinite space between people, you can still feel
connected to them, right?"

He nodded.

"Like you can never *be* another person, obviously. And

so you can never really get as close to someone as they are to themselves. But you can get pretty close."

"Like with whom?" he asked.

"What do you mean?"

"Who are you close to like that?"

My face went flush. "I don't know."

"Your parents?"

"Sure, I don't know. "

"Your sister?"

"Yeah, maybe."

"Who else?"

Another unpleasant pause. My throat so tight. *Please don't say it*, I thought. *Don't say his name.*

But I knew he would.

"Amir."

A silent minute passed. Passed slowly, painfully. Father Joe wheeled his chair around, popped open the CD player, flipped through a book of CDs, picked a new one, and pressed Play while these big tears dropped out of my eyes. No sobs or bawling or anything like that. Just the tears—like spilled water falling off the side of a table. The music played loud at first, but he lowered the volume to almost nothing. It was a light, plucky guitar—classical, I guessed, no singing. A harmless, calming background melody.

He spun the chair back around. "So what about the infinite space?"

"It's just that . . ." I wiped my eyes and sniffled. Why was it impossible to cry without feeling like a five-year-old boy?

"You can reach out to people, and they can reach back to you, but you can never cross the space, right? That's what you said, anyway. So God *must* be the space. He's like this . . . conduit, or whatever, that transmits the signals between us. He lets us get closer to each other than we can manage by ourselves."

"You know what the key part of that is?"

"What?"

"You said, 'You reach out to people, and they reach back."

"Okay?"

"It takes *two* people to do the reaching. You can't just sit back and wait for it."

I wiped my eyes again and tried to think about this, knowing, as with a lot of what Father Joe laid on me, it would take days, maybe weeks—years, even—before I could apply it to all the parts of my life he wanted me to.

"Okay, now get ready," he said, leaning forward with his elbows on the desk. "I'm about to launch into a lot of grown-up priesty stuff. And you're not going to like it. We gotta take our vitamins. Okay?"

I nodded. "Okay."

"You reached out to Amir, and he reached back to you. And it was great. I mean, it's the greatest thing in the world, isn't it? To have a true friend? To love someone like that who loves you back? And I think the God-as-transmitter idea is a hell of an idea. A *hell* of an idea, Ray. But it's just an idea. And that's all God is. He's an idea. A map, let's say. But a map's pretty useless if you don't use it. Amir's gone now. I'm so sorry for that. I can't even begin to put into words how sorry that makes me. But he left you something."

He was right about the vitamins thing. This was too much, and I sat there gripping the arms of my chair, trying to resist the moment's effect.

"Do you know what he left you?"

"The map," I said.

He nodded.

"Suicide . . ." he said. This was the first—the only—time we'd ever addressed my outburst at the mass. The word seemed so offensive when he said. Violent. "*Suicide* is the exact opposite of everything we're talking about here."

I fiddled with my hands and didn't say anything.

"It can happen again, Ray. That connection. Maybe it already has. Maybe it's happening right now. Isn't it worth sticking around for that?"

And so two days later, I found myself no longer wanting to die, but lying, nevertheless, in my Box of Eternal Suffering and Darkness, the emergency string dangling beside me, tickling my ear.

But I wasn't going to pull it.

I wasn't going to die either, though. Because I'd also realized something about Cullen during my time as a ghost. Something I needed him to see for himself—the very reason I'd climbed into the casket. Cullen, unlike me, was a natural reacher. He'd reached out across the Infinite Space to Amir, and to Bri, and, of course, to me.

Bri wasn't going to kill herself. I saw that when I finally calmed myself as much as it was possible to calm myself in that death trap. It was all too perfect. The signs. The pamphlet. The not-so-subtle hints Cullen had dropped. I wasn't buying it. He was doing all this because what happened to Amir was devouring him from the inside out, just like it was doing to me. Here he was trying to make me save myself, but it was too late. I was going to make him do it.

The dirt had long ago stopped falling. But for the thump-thump-thump of my pulse and the whooshing of blood in my head, the silence was almost as total as the darkness. The cold had been replaced by the heat from my body and breath. The casket pinned my arms against my sides, and it seemed to shrink with each passing second. A weightless feeling rolled like fog through my head, and I realized I was taking shorter and shorter breaths.

Whether he liked it or not, Cullen was one of the good guys.

Any minute now he'd understand.

Any minute now he'd dig me out.

Brielle

HE PROMISED HE'D CALL as soon as it was over. He gave me his cell phone so we didn't have to deal with the possibility of Dad answering the house phone. Everything would be okay. I didn't have to worry. I didn't need to come looking for them.

Too nervous to stand still, I walked to the center of town, one hand wrapped around Cullen's cell phone in my pocket. Families and hungover people in their twenties ate at the diner. The ice cream store was just opening for the day. I passed the music store, where a bunch of middle school kids paraded out, shouting, laughing, chewing gum, comparing purchases, one boy ripping the plastic off a CD case and popping the CD in his Discman. I walked to the end of the block, then turned around. The phone wasn't ringing. *Please*, I thought. *Please ring*. This time, for lack of anywhere better to go, I entered the music store.

A girl at the counter nodded a hello at me, and I nodded back. I paced the aisles, peeking at the genres and band names. The clerk—she was maybe ten years older than me—stepped out from behind her perch and came toward me. I stopped and immediately flipped through a batch of CDs, hoping to keep her away.

"Can I help you find something?" She had a tattoo of a star on her wrist and a silver nose ring.

"I'm fine," I said. I didn't want to talk to anyone. I didn't want to buy music.

The phone was not ringing.

"You like country?"

"Huh?"

The girl nodded at the cases I was so intent on pretending to study instead of talking to her. I looked at the names: Garth Brooks, Willie Nelson, Keith Urban.

"Oh," I said. "I don't know."

I flipped open Cullen's phone and stared at the screen like it held some grave message that required my immediate attention. The girl drifted back toward her counter. I took one more lap around the store, eyes fixed on the screen. The problem with having Cullen's cell phone, of course, was that there was no way for me to reach him. I was almost to the door of the store before I realized Cullen had, of course, planned it this way, for that very purpose.

"I like your hair."

I paused before stepping outside. The girl smiled at me. The eyebrow ring was hard to forget because it had swelled and bruised after the piercing, and I had to ice it for two days. But I kept forgetting about my hair, which I'd dyed on my own, after school, without Cullen, in the upstairs bathroom. The box had featured a smiling girl with a brilliant purple head of hair—the kind of violet you find in a cartoon rainbow. But I was afraid of using too much dye, and so the half dose I had used, combined with my already dark brown shade, had resulted in a wine-colored tint.

The girl pointed to her head. "I did a sapphire thing once, but it washed out a while back."

"Oh," I said. "Yeah. Thanks."

"You in a rush?" she said.

"I'm waiting for a call. Sorry . . ." I took one step out the door.

"Here, wait." She stepped out from behind the counter. "You like sad music?"

I couldn't think of anything to say. I wanted to run out of the store, but I didn't have anywhere to run to, so I let her take me over to a pair of headphones that were hooked up to a CD player mounted on the wall. I opened and shut and reopened the phone. I checked the ring volume, barely listening to the girl, who was saying, "This is a couple years old, but I've been playing this for everybody I know. I just can't get enough of it."

She planted the headphones on my head and pressed

play. The music faded in, and I was instantly dropped into a dream. Everything else faded away. The cell phone and Cullen and Ray and Mom and Dad and Katie Kinney and even this music store girl . . . they didn't exist. There was only the music and myself. The singer sang with such soft, hollow sorrow. His voice was almost a whisper. The guitar was slow, quiet, and the whole song moved through me like it was melting in my bones. I closed my eyes, and it seemed like, if I'd wanted to, I could have reached out and touched the surface of time with my fingertips. There weren't many lyrics—it was mostly just a refrain sung over and over, each syllable moving one note higher up the scale:

"Everything means nothing to me.

"Everything means nothing to me.

"Everything means nothing to me.

"Everything means nothing to me."

It was like the music knew me. Like it had somehow existed inside me before this guy ever sang it. This was all I ever wanted—something for myself.

I thought about Ray and felt a shiver of panic.

"So?" she said.

I nodded, unable to talk.

She reached into the rack, dug out the CD, and held it out for me to take.

"Oh," I said. "I don't have any money."

"Gotcha. No worries. Come back when you do."

I told her I would, thanked her, and rushed to the door. I suddenly knew what I had to do and felt a violent panic that I hadn't done it right from the start. I never even thought to look at the singer's name. But at least now I knew where to look.

I ran home, hand clutching the phone, which still wasn't ringing. I stepped into the kitchen, distraught, looking for Dad, but found Mom instead. She was on the floor, in the fetal position, hugging her knees. For a blinding, panicked instant, I thought she must have collapsed, was maybe even dead, but then understood that she wouldn't be positioned like that if she hadn't put herself that way.

"Mom?" I bent to her. A band of sunlight cut through the kitchen window, shining on her face and eyes, which she'd shielded with her hair. The sun lit the red of her hair so that it seemed to sparkle. I loved and hated that hair. It always made me believe in impossible things.

"Mom?"

I nudged her shoulder. She stirred awake. Looked at me. Blinked. Pushed the hair from her face.

"Hi, honey," she whispered.

"Mom, what are you doing?"

She looked around, trying to hide her surprise. "Oh."

"You're on the floor."

"Yes." She pushed herself up to a sitting position. "I wanted . . . I was making tea."

"Yeah?"

She leaned against a cabinet door and sighed.

"And then what?"

"Huh?"

"You wanted tea. How did you end up on the floor?"

"Oh, I was waiting for the water," she said. "I'm fine, honey. I was just . . . a little tired. Needed a rest."

I checked the stove to make sure she hadn't left a flame on. Mom sighed again, rubbing a fist into her eye. She wore an old T-shirt and sweatpants. I felt her forehead and neck, but she didn't seem to have a fever. Her hands felt, as they'd always felt for as long as I could remember, very cold.

She closed her eyes. I held her hand and suddenly saw my mother, and myself, and my family more plainly than I ever had before. I admitted something to myself that I'd been trying to ignore for a long time.

"Here, Mom." I put a hand under her arm and lifted her up. "Let's go upstairs, okay?"

I helped her up the stairs and put her to bed, drawing the blinds in her room, folding layers of blankets over her. I did all this gently, but also quickly, my mind still on Ray. As I was about to hurry out of the room, Mom grabbed my hand.

"Brielle," she whispered. "Your eyebrow."

"Oh."

She'd seen it before. I was sure of it because I remembered so clearly her not saying anything about it the first time, after that night Dad found me in Cullen's basement and I'd had to sit at the kitchen table and suffer another one of his lectures, while Mom sat next to him, staring into a mug of coffee, unable to participate, incapable of comforting, encouraging, punishing, or scorning.

"Who'd you do that for?" she mumbled.

Maybe I misheard her. I don't know. Maybe she said, "What'd you do that for?" Maybe "Why?" Either one of those questions would have made more sense than "Who?" But it was dark, the covers were drawn up to her chin, she was deeply fatigued, and I was in a rush. What I heard was "Who?" And when I heard it, I felt so dumb for not having known the answer to that question sooner.

"You," I told her.

I sprinted through the house and found Dad in the garage, cleaning out two childhoods' worth of balls, bats, skate-boards, scooters, and whatever else we'd accumulated in this storage room over the years.

"Do you want this?" he said when I opened the door. He held up a toy stroller in which I used to push my dolls and stuffed animals around the driveway.

"Dad."

He let the stroller down, catching the distress in my voice.

"It's Ray," I said. "I think he's about to do something really stupid."

Cullen told me where it was going to happen. He even showed me on a map the exact spot in the woods where they planned to hike to and start digging. So Dad and I drove to Jockey Hollow and parked near the cabins that Cullen and I had sneaked into that day I'd skipped practice. We jogged past the cabins, down a wood-chip trail, follow-ing Cullen's map off the trail and into the middle of the woods. We peered through the trees. We shouted for Ray. For Cullen. Nobody was there.

"God, they could be anywhere," Dad said. "We should split up."

"No," I said.

"They have to be somewhere."

"No, Dad. They're not."

"What do you mean? Cullen told you—"

"He lied."

"He—"

"He lied. I should have known. Of course he did."

I said this last part mostly to myself, but it didn't matter because Dad wasn't listening anyway. He'd already taken out his phone and was dialing the police.

Cullen

Honestly, I didn't think he'd last more than one minute in that box. And so even though I went into it intending to pile the dirt loosely atop the coffin, allowing for a minimal-effort excavation, I started thinking that the more I played up the illusion, the more quickly he'd bail. I got carried away. I found myself tossing in more and more dirt, occasionally wheeling a shovelful above my head and slamming it down, hoping to send horrifying reverberations through the earth that would rouse, once and for all, Ray's ultra-depressed soul.

Unquestionably, he would want to live. No reasonable person could withstand this kind of terror. Leaping off a building, shooting yourself in the temple, swallowing a fist-ful of pills—all that stuff was different. Just one step. Simple as batting an eyelid. But this thing with Ray was a deliberate, drawn-out piece of sustained, bone-drilling horror. Every single person who ever lived—no matter how screwed up in the head they may or may not be—would pull that string. Nobody could lie there and let this gruesome nightmare be their last moment on earth.

By the time I looked up from my business with the dirt and the shovel, realizing that Ray wasn't flinching, I found the coffin pretty decently buried. Much, much too decently buried.

And the bell was not ringing.

How long could a person live without oxygen? When did brain damage become part of the equation? Had he underestimated how long he could last? Passed out within moments before he could ring for help? Before he could even hear the dirt piling up? Before he could see I wasn't bullshitting him?

"Pass the test, Ray," I muttered.

My voice sounded strange in the silent woods. If Cullen talks in the forest and Ray is too buried-alive-in-the-freaking-ground to hear it, does anybody give two shits?

A cold, moonless forest in the middle of nowhere. The air misty and wet. A vapor had hovered above the pond before the sun blinked out for good a few hours earlier. If I picked up that shovel, he'd always need digging out. If not by me, then by someone else who came along. He'd always be latching on to whomever, always in search of his One True Savior. Your classic teach-a-man-to-fish scenario.

"Fuck!"

I paced a lap around the mound. Inspected the emergency bell, giving the string a gentle pull. Everything in working order.

"Come on, Ray!"

I smashed the shovel into a sticky, sap-oozing tree over and over again, even as a penetrating ache exploded through my hands. "Coooooome oooooon!"

A cold wind blew across the pond. Pine trees rustled. Ash floated up from the coals of the snuffed-out fire.

"What a stupid thing, Cullen," I announced. "One more stupid, stupid plan."

I was so disappointed I wanted to cry. I expected so much more from Ray.

I raced to the generator, flipped on the lamps, skidded back across loose, ashy sand, and dug.

"Fuck, fuck, fuck, fuck, fuck." Hammer slung in my belt loop, trying not to step where the coffin was, imagining a gory B-horror-movie situation where the wood gave way and I stomped a boot right through Ray's lungs, which, in their weakened state, would pop and turn to mush like two moldy peaches, I dug and dug and dug.

There were only four nails, each one hammered halfway. The rest of the hammering had been done only for Ray's benefit. In my panic, I yanked out the one nearest his head and tried to pry the lid up to give him some relief, but it was a no-go. I scrambled across the lid, sweeping away dirt that was still warm from the thawing fires, feeling for the other nails. When I'd released the two middle ones, I crawled to the foot of the box, fingernails stuffed with dirt, and hauled the lid up to my chest, peering around the side to see Ray. The work lamps lit him up and colored him like a painting. Some classic from the old masters or something. Eyes closed. Waxy face. Unconscious. No breathing. Dead fingers interwoven on his chest.

"Fuck, fuck, fuck, fuck, fuck, fuck!"

I wrestled with the stupidly, awkwardly shaped lid, prying it from the hold of the final nail, and tossed it out of the hole.

"You stupid asshole, Ray, you fucking stupid idiot, Jesus Christ."

There was no way to give him CPR without sitting on his chest. I flipped him, limp and heavy, in a fireman's carry over my shoulder, and then, as I was trying to lift him out of the hole, one of his heavy arms swooping down and smacking me in the face, his whole body, once an impossible-to-lift bag of potatoes, seized up at the middle, and I heard a grunt.

I paused.

Another grunt. Stomach muscles trying and failing to relax against the pressure of my shoulder.

I shifted the body to the ground, balancing him on his feet, my hands on his shoulders, and he looked at me. Eyes open. Very much alive. Lips twisting, against all efforts otherwise, into a smile. The beginnings of a laugh.

I let go of the shoulders. He did not fall.

"The fuck?" I said.

He laughed, for real this time, and it sparked an angry fuse within me, and I hit him. Right hook to his left cheek.

"Asshole!" I shouted.

He came for me. A fist slapped my ear. Knee in my groin. Blistering-hot anger rippled through me, and I grabbed him by the throat, lifted him off the ground, and slammed him into the box. He squirmed beneath me, but I pinned a knee into his gut and tightened the grip on his throat.

"You think that was funny?"

I held the grip until his face looked like a zit about to pop pus and blood all over the place. When I released him, he coughed and sucked in huge gulps of oxygen, and I sat on my haunches, and I must have blinked or glanced up at the blinding lamps or closed my eyes to the horrible red mark my grip had produced on his neck, because I didn't see him snatch my hair. I felt the tug and then looked, too late, as he yanked my head down and swiftly smashed his forehead into my nose.

"Aww." I tilted back, seeing red—dark, oozing, boiling shots of red—and tasting rusty metal. "Awwww."

Finding the edge of the box, clawing at the side of the hole, thinking Ray was still coming for me, thinking if I were him I'd sure as hell be coming for the guy that just choked me, but then letting my head tilt back against the dirt, understanding it was over, I curled up in whatever corner of the hole I'd found and brought a sleeve to the torrent of blood gushing from my shattered nose.

"Head-butt," I said, shaking my head. "Holy shit, Ray."

His wheezing was quiet against the buzzing generator, but I could hear enough to know he wasn't ready to talk. At some point I managed to open my eyes against the tears and blood to see Ray propped up, like I was, at the opposite end of the casket. We sat for a long time. The generator and the lights and Ray's breathing and my sniffling of blood. Intermittently, my eyes would close and my head would drop before I'd catch myself and wake up. Minutes passed. Twenty. Maybe thirty.

"Feel like you made your point?" I said finally.

He nodded, head loose on his neck like a jack-in-the-box.

For a while longer we sat in silence. I titled my head back against the lip of the ditch and watched the trees above: Ray's view before I'd brought the darkness down on him. The pine trees were fuzzy against the sky—wooly bear caterpillars crawling over my eyes.

Sweet Jesus Christ, did my nose hurt.

Ray

I DOZED FOR MOST OF THE DRIVE HOME, waking to see that Cullen had pulled the truck up to his own house. I yawned and stretched. Outside, wind gusts pushed against the car.

"Cop car was pulling away from your house when I got there."

I tried to nod casually, but he could see I was nervous.

"It's fine," he said. "Go through the woods. You didn't do anything wrong."

"Is my neck . . . ?"

He clicked on the cabin light and inspected my throat. His nose looked awful—swollen and crooked, with dried blood at the edges.

"Not too bad," he said. "Redness went down."

"Is your nose okay?"

"Hurts like hell."

"Sorry."

"Don't be sorry. It's not about that."

I opened the door and dropped one leg to the ground. The wind was so strong it blew the door shut against my thigh.

"Oh, wait." Cullen dug into his back pocket. "I have some things for you."

He pulled out a crumpled pile of cash and shoved it into my hand.

"What's this?"

"I never wanted the money. Tried to tell you that."

"Cullen—"

"Take it," he said. "This is what you would have stolen from the store anyway. Take this too."

He handed me the Caravaggio print he'd stolen from my locker. It was crinkled from being in his pocket. One deep crease cut vertically through Peter's torso and another horizontally through his face. I always thought he looked so hard and poised, prepared to endure his honorable fate. But tonight, in the low glow of the cabin light, in Roman's beat-up truck with its weak, rattling heat system and its cracked, cold leather seats, St. Peter looked terrified. He seemed to be looking off to some approaching horror that was even more hideous than crucifixion. Like maybe a pack of rabid dogs was coming to tear his face apart while he hung upside down. He looked tired. Weak. Defeated.

I handed the picture back to Cullen.

"You don't want it?"

"Nah."

"Why not?"

"I don't need it."

"What is it, anyway?"

"St. Peter. His crucifixion."

"Oh yeah? The pearly gates guy?"

I cocked my head. "Huh?"

"St. Peter. Dude's like the Santa Claus of Heaven, right? Decides who's naughty and nice."

"Oh." I put a hand to my neck, thinking.

"You all right?"

"Yeah, yeah." I laughed, leaning over to look at the painting once more, blinking against the glare of the dome light. I hadn't thought about that. I don't know why, but it was so funny to me that this St. Peter was the same one you see in cartoons about people trying to get into Heaven, the ones where St. Peter always has some great punch line. As though getting into Heaven—the possibility of living forever, the eternal stakes of having faith in God and honoring God and loving God, whether or not our lives actually have any purpose at all—like these things were all just a big joke. And meanwhile here was Caravaggio's St. Peter.

"Sure you don't want it?" Cullen asked.

"You keep it. Or toss it, I don't care." I rubbed my eyes and stepped out of the car, looking over Cullen's yard, which had never been put back together after Bri's accident.

"Anyway," I said. "I guess you'll be over to see Bri or whatever."

"Yeah, maybe," he said, but he didn't exactly sound convinced this would happen. "Hey, Ray. What would you have done? If I didn't dig you out when I did?"

"You did dig me out."

"I know, but I'm saying . . . if I didn't?"

"But you did," I said.

"Okay, but . . . that's a hell of a gamble hoping someone will save you like that."

"It wasn't just someone, though, was it? It was the almighty Cullen Hickson." I smiled at him in what I hoped was a not-too-corny way. "You did exactly what I knew you would."

I moved through the dark woods from Cullen's house to mine, shoulders drawn in tight against the wind. I walked slowly and thought about my life and all the things I wanted to tell Amir. I wanted to tell him about the Infinite Space, about building the casket, what it felt like to be buried alive, that it was even scarier than the subway tunnel, that my favorite moments with him weren't when we were doing all those stupid, crazy stunts but were instead the quiet moments, the still moments, the real moments. That I wished he were here with me right now, in these woods.

I wanted to tell him that I finally understood the thing I'd been searching for all along wasn't something you found at all. It was something you built.

The wind seemed to shake the whole forest. Saplings bent almost to the ground. Leaves whipped at my ankles. I stopped walking and looked up to where the bare branches rattled against each other in a loud, shadowy tangle. A few scattered stars were visible.

I shouted into the trees. Shrieked as loudly as I could until my throat felt shredded. I screamed and screamed, but the wind kept taking it away.

It was hard to understand that he wasn't coming back. Ever. I wondered if that feeling would ever go away. Or if I even wanted it to go away.

At our yard, I stepped over the fence. The ground floor of the house was lit, the blinds drawn up.

She's in there, I thought. *You can talk to her.*

I stepped onto the deck and peered through the sliding glass door into the living room. Bri lay on the couch. She clutched a blanket to her chest. The TV blinked shades of blue and yellow across her face, but she wasn't watching it anymore. Her eyes, I could see when I cupped my palms around my face to limit the glare, were closed. I watched her for a long moment to be sure she was sleeping, drawing my collar up against the wind. She didn't move. I could hear the TV from outside. The volume was cranked, probably to help her stay awake. She must have waited a long time

I walked to the other end of the house, where, at the kitchen table, Dad waited. When I approached the window just beside the door, he turned to look at me, as though he'd been expecting me at just that very moment. His eyes were red and puffy, and he leaned on his elbows with heavy, rounded shoulders. His hands were folded near his chin, like he'd been—and maybe still was, even as he was looking right at me—praying.

I hadn't looked in a mirror all day. There was no telling what I looked like, but it couldn't have been pretty. No one comes back from the dead fully healed. Dad didn't offer much of a reaction, though, and I had the thought that maybe it was so dark out here he couldn't even see me. I shivered and kicked dirt off my shoes. My legs wouldn't stop shaking. I put one hand in my jacket pocket, wrapped the other around the doorknob, and pulled. The wind still beating and clamoring outside, I stepped into the light and shut the door.

Acknowledgments

To be a writer is to walk a foolish, occasionally reckless path that requires a lot of faith and more than a few allies. The following list is a hasty, incomplete attempt to express gratitude to the many true believers I've encountered along the way. Everyone here has helped keep my creative wheels turning in one way or another—in many cases by offering a candid opinion when it mattered most, but in other instances, and just as important, by withholding one.

My Family: Via (my love and secret coauthor), Finn (my biggest joy and best buddy), Mom and Dad (who only gave me everything), Erin and Colleen Strong, MMM&K, the Allmans, Chuck Osgood, Zac Osgood, and Carol Bobrow.

My Book People: Peter Steinberg, Ben Schrank, Marissa Grossman (Dream Makers Three), and everyone at Foundry and Razorbill.

My Teachers: Mrs. Pehowic (Central Ave. School); Martin Berman, Harry Dawson, and Richard Binkowski (Seton Hall Prep); Norma Tilden and Steve Wurtzler (Georgetown); and Gina Nahai, Janet Fitch, Lee Wochner, and Coleman Hough (USC).

My Readers: Via Osgood Strong, Andrew DeSilva, Yance Wyatt, Neelanjana Banerjee, Yvonne Puig, Mitra Parineh, Andy Bailey, Christopher Varley, and Gregory Spatz.

My Day Job Employers: Patty Kiley, Jack Blum, and John Holland.

My Riffraff: Russo, Fanning, Quick, the 1400 Club, Doug MacLeod, the A.W.S.O.M.E., the MPW gang, Kevin Long, 2256, Fort StrongFort, the Words that Speak crew, everyone at Moving Arts Theater in Los Angeles, Andrew Tonkovich at the *Santa Monica Review*, the Community of Writers at Squaw Valley, and—by way of fulfilling a promise to my eighteen-year-old self—Jack Kerouac.